Footsteps

Kirsten Johnson

Plain View Press
P. O. 42255
Austin, TX 78704

plainviewpress.net
sb@plainviewpress.net
512-441-2452

ISBN: 978-1-935514-25-1
Library of Congress Number: 2009931506

Cover art by Alex Mbugua
Cover design by Susan Bright

Acknowledgments

There are many people I would like to thank for helping me see this novel through to its publication. First are all those who gave me the factual background I needed, including Celina Kanini Kinoti, Kithure Nyaga, Joseph Kiria, Edwin Kiria and Brother John, from Materi Girls' School. I would also like to recognize the folks who advised, supported and encouraged me in so many ways, from reading through versions of the book to lending a listening ear or an understanding shoulder to cry on. These include: Cynthia Green, Tamara Guirado, Imad Rahman, Joan Abbot, Duncan Chaplin, Scott Zesch, Howard Hoffman, Christine Desmet, Christel Preuss and Diana Keyes. I would also like to thank my family for putting up with my crazy moods, late nights and the endless revision process, which lasted for over six years, as I slowly put together this story, which has become so much a part of who I am.

Contents

Foreword To *Footsteps*: A Cultural Exploration

Celina Kanini Kinoti, January, 2009

Many years have passed since I first wished to put into writing the tribulations borne by Tharakan girls in my country, Kenya.

I was born in Tharaka, a hot, dry place to the east of Mount Kenya, in 1963. My parents were Christian, yet believed in the tradition of female circumcision. All the provocative talk around me at such a young age—I was ten or eleven at the time—frightened me, but there was nothing I could do to prevent what was coming.

In 1975, my older sister and I underwent the initiation rite. My bleeding would not stop, making me very weak. I am fortunate that my parents took me at last to the mission hospital at Nkubu. At the hospital the nurses gave me a blood transfusion. Their conclusion was that my extreme anemia was caused by the malaria that I had on a regular basis. Nothing was said about my circumcision, which had been so badly performed. As I lay in that strange place, I wondered why it had been performed at all. The nurses attending me were educated and not circumcised. At this young age I began to wonder what the significance of the rite was if these educated people hadn't undergone it. Instead of feeling that I had become a woman in my culture, I felt angry at the traditions of my ancestors.

Due to my awful experience, my parents did not force my younger sister to be circumcised. At least I could take some comfort in that. But still I felt an intense hatred of the act, so much so that my personality changed. I now felt at war with anything the culture forced upon Tharaka women and girls. I made a decision to personally improve myself through education and absolute denial of any cultural ties. I thought that if I were to embrace a Western education, I must, at the same time, give up anything to do with my traditional culture.

One of my particular and deliberate interests has been to break through the bondage women bear in Tharaka. I say "bondage" because, like many places in Kenya, Tharaka is a traditional place, where women have few rights to do what they feel moved to in life. Historically, we have been controlled by our fathers, our brothers or our husbands from the time we are born until we die. Education has enabled me to choose not to be a "traditionalist", that is, a woman who must submissively go along with every outdated tradition of the culture, and to fight the stigmatization I might have suffered as an orphaned child. (I say "orphaned" because, even though my mother is still alive, my father died while I was thirteen. My father had practiced veterinary medicine and been the sole bread earner in the family. Without knowing her father, a child in Kenya loses some part of her identity.)

Education has brought women dignity and freedom, however it comes at quite a cost. For poor people in areas like Tharaka, it is impossible to afford schooling much past the primary level. I am eternally grateful to Brother John at Materi Girls Mission School, who paid my school fees (via donations from people in foreign countries) from "form one" through "form four" at Materi Girls, where I went for my "O Levels". (At this time, Kenya followed the British system of education.) Thanks to him, my "A Levels" were also paid for; thus I finished "form five" and "form six" at Njonjo Girls High School, a place far from Tharaka, in the cool highlands of Kenya. I took the following subjects: Geography, History and Christian Religion. Though I wasn't officially "trained" as a teacher, I was considered adequately trained to teach at any Harambee school in Kenya.

Harambee schools are located in impoverished rural areas. "Harambee" means "let's pull together", meaning that poor parents need to come up with the full amount of fees for their children to attend these schools. This is in contrast to the private schools, like Materi Girls, where sponsors (and wealthy parents) pay the fees or the government schools, which are supported by Kenya's government (and also the parents). Even though government schools have lower fees, they are tougher to get into and the standards are higher than Harambee schools.

It was at Kajuki Harambee Secondary School in 1983 that I met Kirsten Johnson, an American Peace Corps volunteer who was also teaching there. Kirsten and I lived together as housemates. During our time together, we thrived on having sometimes conflicting, but usually interesting discussions until late into the night.

On one of our first days living together, we planned to clean the house. As she went to get a bucket of water from the pump, I collected the rags, with which I planned to mop the floor. As she re-entered the house, I heard her say, "We don't have to squat down to wash the floor. I bought a real mop so we can mop like civilized people do."

I stopped short and looked her right in the eye. "And just what does a style of cleaning have to do with being 'civilized'? Does squatting down to mop mean I can't live in a community? Does squatting down to mop mean I can't follow the laws made by a society? Just what is your definition of being civilized, Kirsten?"

I know now that she probably didn't mean for her statement to sound like it did. However, this example shows that, despite not being a

Tharakan traditionalist, I have not embraced all Western assumptions; to do so would deny everything that I am. I will always defend the African way of life and be proud of most aspects of my heritage, never just buy into every Western idea of "civilization" or start thinking like the wazungu. Not only would I refuse to accept anything they do or say without a debate or at least a discussion, but I would never agree to a hand-out without working my fingers to the bone to pay it back or to make the benefactor proud that he or she has donated to my cause. This is the dignity with which I have tried to live my life. I will hope to my dying day it has not been in vain.

I left Kajuki in 1985, but I continued teaching school in the area. My sister had married and had her own family; thus, I was the only one who could help my poor mom pay the school fees for my brothers and younger sister, as well as buy food during periods of drought. I had always been of small stature; from the time of my circumcision to the present I have battled various illnesses. Either I suffered from malaria or the cold weather I wasn't used to or I had an amoeba from the river water that we drank. I usually would not sacrifice my pay to buy medicine because I always prioritized my family's expenses and needs over my own.

It was in my twenties that I refused many young men's offers for marriage. It seemed like all they wanted was to prove that they could support me better than I could support myself. I heard many rumors that they were saying things to people I knew, such as, "What is this woman trying to show us? She thinks she can single-handedly pay all these school fees for her brothers?" I ignored what they said and continued living in the way I believed in.

In 1991 I decided to venture into what was considered a "man's job" by becoming the first unmarried lady education officer in Tharaka. Old mens' delegations were sent to my house to advise me against taking on such a position, but they didn't sway my determination. These wazee worried that I must not have been "decent" enough to get a husband, which, at the time, was still thought of as a woman's ticket into proper society. Within a few years of landing this job, however, I did become married to my current husband, Kinoti.

Although a man, Kinoti is not typical, and we have worked through our differences to build a relationship, which at present is as strong as it's ever been. For many years, I suffered from clinical depression. He supported me by helping pay for the expensive treatments. A few years ago, I thought I might have breast cancer. The lumps turned out to be benign, but the doctor told me that maintaining a calm and peaceful life was key to complete recovery. My life has been anything but calm or peaceful. My job with the Department of Education makes it necessary to travel by foot or public transport for at least three hours daily on unpaved roads, which become washed out and dangerous during the rainy seasons. Through all of this, Kinoti has been supportive, both financially and emotionally. We have had our ups and downs, but after fifteen years and four children, I finally feel as though he treats me like an equal and we are now truly a married couple.

At the age of forty, I started at Kenyatta University in Nairobi in order to complete a bachelor's degree in History and Literature. This I completed in July of 2008. I would now like to pursue a masters degree, but I will put this dream on hold until my children are finished with their schooling. I still need to pay back loans to the tune of half a million shillings; I can only conquer this enormous expense a small amount at a time.

I am pleased to say that throughout my lifetime in Kenya, the outlook for women has improved and is continuing to improve. Many women have taken up jobs they would never have been allowed to do in the past, especially in education, and the men have stopped underrating our strength. When women become educated, men start to respect us more and allow us to make better choices for ourselves and our families.

When Kirsten first approached me to help her with the novel she was writing about Tharaka, I gladly accepted. I have a sincere interest in getting stories about women from my culture to the rest of the world. It is my hope that what is depicted in this fictional work will improve the reader's understanding of a part of Africa that is filled with conflict and controversy, but also beauty and integrity.

Tharaka, Eastern Kenya
1985-1986

Chapter 1

It was the night before Kanini's brother would undergo circumcision. The following morning relatives would bathe him in the river then bring him before the circle of villagers, where a circumciser, with a swipe of his knife, would remove the flap of skin that for fourteen years had kept Njagi a child.

Nyambura, as circumcision was called in their native language, was one of the most important traditions in their culture: it initiated a young person into maturity. Kanini remembered Njagi's face at the butcher's earlier that day, illuminated with anticipation. Her own *nyambura* would take place in a year when she was thirteen, but all she felt now was dread.

Inside the family's main hut, she sat up groggily, her eyelids heavy from her late afternoon nap. She looked down at her faded dress, creased and dirty from the day's activities. She'd been planning to change into her clean one, but it was probably still drying on a nearby thorn bush. She touched a handful of her dusty, wispy plaits, which she'd hoped to wash and grease. She would just have to cover them with a head square. At the very least, she could scrub her ankles and feet.

The rattle of pans and thwack of a *panga* lured her to the door. She wrenched it open to reveal a gaggle of village men looming in the shadows, their bandy legs and splayed feet coated with dust. They were singing in low toneless voices, accompanied by the occasional beat of a drum and clop of coconut shells. Some of them gyrated their hips to the rhythm, while others sat on their haunches or hovered in a tight knot around the fire pit. A few wore grass skirts tinkling with bottle caps, while most had on everyday clothes: tattered pants, a patched sweater or jacket, and sandals made of old tires.

Njagi approached her, straw hat cocked jauntily over one eye. "Stop staring, Dada," he commanded. "You look like a dying fish."

"Sorry, Brother," Kanini mumbled, her eyes dropping. "I shouldn't have slept so late."

"Yes, you would have missed my *nyambura* and then what would you tell the girls at school?" Kanini looked up at his charcoal-smudged face and shrugged. "Anyway, I need you to get us another gourd of *uki*. They're down by the river, keeping cool."

Kanini stumbled down the stony hillside in the semi-darkness, hoping the gourds would be visible in the fading light.

"Where are *you* going?" The sudden, shrill voice nearly caused her to trip. Her little sister, Gatiria, was hurrying to catch up, rubber slippers slapping rhythmically on the hard earth.

"To the river. To get Njagi a gourd of *uki*. Why?"

Gatiria shrugged. "I can't believe *you're* going to fetch it. It's nearly dark. What if the wild dogs get you while you're down there, all alone?"

"So, you think Njagi should get his own *uki*?" Kanini asked.

"Of course. It's his party. He's the one drinking it."

"Yes, well, maybe I thought I'd lend a hand, since it is his big night." Kanini had always liked being helpful, even though it seemed like Njagi was ordering them around more than he used to.

"How'd it go at the butcher's this afternoon?" asked Gatiria, jogging to keep up with Kanini's longer stride.

"Oh, it wasn't so bad," Kanini said. "Njagi was his usual self. Friendly enough as we walked to market, but—"

"But on the way back he wouldn't talk to you."

Kanini nodded.

"Did he help you push the cart?" In the dim light, Kanini could see on her sister's face that she already knew the answer.

"I tried to get him to, but he was too far ahead." Kanini remembered ramming the unwieldy cart through the powdery dirt and crashing into a few stubborn boulders. Thorn bushes had reached out to scrape her legs as she struggled to follow the footprints made by her brother's giant feet.

"He should've helped you. He's the one who wanted two whole goats. I bet it was heavy." Gatiria's voice held more contempt than sympathy.

"It was, but I'm strong, so...it wasn't a problem." Kanini tried to keep her voice light. They had arrived at the river's edge. Kanini spied the large gourds hidden in some rapier grass and hauled one out of the water. She made sure the plug was in tight. Then, heaving the gourd onto her shoulder, she started back up the hill, hoping Gatiria would stop her verbal spewing.

"You shouldn't just keep doing everything he asks, Kanini. He'll treat both of us worse once he's healed from *nyambura*." Gatiria blocked one nostril and blew out of the other. Then she wiped her nose with the back of her hand.

"Don't you have a handkerchief, Gatiria?" asked Kanini. With her spare hand, she tried to pull hers from her pocket.

"Never mind," said Gatiria. Tossing her head, she broke into a run and sprinted the rest of the way up the hill.

The flash of a waving cow tail caught her eye. Kanini noticed the chief of their location flicking the tail about with authority, as the Kenyan statesmen did. One wizened *mzee* had fashioned a hat out of an actual colobus monkey tail. His younger companion carried the horn of a cape buffalo, dripping with ragged fringe and beads.

Mama emerged from the bamboo *riko*– the kitchen hut—and called out to Kanini, as she stooped to swing a load of firewood onto her back. Her mother was a tall, stately woman with thin, hard calves and proud shoulders. Her cheekbones glowed in the firelight as she approached. She set the load of wood down at Kanini's feet and without a word, turned back to the *riko*, where she'd been chopping goat meat.

Kanini set the logs on the fire and the flames leapt and danced, causing more of the men to follow suit. They jutted their pelvises in and out and lurched their shoulders from side to side as the drum kept up its steady pulse. Kanini picked an old scab on one elbow as she watched. It made her a little nervous to see her elders like this, especially when she pictured herself the center of all the attention next year. So sedate and reserved whenever Kanini saw them—usually sipping tea in the marketplace—the men finally had their chance to let loose and become one with the night.

At least only women would be around when it was her turn, she thought with relief.

A pack of the women paraded in with the rising of the moon. Many carried babies on their backs or hips and bore trumplines across their foreheads. These braided ropes held more gourds of the alcoholic *uki* as well as *ucuru*, a fermented millet gruel. Their voices were high-pitched and cheerful. Some joined in the dancing, while others stood by, watching and clapping.

The pulse of the party quickened. A woman trilled loudly, "Ayeeeeeee!" Kanini realized it was the voice of her own grandmother, her *cucu*, who had attended countless circumcision ceremonies.

Shrouded by smoke, Gatiria danced lustily, her bare feet kicking up the dust. She was only nine, but had always been more willing to plunge with abandon into unknown territory. Kanini watched in envy as her sister's lithe, slender form copied the movements of the women, her eyes wide and clear in her pert, egg-shaped face. Kanini looked down at her own body, which was blunt and stocky by comparison. Kanini had muscular arms and hips that were already developing the shape to bear children. She knew the men of her culture admired these traits and she should be satisfied with her build. Why, then, did she often feel so clumsy and awkward within her own body?

The aroma of roasting meat blended with the pungent smell of the smoke. Kanini took refuge with her mother in the *riko* and helped her cook the goat meat on spits over the kitchen fire. She cut them into bite-sized pieces and then carried platters outside to serve the dancers. Most were now quite inebriated. One of her father's cousins grabbed her hands and said, "Come on, Kanini! Next year it'll be your turn!" Kanini backed away, an unexpected tightness gripping her chest. She returned to help Mama prepare more meat.

It was hard to believe most of the adults would stay up all night. Long before dawn, Kanini dragged herself to the main hut and fell asleep on the mat next to Gatiria.

It seemed as though she had barely closed her eyes when the pink glow of daybreak woke her, streaking through the tiny window and across the wall above her head. Now was the time when the circumciser would cut Njagi.

Gatiria's voice was at the door. "Kanini! Hurry! We're going to the *kigiri!*" The *kigiri* was the field that had been sanctified early the day before by the sprinkling of goats' blood. Njagi and Baba had done the task as soon as the goats were slaughtered.

Kanini wobbled to her feet and floundered about for her rubber slippers. Outside, the gray light of morning revealed a vacant compound, strewn with tin cups and empty gourds. A thin wisp of smoke drifted up from the fire pit. Mama was adjusting their little brother, Gitonga, on her back with an assortment of blankets and thin cotton *lesos*, since he was too sleepy to walk. Tying a faded head square over her plaits, Kanini linked her arm in Mama's. The four of them set off for the open field atop the riverbank.

The people of the village had gathered in a huge ring, their chanting reduced to a hoarse croaking by this time. Faces were ashy and drawn. Kanini felt groggy and envied Gatiria's vivacity. It seemed that no matter how little sleep her sister got, Gatiria always had plenty of energy.

Kanini watched the circumciser, the *mutaani*. The *mzee's* face was painted blotchy white, and his tail plume hung in his shadowy eyes as he skulked around inside the circle of people. He brandished his knife for all to see.

Gatiria gasped, "It's *Mwalimu's* father!" The father of Gatiria's teacher. Unsurprised, Kanini did not answer.

Suddenly, a loud shriek drew their eyes toward the river. Outside the ring, Baba and his uncle, Bwana Mkubwa, were escorting Njagi across the stones toward them. His naked form gleamed with sweat or river water, or perhaps both. Kanini looked away, out of shame, imitating some of the other women. Gatiria continued to stare, unabashedly.

When Kanini looked up again, she saw Njagi's writhing form as it was pushed into the ring. He fell to his hands and knees then rose up, leaping and dancing as though possessed by demons. Kanini stared at his face, trying to catch a glimpse of the boy she had known as a child, a boy she knew had all but disappeared.

Baba and Bwana Mkubwa caught Njagi once again and brought him, still twisting and arching, before the circumciser. They forced him to his knees and as he leaned back, Kanini squeezed her eyes shut. She couldn't watch as the knife bit into his flesh.

In the split second that Njagi was cut, the women began fiercely ululating, as all turned and ran shrieking from the scene. Some dragged young children by the hand, while others lugged babies on their backs. Kanini slowed to wait for Cucu. They did not catch up with Mama and Gatiria until they had neared the village. Kanini's heart throbbed, though the walk had not exerted her. She breathed deeply of the already sweltering air.

Women appeared everywhere, their dark faces split with smiles, an odd sense of relief binding them together. Mama ordered cups of *chai* for both Gatiria and Kanini, though the locusts swirling around in Kanini's stomach made it hard to drink.

"How're you doing, Kanini?" Gatiria settled onto her haunches under the shade of a scraggly acacia and slurped her *chai*. Her impish face was cheerful, her dark eyes sparkling.

"I'm all right," Kanini answered, then paused to consider. "Actually, I'm not sure how I am. It made me nervous when I saw Njagi fall before the *mutaani*."

"Really? Njagi wasn't nervous. He didn't make a sound."

"Didn't he? I wouldn't have known," said Kanini, staring through her half empty glass. "The women made such a racket, I had no idea what Njagi was doing."

"I'm sure they'll make at least that much noise next year...at your ceremony."

Kanini winced and darted a look at her sister. Gatiria's gaze bore into her.

"I'm sure they will." Kanini's heart beat harder as she tried to shrug off the familiar shawl of angst. "Too bad you won't be around to hear it. You'll just have to wait for your own."

"My own?" snorted Gatiria. "I don't intend to go through it, Kanini."

Kanini's head had started to throb. Leave it to Gatiria to make this proclamation right after their brother's *nyambura*. She blew her nose and stuffed her handkerchief back in her pocket. "You think you know so much, Gatiria. How can you seriously believe you can get out of being circumcised? What would become of you? Who would marry you?"

"Kanini, I've heard of girls who never recover from circumcision," Gatiria said in a lowered voice. "They bleed to death, or they get infected and die after a few weeks. Even the ones who survive, some die later in childbirth. Haven't you heard the stories? What do I care if no one wants to marry me? I'd rather be a childless old woman than die from *nyambura*!"

Kanini gaped at her sister. How had such a young kid, only in Standard Four, found out such things? She squeezed her eyes shut, trapping the tears that threatened. *I've got to think of something that will scare her about not getting circumcised*, she thought.

"Haven't you heard the story about the girl who refused and ran away?" Kanini blurted. "She was tracked down by her family and killed."

"I never heard that, Kanini! You're making that up!"

"No I'm not! It happened a few years ago. The girl was from over by the Tana River. I remember people in town talking about it for weeks. Her parents were very conservative, more than Baba and Mama, but still... You never know what could happen if you don't follow the traditions, Gatiria."

For once, her sister was quiet. She bit her lip as she stared off into the distance. Kanini felt a tiny insect bite of satisfaction, but she dared not scratch it.

Mama appeared again, fanning her face with her handkerchief. Gitonga was no longer on her back. She leaned against the shady wall of a nearby shop, arms folded in front of her.

"Why did the women all run away like that, Mama?" Gatiria asked. "After Njagi got cut, I mean."

Mama bit her lower lip. "We are leaving the men to welcome Njagi into their circle, Gatiria. He's one of them now. His power has been released. He no longer needs us—mothers and grandmothers, or sisters—in the same way he did before."

Gatiria's face remained serious; a faraway look gleamed in her eyes. "Maybe the women run away because they're scared of the power he has over us. We're worried—now that there's another man around."

Chapter 2

Prior to his circumcision, Kanini had tried to keep out of her brother's way as much as possible. Njagi's moods had fluctuated: excited and upbeat one minute and sullen or quick-tempered the next. When she asked Mama about it, Mama told Kanini that it was because of a job offer Baba had received a few days before. A group of the village men were going to Mombasa for a few weeks to harvest tomatoes; Baba was therefore leaving town the day after Njagi's ceremony. Kanini knew work was in short supply and Baba was desperate for anything. She couldn't imagine worse timing, however.

Without Baba's presence, Njagi would not be able to recuperate in the brand-new hut he'd just finished building on the family compound. Instead, he was obliged to go where there would be other men nearby to care for him. Kanini knew Mama was disappointed that Njagi wouldn't be around, but she secretly felt relieved and knew Gatiria did too. With only women and their four year-old brother on the family compound, life would be fairly placid.

Immediately following *nyambura*, the men escorted Njagi to the compound of Bwana Mkubwa, Baba's wealthy uncle and the sub-chief of the location, where he began the healing process in a vacant hut. His *mugwatani*, or caregiver, was one of Baba's cousins. His job was to help Njagi tend his wound, take food to him and begin instruction on the fine art of becoming a man. Njagi was not to be seen by anyone except this cousin until his *mpumiro*, or "coming out" ceremony, three weeks later.

Mama cooked delicacies, such as rice laced with beef, and carried it to Bwana Mkubwa's place, almost on a daily basis. Once she asked Kanini and Gatiria to walk the pot over instead, and it was such a fine break, that Gatiria clamored to do it every day afterward. "I'd much rather stroll over to Bwana's place than slave in the *munda* all afternoon," she told Kanini. Though they had not yet seen any rain, the change of season had already brought more humidity than they were used to, and planting had become nearly unbearable during the heat of the day.

One evening, Kanini noticed that the red-brown river had risen and was churning along the banks, like roiling *chai*. The rains had started higher up on Kirinyaga, or Mount Kenya, as the *wazungu* called it, and would hopefully move their way soon. Kirinyaga was the home of Ngai, the deity worshipped by the Meru people. Ngai had always had their best interests at heart; He knew their beliefs and desires and their values in life. With the coming of the white missionaries, the Meru were supposed to worship the Christian god, but she knew her elders continued to pray to Ngai. Perhaps, in the end, the two gods were really the same thing. Or perhaps it was because so many had converted to the *mzungu* religion that Ngai had become angry and was no longer sending as much rain.

That night she heard thunder and lightning for the first time in nearly a year. The pounding on the thatched roof made it sound like a heavy dousing, but in the morning, the ground was barely moist outside the hut. Nevertheless, Kanini and Gatiria did not head to the *munda* as usual. While Gatiria took the goats out, Kanini sat with Gitonga outside the *riko*. She watched Cucu for a few minutes as the stooped old woman used a bundle of twigs to sweep the compound—the dust had finally settled due to the rain—then turned to help her little brother scoop together some dirt for building.

"I wish it would rain enough to make lots of mud." Her brother squatted on his plump thighs as he dug, his bare little manhood hovering a few centimeters above the ground.

"If it rained that much, it would be a special gift from Ngai." Kanini added a handful to his little pile. Gitonga got up to look for sticks to make a tiny house.

"Kanini, where does Ngai live?" Gitonga asked suddenly, turning to look at her.

She pointed toward Kirinyaga.

He squinted and gazed at the distant mountain. "It's green at the bottom and silver at the top."

She brushed a fly off her brother's forehead. "That's because Ngai lives in a lovely stone house with a tin roof. The folks in Chuka and Meru live in the green lands at His feet."

"What land do we live in?"

"We live in the brown lands that spread out all around Him."

Gitonga looked thoughtful for a moment. "But our land will turn green when the rains come," he stated.

"Yes, our turn will come soon. The ones who live further up just get the rain first."

"I know," the boy added solemnly. "They must be really special because they live so close to Ngai."

Njagi's *mpumiro* was planned for the Friday before school started. Mama griped because Baba had not yet returned from Mombasa, nor had they even heard from him. The night before the ceremony, Kanini lay awake behind the curtain that divided her sleeping area from Mama's. She could hear muffled sobs coming from Mama's mat and a wave of sympathy washed over her. How she must miss Baba, Kanini thought. And yet, Baba was making money in Mombasa, wasn't he? Why couldn't Mama get some comfort from that?

Kanini got up the next morning, her limbs stiff and sore. She had spent the previous day bent over in the *munda*, weeding the cotton. Back in March, they had planted some of their land in the lucrative cash crop, which Baba said would give them a fine stash of money to send her off to school next year. Cash crops. How much tending they needed! Every weed had to be pulled and periodically, special *dawa* had to be applied. Kanini knew it was an investment for her own education and she was glad it was something they could depend on. This morning she just felt so weary.

Mama sighed as she stoked the fire. She settled a *sufuria* of water over it for gruel. "I can't believe Baba isn't here for this day," she muttered. "It's not right for fathers to be gone when their sons are going through such important rites. Especially first-born sons."

"Maybe Baba will bring home enough money to pay Njagi's school fees," remarked Gatiria, who'd come in with an armload of sticks. She dropped it at Mama's feet. "Then it'll make up for him not being here." Mama picked through the pile, a doubtful expression on her face. She turned back to the fire in silence.

Later, as Kanini ground millet for the *ugali*, she sensed Gatiria's presence behind her. "I know why Mama's so upset that Baba's not here."

"You do! Why is she so upset?" Kanini looked up at her sister, who was toying with a hair pick.

"Njagi told me one day while he was building his house. He said there are all sorts of distractions in Mombasa that might keep Baba from making money." Gatiria gave a furtive glance around.

"Distractions!" exclaimed Kanini. "Like what?"

"Well, there's *miraa*," Gatiria slowly dragged the comb through her short hair and then looked at it to make sure the tines weren't coated with too much grease.

"What's that?"

"It's something the men chew to make them feel good. Some kind of drug. They get it at the clubs where they drink beer and—" She paused and chewed on her lip.

"And?"

"Well, they can buy a woman."

"What do you mean?"

"You know, Kanini. For a man's pleasure."

How did Gatiria know what a man's pleasure was? Kanini barely had any idea herself. "But I thought that was something between a man and his wife."

"I guess these women get so bold they even tempt the married men."

"How do they do that?"

Gatiria shrugged her narrow shoulders and pursed her chapped lips into an O. "I don't know, Kanini. I guess that's their job."

Conflicting thoughts swirled around Kanini's brain. She hardly knew how to respond. "So, you think these things would make Baba forget his family, or...what?"

"I've heard about other men who've never come home."

"Never come home! Gatiria, how can you say such a thing? We're his family! This is his family's land—" Kanini sucked on a knuckle she'd just scraped across the grinding stone. How could Gatiria talk this way, so unaffected, as though nothing Baba did would surprise her? Kanini turned her back on Gatiria's smug look and continued grinding.

The afternoon was windy and hot as Cucu, Mama, Kanini, Gatiria and Gitonga set off for Bwana Mkubwa's compound. Kanini carried the pot of *ugali*, which she balanced on her head with one hand, while Gatiria hauled a gourd of *ucuru* fitted inside a woven *kiondo* on her back. She complained because the bag's rawhide strap chafed her forehead. As they walked, Mama shielded herself and Cucu from the sun with the umbrella. Cucu held Mama's strong arm, while Gitonga ran ahead exploring and jumping in shallow arroyos, shrieking with glee whenever he scared up a lizard or garter snake.

Kanini looked out over their area, so sparsely populated with humans, but so well endowed with rocks, cactus, thorn trees and spindly bushes. The huts that crouched behind their brambled fences blended into the tawny background; only the bright dresses and shirts drying in the sun lent the landscape any color. Kanini's heart was full as she gazed upon the smudge of purple hills melting into the clear blue of the sky. This was her land,

Tharaka, and as tough as it was to eke out an existence here, she knew she would never stray far from it. She had never wanted anything more than to live a quiet life with a family of her own, in a place just like this one. Her only hope was that she and her husband would always have enough food and maybe a little money left over for luxuries, like school fees for the children.

Gatiria's voice pierced the hum of her thoughts. "If Baba were home, would we be hosting the *mpumiro* instead of Bwana Mkubwa?"

"What difference does it make, Gatiria?" snapped Mama. "Baba's not here and we're not hosting it. So, why ask?" Kanini wished her sister would keep her mouth shut; she hated the idea that Gatiria might embarrass her at the ceremony. "Gatiria, at the *mpumiro*, the boys will be behaving like grown-ups," Mama continued. "You should not interact with them or speak to them. Do you understand?"

Gatiria shifted the strap of her *kiondo* so that her gourd of *ucuru* swung precariously on her back. "Yes, Mama," she mumbled.

Friends and relatives had already assembled at Bwana Mkubwa's when they arrived. A parcel of *cucus* greeted Kanini and her family as they entered the compound; Kanini recognized Bwana's older sister and two of his wives. She gravitated over to her cousin, Bahati, a girl her own age, whose name meant "luck" in Swahili. Gatiria followed along, though Kanini ignored her. "Are those the recent initiates?" Gatiria asked Bahati, staring at a clump of boys bunched together next to an enclosure of thorns.

"Yes," said Bahati. "Most of them were initiated last December. They're the ones who'll take Njagi around and show him off."

"Njagi's really going to feel like a big man today," Gatiria mused. Kanini darted a warning look at her.

Njagi did not emerge for many hours. Kanini knew that Bwana Mkubwa and the other male elders were counseling him in the responsibilities that awaited him. These included becoming a leader in the community, the intricacies of courtship and marriage and showing respect for his elders. He would be reminded over and over to never again enter his mother's kitchen or his parents' hut. From now on, he would sleep and be fed in his own hut, alone while he was still young, and by his wife when he later married. Kanini wondered how Mama was coping with the fact that Baba was not present to be part of this counsel.

The girls spent the time playing quietly outside Bahati's parents' hut. Kanini kept an eye on Gitonga who ran in and out and finally lay down and dozed off for a while. She noticed her mother sipping *uki* and wondered if the drink would alter her mood. She was happy to see her able to relax, at least.

"Do you ever think about our own ceremonies next year?" Bahati broke in on her thoughts.

"All the time," Kanini said without hesitation, glad that Gatiria had finally left. "I keep comparing what Njagi went through with what'll happen to us."

Bahati sniffed. "I've heard ours is worse."

"Do you think so?" asked Kanini, her heart pounding. "I've heard they're about the same."

"You probably heard that from a boy. Boys will make you think theirs is just as painful or worse. But we girls must heal for a longer time. After *nyambura*, we can hardly stand. I've heard…I've heard you can lose up to a liter of blood." Bahati continued to toy with a *mzungu* doll she'd dressed in an old head square. The grimy plastic skin was the color of vomit, and one of the blue eyes was missing. Kanini swallowed the bile that had risen into her throat.

Suddenly, Gatiria appeared. "They're bringing Njagi out!" she announced. The older girls hurried to their feet just as the women began to ululate, their voices a shrill warbling that vibrated on the air. Escorted by his caregiver and his agemates, Njagi appeared at the door of the hut he had been healing in for three weeks. The relatives surged towards him; they patted his back, shook his hands and handed him coins and cups of *ucuru*. One person thrust a plate piled high with meat and *ugali* at him.

Kanini and Bahati hung back and watched most of the activity, while Gatiria pushed forward with the grown-ups, poking coins at her brother and trying to grasp his hand. Njagi was taken away by the other initiates to eat in privacy, and the girls didn't see him again. As the crowd dissipated, Gatiria returned to Kanini's side.

"Maybe now that Njagi's a man, we'll get along better," she said, irony peppering her voice. Kanini wished she were serious. Gatiria and Njagi had been known to quarrel like cats. Now that Njagi had been made aware of his manly responsibilities, Kanini hoped he would set a mature example for both Gatiria and Gitonga, especially with Baba away.

Kanini and Gatiria awaited plates heaped high with delicious chicken, greens and *ugali* and ate in a little circle with Bahati and another cousin, Mary, who'd just arrived. By this time, Njagi had already left the compound with the group of boys. They would traverse the area for the next few nights, stopping to eat and relax at the various homes of the newly initiated sons.

After the sun had set, Mama approached them, her mouth set grimly. She indicated without speaking that it was time to leave. After thanking their hosts, they set off. Mama carried a sleepy Gitonga bound to her back; his head lolled about as she walked. Cucu toted the closed umbrella and Kanini and Gatiria their empty vessels. Kanini was happy for the walk home; it felt good to stretch her legs and breathe deep gulps of the sweet evening air.

They were nearly halfway when Mama spoke, her voice so low Kanini could hardly hear it. "I worry about Njagi running with those boys all weekend."

"Kambura, you worry too much," her grandmother answered. "Boys have followed these traditions for hundreds of years. What harm could come?"

"Years ago, boys were not returning to secondary school three days after *mpumiro*. Everything is so rushed these days. I feel like Njagi will hardly have finished healing before he's got to sit in a chair eight hours a day studying. It doesn't seem right." Mama clicked her tongue as she shifted Gitonga's weight inside the *leso*.

"I think the real reason you're troubled is because Kagwima is still gone," Cucu said softly. Mama said nothing, but Kanini could hear her belabored breathing in the still twilight. They walked the rest of the way in silence.

Chapter 3

The first time Kanini got a close look at Njagi was Sunday evening. The sun was casting long shadows as she herded the goats up from the river. As she struggled with the thorn gate, she didn't see him standing behind the scraggly mango tree. He stepped suddenly forward to wrench the gate open. Like fresh milk into a calabash, a grin spilled across his face at her startled look.

"*Ngai*, Njagi, you could give me some warning!" Kanini said, but she couldn't resist returning the smile. She was surprised at how her brother had actually grown in just the past few weeks. He was taller and knotty muscles had appeared in his forearms and thighs, where before only bones had been visible. The recent lengthening of his face emphasized the fine planes of his cheekbones and chin. His hair was closely cropped and looked smart, unlike the nappy look he'd sported before *nyambura*.

"Where's Mama?" Njagi asked, as he followed Kanini into the compound and closed the gate behind them.

"Just there," Kanini pointed at the *riko* with her pursed lips.

Everyone burst from different areas of the compound—Mama from the *riko*, Gatiria from the goat pen, Gitonga from the tiny chicken hut, high on its stilts, where he'd just discovered an egg and Cucu from her mangy little hut, squeezed between the main hut and the bamboo shed where tools were kept.They shook Njagi's hands and patted his shoulders. Njagi held his head high, enjoying the attention. "Good news, Mama," he proclaimed. "Bwana Mkuu has given me the money for next term. No being expelled to come home and search for money. I have it here in my pocket!"

Mama beamed—a rare occurrence. "What a wonderful circumcision gift, my son. That money will be a lifesaver. We haven't heard from Baba—"

Kanini's quick glance caught the fading of her mother's smile.

The next day saw Njagi leaving on an early morning *matatu*, his trunk and slender mattress slung on top of the covered pick-up and lashed down with rope. His boarding school, Karamugi Secondary, was twenty kilometers up the mountain, past the town of Chuka and nestled in the coffee groves of a village called Chera. They would not see him again until the term was over in August.

The first day of primary school dawned like any other for Gatiria and Kanini. Pale watery sunlight seeped through the space between the roof and the walls and penetrated Kanini's sleeping brain. Her sister was already up and washed. Kanini could see her shedding her faded rag dress and donning her aqua-colored school uniform, now almost too small.

"Miss Lazy, you need to be waking up!" Gatiria commanded in *Kizungu*, the white people's language, which always jarred Kanini's senses at first. "*Mwalimu* Mugambi will be angry with you for your lateness."

Kanini dragged herself up without a word and pulled her faded blue uniform from the line of clothes where she had tossed it nearly a month ago. She put it on and pushed her way out the door into the sunlight. Adding some sticks to the fire in the *riko*, she blew the ash from the flickering embers. Before long she had a *sufuria* of water settled over the fire for their morning *uji*.

The girls sat on their usual stones, sipping the hot gruel, saying little. Kanini scanned the distant horizon, where the purple hills had begun the morning begging the cloudless sky for more rain. She watched as Mama entered the compound with a *mtungi* of water on her back. "Kanini! Gatiria! You're going to be late!" She set her jug down and clapped her hands in their faces. Dropping their cups with a clatter, they dusted off their skirts, grabbed their exercise books and pens and hurried down the path.

From a distance their primary school appeared to be an enormous mud brick, covered with an ailing roof of fluttering tin. As they got closer, Kanini was not surprised to see that the gaping holes in the walls had not been fixed as the headmaster had promised. The kids on the field were bouncing figures of turquoise on pencil-thin legs. Gatiria joined a game of tag, while Kanini looked around for her friends. She found Kagere and Mukami and sat down beside them in the shade of the school wall.

"How is your vacation, Kanini?" Mukami asked in her stiff English.

"*Was* your vacation, stupid!" said Kagere with a short laugh.

"It was fine," replied Kanini, looking from one to the other.

"Now your brother is circumcised, isn't it?" asked Mukami. Kanini nodded. "My cousin will go next year."

"My brother in two years," added Kagere.

Kanini drew a deep breath before asking, "And what about yourselves? Are you not going for circumcision next year?" She felt her heart beat faster. This was the first time she had brought the subject up with her friends.

Mukami nodded, staring at the ground. Her eyelids, ruffled in thick lashes, gleamed like dark pearls in the morning light, and the soft shadows accentuated the curve of her cheek and the fullness of her lips. *Mukami has grown even prettier over vacation*, Kanini thought. Not having glimpsed an image of herself in months, she wondered fleetingly what she looked like now. Both she and Kagere had much darker skin than Mukami, which many Bantu people deemed less attractive than the lighter skin. Kanini knew her eyes were striking, though her lashes were nowhere as thick as Mukami's. Maybe her nose had become more prominent; it had always been her worst feature. If she were invited to Kagere's house again, where a mirror hung on one wall, she would be able to see for herself.

Kagere spoke up with a hint of superiority. "Circumcised? We girls? That is a barbaric custom, only practiced by uneducated types. I will not be done that way."

Mukami looked over and Kanini met her eyes. The girls knew that Kagere's kinsfolk came from the Chuka area, up the mountain. Though also of the Meru tribe, they considered themselves superior to the Tharaka people, who literally lived beneath them at the lower elevation. Kagere had never resided near Chuka—her mother had married a man from Tharaka and moved down there—but her mother's people had influenced her with their beliefs.

"Do you not know it is illegal to circumcise girls? Illegal!" Kagere emphasized. Kanini and Mukami both stared at the ground. Out in the bush, where they lived, the arm of the law rarely penetrated. Traditions continued much the same as they had for thousands of years.

"But it is our way—" Kanini began.

"Your way is the way of barbarians!" blurted Kagere, just as the headmaster rang his brass bell. The girls stood up and went to join the line of standard seven students. They filed into their room and sat solemnly at their tables.

Throughout the rest of the morning, Kanini felt the same heavy feeling of foreboding she had felt so often over the past month. She and Kagere did not speak again, but a few times she saw the girl cast looks of contempt her way. Maybe she would not be invited to Kagere's place anymore.

After school, Kanini avoided Kagere and sought out Mukami. They walked home together, ahead of Gatiria. At first, they said nothing. Finally Mukami spoke.

"Why does it bother you what Kagere says? She's always considered herself superior to us. So she believes circumcision for girls is wrong. Maybe for her, but not for us. Who would want to marry us if we weren't circumcised?"

"Do you think Kagere will find someone to marry, even if she stays uncircumcised?"

"Maybe, but not from around here. The men from other areas aren't so choosy about their wives." Mukami reached down to pull a thorn from the heel of her rubber slipper.

"But if circumcision is really illegal in Kenya, don't you think some men will worry about marrying a circumcised woman?" asked Kanini.

Mukami looked at Kanini uncertainly. "I'm not sure. I don't think that'll happen for a long time, maybe not until our children are grown. You know how it is to stay uncircumcised, Kanini. Remember that girl from—I don't remember where—who was never circumcised, and she ran around in the bush, going with any boy who asked her?" Mukami's pretty eyes glittered as she spoke. "She had two babies before she was seventeen, and *no one* would marry her after that! Getting circumcised keeps you acting more...proper. It's better like that."

Kanini wondered if Mukami had heard of the girl who'd been hunted down after refusing circumcision, but decided not to bring it up. "So, maybe Kagere will have to move to Chuka if she wants to stay uncircumcised," Kanini mused. "She might get into trouble if she sticks around here."

Mukami nodded, a grim look on her face. She turned off onto the path that led to her place. "See you tomorrow, Kanini."

Kanini waved good-bye and waded the rest of the way home through the ruddy dust.

Chapter 4

The rainy season did not last long. After two or three weeks of intermittent cloudbursts, thunderheads hovered over Kirinyaga for a few days and then disappeared altogether. Only the mosquitoes continued their nightly attacks, a lingering reminder of the wet season that had come and gone so quickly.

Cucu came down with a bad case of malaria and lay moaning on her mattress for more than a week. Kanini brought back chloroquine from the dispensary, but it didn't seem to help. Finally, Mama and Gitonga took her by *matatu* to the clinic at Ishiara, the nearby market town. At the clinic, they were told to hang mosquito nets over all their beds, especially the beds of Cucu and Gitonga. They could purchase the nets in town for fifty shillings apiece.

Mama just rolled her eyes. How she wished they could cover all their beds with mosquito nets! To do so would require beds, first of all, since everyone but Cucu slept on woven mats on the floor. They would have to sell their entire herd of goats. Mama did return to Ishiara a week later to sell a few chickens in order to purchase a net for Cucu. After receiving an injection at the clinic and sleeping for a few nights under the net's protection, their grandmother improved.

At the end of May, Kanini brought home a letter from Baba, picked up at the market place. Mama, Cucu and Gatiria gathered around to hear her read it.

"'My family'," Kanini began. "'I am writing to report that I am out of money and can no longer remain in Mombasa. The tomato harvest has not been as good as we hoped. Staying here costs too much, most of what I have earned. At least I have not gone into debt. I will be home by the start of June. Regards, Kagwima'."

When Kanini finished reading, she noticed a glistening in Mama's eyes. For a few moments the only sound was of breathing. When Gatiria spoke up, her voice was brittle. "So, Baba went all the way to Mombasa for work and he's not returning with anything? He could've stayed here and helped us! He could have gone to Njagi's—"

Mama's hand shot out and slapped Gatiria's cheek. "Get out, Gatiria! Take the goats and go! And don't come back till sundown!" Gatiria scurried off, leaving a vacuum of quiet, a hollow shell that continued to echo with Mama's words.

June arrived and brought the cool season with it. After school these days, Mama sent Kanini and Gatiria out to harvest what they could of the *munda*. The cowpeas had not fared well, nor had most of the mung beans, or "green grams" as they were called. Millet and sorghum had done all right as well as a little maize, which had been planted in a lower area. This food would have to last until at least November or December when the next rainy season came.

Baba arrived home, no longer his old easygoing self. From the start he seemed defensive and tense. Kanini often heard her parents arguing even more viciously than the previous year when the drought had been one of the worst in Kenya's history.

One night after everyone was in bed, Kanini lay awake listening to their voices hissing back and forth from the other side of the curtain.

"You know the reality, Kambura. I am uneducated. No one wants to hire me. There are thousands of men in my situation. What should we do? Compete for jobs with Form Four and Form Six leavers?"

"Of course you can't compete, Kagwima," Mama said. "But there are many jobs those educated ones will not do. What about road building? That cousin of mine was making twelve shillings a day working on the Chuka road. For over two years he never went without wages."

"Where is the road that needs building now, Kambura? I saw one near Mombasa, but where would I stay? Just to rent a small place costs one hundred-something a month. That leaves very little."

"Well, we have to do something. The children are growing. They have more needs than before. I want them to continue their schooling. Maybe we could raise more chickens..." As Mama's voice trailed off, Kanini heard some scuffling noises. Baba was moving restlessly about.

"You don't really understand how good we have it here, Kambura. At least we own our home and our land. Our children aren't begging on the streets. You would not believe the hunger in Mombasa. Whole families living in tiny shacks in slums or right on the street, with nothing."

"I know our life is better than some. But what will we eat once this small amount of *unga* and *nthoroko* runs out?"

There was silence for a moment. Then Baba whispered hoarsely, "We'll be eating whatever cotton money is left after paying Njagi's fees."

Eat the cotton money! Tears burned behind Kanini's eyelids and she scratched hard at her hardened callouses, hoping one would pop open and bleed so she could truly feel sorry for herself. That cotton money was to pay for *her* school fees next year! What to do? She would work as hard as possible. She would pass the Certificate of Primary Education, the CPE, as well as she could, even better than Njagi had. Maybe she would be called to attend a government-sponsored school, which wouldn't require as much tuition. Inside, however, she knew that students at these schools still needed money for various expenses, and if her family had none, there was no school to which she could go.

The next morning, Kanini donned an old cardigan Cucu had knit her before her eyesight gave out and joined Mukami on the path to school. The girls walked in silence for a few moments before Kanini felt her friend's eyes scanning her with questions.

Kanini took a deep breath. "So...I found out last night that I won't be going to secondary."

"Really?" Mukami grasped Kanini's hand and squeezed it. "I'm sorry, Kanini. I know how you've been looking forward to going."

Kanini blinked tears away. "I still want to go, but....Baba and Mama can't afford it."

"What about all that cotton you're growing?"

"It won't bring enough money. Just enough for expenses and Njagi's fees for third term. Even if we sell all the goats, which we could never... There's just no way."

Arriving at the schoolyard, they noticed Kagere talking with another girl. Kagere's uniform was neither too tight nor faded to a nondescript color, like Kanini's was. Shiny leather shoes adorned her feet. "I suppose Kagere will be going to secondary," Mukami murmured, reading Kanini's mind as she often did.

"Oh sure," answered Kanini. "She's always planned to go. Her grandparents have that coffee plantation up the mountain, remember? Coffee doesn't bring a lot of money either, but a bag of coffee beans sure weighs more than a bag of cotton!"

"Well, you and I can have our *nyambura* at the same time, and we can celebrate together afterward," Mukami said in a voice Kanini knew was supposed to sound comforting.

A chilly wind blew through the thin fabric of Kanini's uniform. She removed her hand from her friend's grasp and clutched her sweater around her, the better to keep out the cold.

The next month brought exam preparation for the pupils in standard seven. These "mock exams", as they were called, were to prepare them for the actual CPE exam to be taken at the end of third term.

"Are you nervous about mocks, Kanini?" Mukami asked Kanini one day on the way home.

Kanini shrugged, attempting nonchalance. "I don't know. I do care about them, but what does it matter if I do well or not? I'm not going to secondary anyway."

"Well, what if you get a sponsor or your uncle finds some money to send you? You'd feel bad if you didn't put out much effort."

"I wish there was a possibility of that," Kanini sighed. "I feel like if I study for CPE it'll just wear me out so much I won't be able to plant and weed and harvest. Baba will probably get annoyed with me since I'm not working hard enough, and it'll all be for nothing."

Mukami nodded. "I'm not going to study myself. I'll just do as well as I can. There's too much work to do at home." Kanini felt a pang of sympathy for her friend. Mukami's mother was her father's second wife. Her father was much older, having married his first wife a long time ago. Now, his original children were grown up, his first wife was dead, and he was ill with tuberculosis and needed constant attention. Mukami, her mother and older sister were obliged to wait on him constantly.

"So neither of us will study then," Kanini said. She felt more of a sense of solidarity with her friend when discussing the CPE than when discussing *nyambura*.

Due to Kithinge being a poor country school, there was no secretary to type up and duplicate the mock exams. Thus, the teachers simply copied the questions onto the peeling blackboard and the students wrote out the answers in their exercise books. The teachers proctored their own classes, walking around the crowded classrooms of forty to fifty pupils to make sure no one cheated. This process took nearly two weeks to complete.

Kanini had not studied much, but she did well. Flushed with excitement, she brought her results home to show her parents. Mama looked them over, a flat expression on her face. Without speaking, she passed them over to Cucu, who, despite her fading eyesight, grinned toothlessly in recognition.

"Kanini will be the smartest girl at secondary next year!" sang Gatiria after looking over Cucu's shoulder at the paper. "Kanini, which secondary do you want to go to?"

A hush dropped over them with the grip of a shroud. Gatiria looked at Kanini and then at Mama. Kanini glanced past Cucu toward the light coming in the doorway.

"Perhaps if the crops do better, Kanini can attend secondary the following year," said Mama, staring down at the slip of paper.

Gatiria gaped at Kanini. After a pause she stated, "You knew you weren't going, didn't you, Kanini?"

Kanini nodded. "I knew there wasn't any way this year."

Later that evening, Baba passed her outside the hut, as he returned from checking on the goats. Although it was too dark to see, she could hear his hoarse whisper. "*Yajayo yapokee.*" Accept what comes. Kanini bowed her head and ducked inside.

Chapter 5

A heat wave ushered in the August holiday. During the afternoons, everyone remained under a roof or in the shade of a tree. Eight months after beginning to build his hut, Njagi was finally able to reside there. He moved his things in with great fanfare and made no secret that he was the second lord of the manor.

Kanini regularly did his bidding without question, while Gatiria often sparred with him, especially if she was tending Gitonga or taking the goats out. "Get your own *chai*!" or "I don't know where your rubber slippers are! Find them yourself!" she would bellow, as she continued with whatever she was doing. Mama appeared more tired than usual; thus it didn't surprise Kanini when she rarely intervened.

One evening Kanini returned from the river to hear Njagi and Gatiria engaged in an especially heated quarrel.

"All you do is sit around all day and eat the food that we cook, and then you tell me that I don't do enough for you!" Gatiria stood akimbo; her ragged dress torn at the waist. "Why don't you take care of yourself and leave us alone?"

"It's your job to do as I say! You're a younger sister. Have you never been taught that?" Njagi retorted. "And believe me, I do plenty around here. Who was it that mended the fence yesterday? And who went for firewood this morning, though it isn't a man's job?"

"Well, then it's a good job for you since you are not a man!"

Kanini breathed in sharply and glanced at Njagi. He looked as if he might strike Gatiria. Instead, he grimaced and backed away, realizing in time that it would be beneath him to hit his sister.

Mama passed them, coming from the *riko* with a steaming pot of vegetables mixed with goat meat, one of Kanini's favorites. She tsk-ed at them to stop squabbling.

"Is something special happening tonight, Mama?" asked Kanini.

"We have a guest coming for supper," Mama said.

"Who is it?" asked Gatiria.

"Your Aunt Njeri," Mama said with a sigh.

Kanini looked up at her mother. Her face was impassive, the lines around her eyes more pronounced than usual. Kanini hurried over to the large clay jar, which held drinking water, and dipped the pitcher in.

Gatiria's face lit up. "Why didn't you tell us! How long will she be here? Is she coming with the cousins?"

"I only just found out. All I know is that she's had some bad luck." The children fell silent and stared at Mama, but she would disclose nothing more. She set the pot of food down on the table outside the main hut and returned to the *riko*.

The previous air of dissent changed to one of pensive silence. Even Gitonga ceased his prattling by the corner of the hut. Baba soon arrived, accompanied by Njeri, whom he had met getting off the *matatu* in the marketplace.

Kanini couldn't even remember the last time they'd seen Njeri. She looked tired; her face was drawn and creased and her arms and neck were thinner than Kanini remembered. She was their mother's younger sister and had married relatively late. She now had two young children and her rounded belly bespoke another on the way. Kanini knew not to mention her condition and hoped Gatiria knew enough as well.

Everyone took a turn to grasp Njeri's hands in greeting and ask about her general state of health, as well as that of her children. Baba settled her onto a chair outside the *riko*, and Kanini went inside to help Mama fill the plates with food. Gitonga carried them out and passed one to each person, while Gatiria lit the lamp and set it in the center of the table.

"So, how was your harvest last season, Njeri?" asked Mama, perched on the edge of her seat.

"It was all right. Not as good as we've had, but nothing like last year." Njeri lifted her spoon and took a tiny bite from her plate. "How was yours, Kambura?"

"Worse than I expected," Mama told her. "We planted the traditional crops, but a lot of them failed."

Njeri shook her head and tsk-ed her tongue, like Mama always did. "I brought you a bag of beans," she told them. "I'd grind your millet for you if you'd give me a little to take back to our place. The children do love *ucuru*."

"Of course. We always have enough for you, Njeri." Mama smiled. "And how is your mother-in-law? Is she still in good health?"

"She's doing very well for a woman of her age. Watching the children for me right now, in fact. She's been very understanding during our...our trouble." Njeri cast her head down.

Kanini got up to stoke the fire in the *riko*. She filled a *sufuria* with water for *chai*.

When she returned outside, Njeri was continuing. "—a disease that was brought over by the American sailors who landed in Mombasa and went with prostitutes. Now, it's passed to anyone who happens to be around these *wazungu*. Mugendi was staying with friends in one of the neighborhoods. Any of them could have gotten the disease from an American or even a prostitute who went with an American. It isn't known."

"I heard something about this while I was in Mombasa. I never really understood it," said Baba shaking his head.

"How is the disease passed?" asked Njagi with interest.

"The Americans have the germs and they contaminate everyone they come in contact with. You can get it from their clothing or by eating a meal with them. Even if you eat a meal in the same place they just were. It's spread very easily, like cholera, only without the flies."

"Do you get sick right away, like with cholera?" asked Gatiria.

"Sometimes," said Njeri. "Other times you can go for a long time, not knowing you have it. Then you get sick and die within a month or two. That's what happened to my Mugendi."

Kanini stopped cold and locked eyes with Gatiria. Their aunt's husband! Dead!

Baba tsk-ed his tongue gravely. Mama shook her head and placed a hand on her sister's arm. "Mugendi was a good man. He helped out all the time and brought home money when he could. It'll be difficult to do without him."

Grim silence permeated the darkness. The lamp sent a spray of dim light onto Njeri's face, which now gleamed with tears.

"Didn't Mugendi have a brother?" asked Baba.

Njeri visibly cringed. "Yes and he's horrible, even though he's a prosperous businessman. He's a drunkard and a womanizer, who leaves the family for long periods to go to Meru and Nairobi. His wife has lost at least two children, either before birth or right afterward, because she's overworked and anxious. It's an awful situation."

"They live right there near you, don't they?" asked Mama.

"Yes. Just down the road."

"Do you think he would try to claim you as inheritance?" Baba's voice was nearly inaudible. Kanini didn't know whether she'd heard him right. The whole compound seemed to hold its breath as a fresh breeze stirred the acacia branches. Kanini scratched at a scab on the back of her hand.

Njeri took another bite of food, which Kanini was sure had long grown cold. "That's my fear. I wanted to ask you if I could stay with you all for a time."

Kanini looked up and caught Mama's eye. "Kanini, you and Gatiria take Gitonga to bed, will you?"

Kanini tried to sleep, but the drone of the conversation creeping into the hut kept her awake a long time. Unable to understand the adults' words, she willed herself to sleep, the sooner to wake up and ask in the morning.

After breakfast the next day, Mama, Kanini and Gatiria headed to the river together. Mama walked between them, her arms linked in both of her daughters'. Their jerry cans and gourds swung from their backs.

"Have you ever heard of the sickness Mugendi had?" Kanini asked Mama.

She shook her head. "No one seems to understand what it is. It sounds like the *wazungu* have brought us a new disease."

"The *wazungu* are the white people, aren't they, Mama?" asked Gatiria.

Mama nodded. "They're everywhere nowadays, not only in the White Highlands, like they were before we gained independence. Though at least they don't own all the best land like they did back then." Kanini had studied this history in school. That was back at the time of the Mau Mau rebellions, in the 1950's, when Mama was a girl.

"Baba says the *wazungu* in the navy go to Mombasa to rest after being out at sea," Kanini added, as they descended into the valley.

"That's true," Mama agreed. "There aren't many other African ports where the Americans are welcome."

No one spoke for a few moments. The surrounding hills had cast them into shadow and a bird piped a lively song.

"What did Baba mean by 'inheritance'?" asked Gatiria.

"Wife inheritance is not usually practiced in our area, but it is legal," Mama explained. "If a man dies, his wife and children need to stay with her husband's family, since they paid the bride price. Inheritance happens when one of the man's brothers claims the widow as his own wife. It's a way to care for and protect single women, and to keep the children in the family." Kanini looked at Mama's face to see whether she approved of this custom or not. Neither her neutral tone nor her countenance gave her opinion away.

"But Mugendi's brother is such a horrible man! She shouldn't have to marry someone like that if she doesn't want to!" Gatiria was indignant.

Mama stopped walking and faced the girls, hands on hips. "Well, I guess he's quite a successful businessman. If he chooses to claim her, there's nothing we can do. Our hope is that if she lives with us for a time, he'll forget about her and she can go on living with Mugendi's parents, where she's lived all these years. She likes it there."

Kanini said nothing. She felt immense sympathy for Njeri and her plight, but she also wondered how she and her children would be able to share their own small space. And for how long? Her thoughts shamed her. It was not their custom to turn away a close relative in need, even if it meant further hardship for their own family.

"I think our people are very backward," Gatiria was saying. "Why should a woman marry a man who would mistreat her? And why couldn't that man's first wife leave him, since she's already being mistreated? It isn't fair."

"Why do you question so much, Gatiria? It is our way. You would do well to accept it," breathed Mama, who, Kanini knew, was trying to stay calm. Why did Gatiria always spout off so brazenly? Kanini tried to catch her eye as they trudged the last few meters to the river, but Gatiria never looked her way.

When they returned to the compound, they found Baba and Njagi working on Cucu's hut, which had been falling apart for many years. Blocks of dried mud had come out from between the bamboo poles and the roof was patchy, like the hair of a child with kwashiorkor. It was about time Baba fixed his mother's hut, Kanini thought.

"If you and Gatiria are going to sleep here with Cucu, we have to get this place reinforced," Baba told them with a grin.

"We're going to sleep with Cucu?" asked Gatiria, glancing at Kanini. Kanini shrugged and pursed her lips together. Once again, she hoped Gatiria would get the message to keep her mouth shut before she caused all of them to lose face.

Within a week, Cucu's hut was in more or less proper condition and Gatiria and Kanini moved in. The hut was small, hardly big enough for their three sleeping bodies, let alone the clothes that they draped over a string tied across one corner. Kanini was especially nervous about the rickety way the walls did not solidly meet the ground, since snakes, scorpions and other vermin could easily crawl in while they were sleeping. It was one thing for Cucu to sleep there: she slept on a bed swathed in a mosquito net. But Kanini and Gatiria would be sleeping directly on the ground atop their woven mats. When she voiced her concern to Baba, he told her not to worry; he would fashion better walls as soon as everyone was settled. Besides, hadn't Cucu slept here for years without any troubles? Except malaria, of course, and mosquitoes would still be able to get in even after the walls were repaired. His words did nothing to reassure her.

Settling in took longer than anyone thought it would. Njeri returned later that week with her children, Silvia and Zacharia, two wide-eyed tots who cried every night until their mother could lull them to sleep. During the daylight hours, Njeri tried to help Mama with the housework, but her children demanded all her attention. By comparison, Kanini was amazed at how mature five year-old Gitonga acted. He took Zacharia on excursions into the bush and shared his few homemade toys with both his cousins. Meanwhile, Mama took up most of the slack, since Njagi, Kanini and Gatiria were soon headed back to school for the final term of the year.

They had been back just a few weeks when Njeri went into labor. When Kanini and Gatiria got home on that September day, Mama met them outside the thorn fence, a load of firewood on her back.

"Where's Njeri?" asked Kanini, burning to tell her aunt something she'd learned during science class. Unlike Mama, Njeri had finished primary school and was often willing to discuss the day's lessons and help Kanini with her homework.

"Njeri's gone into the bush to have her baby," Mama stated, her face stony.

"I thought she still had more than a month to go," said Gatiria, looking Mama in the eye.

"She did. I'm not sure she'll be all right."

"Did she ask you to go with her?" Kanini was unsure how much she felt comfortable asking.

"I tried to accompany her. I told her you girls would care for the children and start supper. But she told me not to bother about her. This is how she gave birth to the others as well. I have to respect her way, though it's hard for me to understand."

Kanini knew that Mama had welcomed other women to assist her in giving birth. She remembered when Gitonga was born. She and Njagi had been walking home from school when Baba had met them on the road, little Gatiria clutching his fingers. He had taken them all to Bwana

Mkubwa's place where they spent the night. Mama had greeted them the next morning with tiny Gitonga curled up in her arms, surrounded by the smiling faces of Njeri and Cucu.

Baba was not home yet and all the children except Kanini were in bed when Njeri came back late that night. She carried a tiny mite of a baby girl, shriveled and purplish gray, wrapped in a hand-crocheted blanket. The baby didn't resemble a living creature, though her heart seemed to be beating solidly. Mama put her sister to bed with a banana leaf soaked in herbs for her private area. She then took the baby to her own lap, holding and comforting the pathetic creature, as the baby grimaced and whimpered. Kanini stayed up and did what little she could to make Mama comfortable. She brought her pillows and made her a cup of *chai*. Finally, Mama bid Kanini good night and brought the baby to her own mat, curling her strong body around the cocoon that was her niece.

Njeri could not nurse the baby, as the baby's suck wasn't strong enough. So, for the next few days she spent hours squeezing first colostrum and then pale milk from her breast by hand into a little bowl. Mama would then feed the baby from a dropper they obtained from the dispensary. In this painstaking way, they kept little Carolina alive.

Though she didn't admit it, Kanini was glad to get away to school every morning, even though by lunchtime she and Gatiria came home to the lion's share of tasks. One would fetch wood and stoke the fire while the other would clean the messy hut and take over cooking. If no one had taken out the goats, they would herd them down to the river where Kanini would fill a *mtungi* with water and haul it back up to start a load of clothes soaking. Sometimes they would just stay at the river and wash the clothes there, laying them out over rocks and thorn bushes to dry. This was the way many of the local women, those who lived too far to haul so much water, washed clothes. There was nearly always a sizeable group down at the water's edge, chattering like birds.

Kanini told Gatiria, "If I was on the road to doing well on the CPE last term, there's no way I can do well now."

"*Sawa sawa*," said Gatiria in agreement. "You know what Baba would say, Kanini. '*Elimu ni maisha, si vitabu*'. Learning is in life, not books."

"I wonder what I'm learning beating these ragged clothes on the rocks and gathering firewood everyday," mused Kanini.

Early one morning, screams from Gatiria's side of the hut stormed in on Kanini's dreams. As she struggled to open her eyes, she made out the form of a scorpion perched on a heap of clothes near their mats, just a few centimeters from Gatiria's face. Cucu was stirring in her mosquito net; Kanini could see the wrinkled pink bottoms of her feet, sticking out over her mattress. She reached over to grab the garment on which the creature perched, but within a split second, it had scuttled away.

A hubbub was beginning in the next hut, as one of the younger children started to cry. Then the muffled whimpering of the baby.

Baba appeared at the door of their shack, wearing only a cloth wrapped around his waist. "What's going on?" His voice was gruff and irritated.

"A scorpion!" breathed Gatiria, sitting up and pulling her *leso* around her. "It could've stung me in the face, Baba!"

"Only a scorpion?" growled Baba. "From all that noise, I thought it was a black mamba. Learn to control yourself, Gatiria."

Gatiria paid him no mind. She tore through the pile of clothes and covers in search of the murderous crustacean. When she couldn't find it, she scampered out of the hut on her bare feet, the *leso* her only garment. Kanini woke Cucu and helped her into her rubber slippers. Then she wrapped a woolen blanket around her grandmother and escorted her outside.

Baba returned hours later with tools and materials to add substance to their walls. The task took him a few days since he didn't work continuously. He took long breaks at the market, claiming that the stress of working among so many women and children was driving him mad. On the final day, everyone helped to slap mud on the bamboo framing and chicken wire. Finally the walls of the hut met the ground solidly, and Kanini and Gatiria felt secure sleeping on their mats in their grandmother's hut.

Chapter 6

By the end of October, they started looking forward to the rains coming again. The crops were all planted: cowpeas, green grams, sorghum and millet. The biggest chore now was weeding, something Kanini usually did without complaint. This year, however, she was exhausted by the extra housework as well as studying for the CPE.

Carolina was now nursing steadily and had begun to grow. All agreed that she would likely survive. She shared her mother's milk with her fussy sister, Sylvia, who, though she was two years old, ate very little solid food. Njeri looked haggard. Nevertheless, she had refused the pleas of the nurse at the dispensary to supplement her milk supply with Lactogen, a powdered milk product sold at the market.

"They just want me to get used to using that product," she told Mama. "Then, after my own milk has dried up, I'll be forced to continue buying it, even if I'm completely out of money." Kanini took her words to heart. She herself had wondered about the milk and cereal supplements she saw on the shelves of the small shops in their town. Who in their community could afford such luxuries?

Then one day Njeri received a letter from Aniceta, her mother-in-law, with the news that her father-in-law had died. Would she attend the funeral? Njeri debated taking only the infant and returning as soon as possible. Then she changed her mind.

"I feel like it's time for all of us to return home. I've heard nothing from my brother-in-law or anyone else that makes me think he would force me to marry him. If I find out otherwise when I get there, I'll turn right around and come back here."

Mama begged Njeri to think it over carefully. It had only been a few months. What if Mugendi's brother was just now coming down from a drunken state and realizing that she could potentially be his second wife? Hadn't he often boasted that he wanted one? Njeri would arrive for her father-in-law's funeral, her brother-in-law would be there, and he would waste no time forcing the inheritance.

Njeri argued that she couldn't just avoid the funeral, especially when a letter had been sent requesting her to attend. She and Mama went round and round discussing the issue. In the end, Njeri decided to proceed with her original plan and return with all her things, including the children.

It was the beginning of November, the week before the CPE exam. Kanini and Gatiria waved good-bye to their aunt and cousins before heading off to school. Despite her concern about her aunt's plight, Kanini's heart felt light as they meandered down the path.

"It's a relief that they're leaving, isn't it?" asked Gatiria, putting into words what Kanini was thinking, as she so often did. "I love Njeri and her kids, but it's hard with everyone around all the time."

"I hope nothing bad happens to Njeri," mused Kanini. "I'd really feel terrible if she had more bad luck."

"Well, as Mama says, '*yakungesha haina wingu*'. What is fated to happen will happen. There's really nothing we can do about it, is there?"

Kanini stared at Gatiria. Was she just spouting Mama and Baba's philosophy in order to placate her family? Or was she actually coming around to their parents' way of thinking? It certainly wasn't like Gatiria to preach proverbs that touted compliance and acceptance.

The CPE exam was given over the course of the next week and a half. Everyday the invigilators, teachers from neighboring schools, would arrive and proctor the tests that the pupils labored over for hours. Kanini and Mukami were glad that primary school only comprised five hours of everyday. Any more time spent test-taking would have completely numbed their brains.

Kanini was confident that she did well on the exam. She would not get the results for months—well into the next year—and by then, secondary school would have begun. For some, but not for her. She tried not to think about it; instead, she tried to dwell on how lucky she was. Lucky to have loving parents, enough food and no one misusing their funds or drinking what little money they had.

She couldn't help glancing periodically over at Kagere while they sat in class, however. The fact that her former friend would attend secondary was enviable in itself. But the confidence she exuded, despite not planning to participate in their traditional rite of passage, caused a crackling in Kanini's heart.

It wasn't that she, Kanini, didn't want to participate in the circumcision rite. Despite the disquiet she often felt whenever it entered her mind, she knew she *should* want to go through with it. How would she feel like a part of her community if she didn't? It was just that Kagere had been given an alternative, while it was taken for granted that Kanini would bow to tradition and undergo what all other Tharakan women had undergone throughout time. For Kanini, there was no choice. She was obligated, whether she liked it or not, to go through with the ceremony. To follow in the footsteps of those who had gone before her.

One afternoon, as Gatiria and Kanini were heading out to search for firewood, Kanini broke open the store of thoughts she'd been keeping to herself.

"I've been thinking...I know circumcision is still a tradition and everything..." Her sister was staring at her as they hiked along, *pangas* in hand, trumplines over their shoulders. "But, like we've talked about before... it seems like the tradition is fading away, sort of like the facial scarring they used to do..." It was hard to reveal what she'd been considering, especially with Gatiria's smug attitude in her face. She breathed deeply, summoning up the nerve to actually put into words what had been pounding around in her head for so many weeks. "Anyway, I'm trying to figure out...how I can get out of it."

"What?" Gatiria exclaimed. "After all this, you want to get out of it? I thought you were excited about it; you couldn't wait."

"I thought I was excited about it, last year, maybe. When Njagi was first planning his." Kanini stared off at the distant hills, hardly seeing them. "Then...I started really thinking about it...and hearing about how common it's become not to have it done at all. At first, I wondered how those uncircumcised girls would be able to find husbands. But really, there are men who'd want to marry one. Maybe not around here—"

"Finally you're talking sensibly," stated Gatiria. "I wondered when you'd figure out what a stupid old-fashioned custom *nyambura* is and stop defending it all the time."

Kanini sighed and stopped to hack at a dead bush with the *panga*. "Stupid and old-fashioned maybe, but Mama and Baba still believe in it and they're not going to let me get out of it. Not unless I have a really good reason."

"Njeri and I talked once about how girls up where she lives never go through *nyambura* anymore," Gatiria picked up the sticks Kanini had cut and laid them over her rope. "It even sounds like she doesn't really believe in it herself, like she once did."

"She told you that?" asked Kanini, trying to catch Gatiria's eye.

"Well, she didn't exactly *say* that, but then why would she go on about those girls not getting circumcised?"

"We talked a little about it too, but I couldn't tell how she felt about it herself."

Gatiria shrugged. "I also heard *you* talking about some girls who aren't participating. That friend of yours...Kagere."

"Kagere'll go to secondary up in Chuka. Her family doesn't believe in it either." Kanini fell silent, and, for once, Gatiria did not interrupt her thoughts. "Why do you suppose Njeri told us how things have changed up there if she still believes in *nyambura*? I mean, she *must* still believe in it, but maybe—"

"Maybe she only says she believes in it to go along with Mama. Maybe she's changing her mind and when her daughters come of age, she won't make them go through it."

"Wouldn't that be fine?" A streak of bitterness seared Kanini. "And maybe by the time it's your turn, she could persuade Mama not to make *you* have it done either!"

Gatiria looked at Kanini with wide eyes. "Maybe I'll just tell Mama myself that I don't want to have it done." She had stopped gathering branches and stood silhouetted against the twilit sky. "You should just tell her the same thing. Tell her times have changed, it's against the law and no one who's educated does it anymore. All of that's true."

"I can't just tell Mama and Baba I'm not going to go through with circumcision. Not when they still believe it's the most important custom in Tharaka culture."

"Who cares about Tharaka culture?" Gatiria spat out. She went back to tying the sticks into her trumpline and stood up. She turned to face the sun, which had burst from behind a bank of clouds and gleamed orange on her skin. "If going along with your culture means you have to endure such crazy pain and possibly death...When it's my turn, if Mama and Baba are still so into it, I'll run away if I have to. I'll go to Chuka or Meru...I'll find protection somewhere. Maybe with Aunt Njeri, or...who knows?"

"It sounds strange to need protection...from our traditions. I wonder what Mama and Baba would do if you did that." Kanini wiped the sweat off her brow with her handkerchief.

Gatiria looked at her. "Kanini, avoiding pain like *nyambura* is worth anything they might do to me."

"What if they disowned you?"

Gatiria shrugged. "If they disowned me, I'd survive. If they stopped loving me, then...I don't know what I'd do."

The very idea of running away! Leave it to Gatiria to think of something so extreme. Kanini couldn't even imagine where she'd go or what she'd do. To reside among strangers! To perhaps never see her family again! To possibly be hunted down and forced into circumcision anyway as an outcast. Or worse. Her mind couldn't even fathom all the potential consequences. She knew she could never run away and doubted whether Gatiria could either.

Nevertheless, discussing the issue with Gatiria filled Kanini with a sense of solidarity with her sister. What if she just told Mama and Baba that she'd given the subject of *nyambura* a lot of thought, she'd realized she didn't want it done after all and she would be willing to deal with the consequences of her decision? She could always have it done later if she decided that was a better option. This resolve should have caused her to feel light and carefree, but deep inside, her stomach still felt like an iron cauldron, swimming with hopes she already knew were futile.

The rains began in early November and continued steadily with almost daily downpours. The girls delighted in walking barefoot into their muddy *munda* to pluck the green leaves off the *nthoroko* plants, which were edible, and tasted delicious cooked with *ugali* or rice. Baba had found out from some local men how to construct mud stoves and he built his family one. Everyone appreciated it, especially during this season when the wood outside was wet and hard to burn. Now, Kanini and Gatiria could go out two or three times a week to gather firewood, instead of everyday, since so much less burned during the amount of time it took to cook a pot of *githeri*, their staple food of maize and beans. Baba helped other families build the stoves and earned a little money this way.

Kanini's primary school career ended at the start of December, as the short rains were coming to an end. They had not yet heard from Njeri, when one day, Mama returned from market with a letter. In it was the sorry news they had prayed not to hear. Though Njeri's brother-in-law, Ezekial, had not claimed Njeri immediately as his second wife, within the first month after his father's funeral, he made it clear that she had no choice in the matter. Had he not been as influential a man, her fate might have been different. Despite her protests, as well as the protests of her mother-in-law, there was nothing to be done. Ezekial was powerful; he would have his way.

"At first, I thought the worst thing would be to have Ezekial marry me," Njeri wrote. "Then I found out that was really the second worst thing. The worst of all was going with a cleanser. I was really horrified to find out that I could not be married by this man unless I was first 'cleansed' by the filthiest *mzee* in the area, if you can believe it. Truly, this is a barbaric custom and I pray that you are never widowed, Kambura, since then you might be forced to go through it as well.

"If you think the children cried when we were with you, they are really crying now. This new husband of mine is not around very much, but his *mucii* is a mess and Endelina, his first wife, is neither a good housekeeper nor a good farmer. She mopes around, mourning the deaths of her babies and hoping to become pregnant again. She never helps with my children and is always making nasty comments. We're all close to despairing."

"I can't believe Njeri has had to cope with such a fate." Mama's voice quavered as she finished the letter. "She could've stayed here with us—I know it would have worked out."

"Kambura, you are denying our traditions," Baba retorted. "In the end, Ezekial would have found Njeri and brought her back where she belongs. Those children are by rights his family's property. You know this. If she'd stayed here longer, it would just have made things harder."

"But Kagwima, you and I both know that not all women are claimed as inheritance nowadays, especially among the Meru people. If she'd really fought it, she could've remained living with her mother-in-law, the children would have stayed in the family, and all would've been fine. The trouble is this boor of a man, Ezekial, who forced her to his way. That isn't right."

Baba was staring off somewhere; he appeared not to have heard Mama. "I can't believe she had to be cleansed," he mused. "Poor Njeri...She was always so pure. *That* is a terrible custom, if you ask me."

Kanini made a mental note to ask about this "cleansing" next time she was alone with Mama. She thought about little else than her aunt's horrible circumstance for days.

Gradually, however, her thoughts returned to her impending circumcision, and how she might raise the issue of thwarting tradition to her parents. She knew they would soon begin organizing the ceremony, if they hadn't already. Unlike boys, girls were passive participants and took no role in arranging things for *nyambura*.

One evening as Kanini was mixing *chapati* dough for supper, Mama herself raised the potent topic.

"I talked to Jacinta today, Kanini. She's arranged for the circumciser to come on the 13th of April, to their place. We discussed her coming here the next day."

Kanini could feel her heartbeat pulsing in her head. A film of sweat broke out on her upper lip. "Mama," she stuttered, weighing her words. "I've been thinking about circumcision a lot. I've talked to some girls who aren't doing it. Even Aunt Njeri told me how so many girls aren't having it done up where she lives." Kanini did not look up as she worked her hands into the warm flesh of the dough. She wasn't using the words she'd practiced; she knew Mama would not find her argument convincing. "I've decided...I mean I hope—" She licked her lips; the familiar chapped place at the corner of her mouth tasted of dried blood. "I really don't want to have it done to me."

The silence that followed was palpable; heat from the fire suddenly seemed trapped in Kanini's face. Her hands stopped kneading.

Mama said nothing for a moment and Kanini wondered if she'd been paying attention. At times, Mama's mind could be far away and Kanini and Gatiria had had to repeat things they'd just said.

"Well, that's something I never thought I'd hear. Maybe from Gatiria, but not from you, Kanini. Why don't you want to be circumcised?"

"I don't understand the reason for it, Mama." Tears welled behind Kanini's eyelids. "It seems like a lot of pain for...for I'm not sure what."

Mama's cheekbones gleamed chestnut in the soft lamplight, while the hollows of her cheeks and throat were shaded in charcoal. A scowl darkened her countenance. Then, she sighed and her look softened. "It is a lot of pain, my child. I want you to know the importance of this pain. It's a very important custom. The most important custom in Tharaka culture."

"How can it be more important than the boys' ceremony?" Kanini asked in a small voice.

"Well, it is. Not only does it make you a diligent and faithful wife, but it welcomes you into our tribe's larger family. After *nyambura*, you are born again, no longer as just the daughter of Baba and me, but as the daughter of our clan." Mama clasped Kanini's shoulders between her strong hands. The sticky dough still clung to Kanini's fingers.

"Another thing, perhaps the most important thing, has to do with the fertility of our land. The sacrifice of blood is a symbol...It fertilizes the soil. It makes Ngai happy, it brings the rains. Have you noticed how little rain we get these days?" Mama leaned against the wall, the wooden masher still in her hand, and looked Kanini straight in the eye. "It was not always so, Kanini. There used to be plenty of rain, and we never had drought or famine. One reason for the droughts is because so many girls aren't performing the ceremony. They're afraid of the pain, they don't see the larger meaning of the custom. Or they think that modern ways are better, modern ways that send girls roaming all around the country, instead of remaining at home where they should be."

Kanini said nothing. Mama had told her some of this before, but it was comforting to be reminded, especially since, as she'd suspected, there'd be no getting out of it. The dough on her fingers blurred through the tears that had managed to spill over. She took a deep breath. "Why has President Moi declared it illegal, if it's so good for our people and our land?"

Mama snorted. She pinched off a lump of dough from Kanini's bowl and toyed with it. "Humph! President Moi and his 'fuata nyayo'. Following the footsteps…Of who, I wonder? The *wazungu* from Europe and America! They say our custom is barbaric, so he declares it barbaric too." Mama tossed the dough back into the bowl and wiped her hands on the *leso* around her waist. "He's supposed to be following in Kenyatta's footsteps, but if he were, he would consider this a great custom like Kenyatta did. The Kikuyus followed this tradition with a lot more ceremony than we've ever had. I wish Kenyatta were still alive today."

"You mean, people in Europe and America don't circumcise?" asked Kanini in surprise.

"They circumcise their boys, I've heard. When they're just little babies. Too young to understand the greater meaning of it. Since the *wazungu* believe in male circumcision, Moi follows along and hasn't made that illegal. Only female circumcision. Doesn't it seem strange to you, Kanini?" Mama tucked a wisp of hair back into her head square.

"So, President Moi is following the ways of the *wazungu* more than he's following in Kenyatta's footsteps?"

"Baba and I believe that, and so does Njeri. Of course, we would never say anything to anyone else." Mama shook her head. "President Moi wants to be rich and respected by the *wazungu*, so he'll do anything they tell him. He claims to want what's best for us Kenyans, but then he eats all the profits this country has, sharing the wealth only with rich parliament members. And do we poor citizens see any of this profit, the profit gained by our hard work? You know how much we get for a bag of cotton. Not enough to buy a can of Kimbo! This country will never get anywhere as long as our government is so corrupt."

Kanini had heard her parents engrossed in this debate when she was supposed to be asleep. Her eyes didn't leave Mama's face. Beads of sweat had popped out on her mother's forehead, which she wiped away with a corner of her *leso*.

"I didn't mean to go on about all that, Kanini. I'm just trying to help you see why Moi has these beliefs about circumcision. I want you to think beyond his stupid laws." Gatiria had used that word to describe *nyambura*. Now Mama used it to sum up Moi's laws. Kanini took a deep breath as Mama grasped her shoulders. "Think about what is really meaningful in life, Kanini. I know *nyambura* is painful. I realize not everyone respects the custom anymore, especially those who cater to Moi."

"If so many people think about Moi like you do, why does he always win the elections?" Kanini asked. Moi had reigned as president ever since her fifth birthday.

"Like I said, there's too much corruption in our government," said Mama with a sigh. "Don't think about all that, Kanini. I want you to try and see past your own selfish pain. Try to look to the greater good that will be gained for yourself, and everyone in our clan, through *nyambura*."

Kanini blinked away the remnants of her tears. She scooped out another wad of dough and started balling it up in her hands. Mama had never spoken to her so frankly before, so much like an equal. She still felt ambivalent about her rite of passage, but it helped to know that Mama respected her enough to talk to her as if she were already a grown woman.

She had not found a good time to ask Mama about the custom of cleansing. Later, she would wonder why Mama disapproved of that tradition, as well as wife inheritance, while upholding the tradition of *nyambura*. These lesser known customs must have also had reasons for existing, back in the days when women were considered the exclusive property of men. Kanini knew she shouldn't just toss all the ancient traditions into one pile, like firewood. Circumcision had to be more significant and necessary for the continuation of Tharaka culture than these other traditions.

She wondered what Gatiria would say if she asked her, then thought, *Gatiria is too young to really understand anything about these issues. She hasn't really given them much thought or balanced her opinions with age-old wisdom. All she does is react to things she finds unjust and gets me to react to them with her. It's better to just avoid her, at least until after I've gone through my initiation.*

Chapter 7

It was the start of the April holiday. It had been a year since Njagi's initiation and he was back to his old habit of ordering his sisters about and strutting around the compound like a cock. Had he forgotten those lessons about taking on a man's responsibilities? His notion of responsibility seemed to focus on getting out of as much work as possible. When Kanini remarked on this to Gatiria, she shrugged and said, "Well, look at what Baba does everyday and *he's* a man."

Gatiria was happy to make her own escape everyday with the goats, though before Njagi's return, she'd complained about it. She began taking Gitonga along in order to train him to herd goats as well as become a more accommodating brother than Njagi.

Kanini was getting used to being at home fulltime now. At the end of January she had received her CPE results. They reflected a high performance, higher than Njagi's. Kanini knew her parents were aware of this, though no one said anything. After looking at the numbers on the sheet, Mama tucked the paper into her skirt pocket. Later when Baba came home, Kanini heard them arguing. Mama was trying to persuade Baba to do something so that Kanini might continue with her schooling. Baba kept protesting that there was nothing he could do, short of taking Njagi out and sending Kanini instead.

He ended his tirade by saying, "Kambura, what you are asking is unrealistic! Yes, the girl is bright. She would do well at secondary. And then what? She would come back here and be taken for hardly more than the same dowry as if she hadn't gone on to school. No one that she would marry around here cares whether she has that education or not!" Kanini could hear Mama sputtering a protest, but she was cut short by Baba. "If we had the money I would send her. I do care that her mind is active. She will not marry for some years, so it would keep her busy. But, what can we do? She will have to be kept busy here at home with you."

She went to visit Mukami one afternoon and found her friend heading down to the river, a *mtungi* on her back. Kanini grabbed another one and accompanied her. It was the middle of the day and the skimpy patches of shade provided no relief from the sun's glare.

"Mama said the circumciser will come to our place the day after she's been at yours," Mukami was saying in her lilting voice. "Njoki is to be done too, since she wasn't done last year."

"The day before she comes to mine, she'll go to my cousin, Bahati's," Kanini said. "I wish we could attend her ceremony before going to our own." Mukami didn't answer. The girls knew that it was taboo to attend a girl's circumcision before they were initiated themselves.

"I can't wait to see the new dress I'm getting," said Mukami, her voice dreamy. "I know my parents went to Embu to buy it."

"Wouldn't it be nice to get some new shoes too?" asked Kanini, whose old ones no longer fit her. She had to be careful to avoid rocks and thorns as she tramped down the less familiar path to the river. Her old rubber slippers were prone to popping apart.

"Yes, but shoes are too expensive. Especially now that we're no longer in school and don't need them anymore."

The river water was chocolate brown and churning, due to the rainfall higher up. The girls filled and plugged their containers in silence.

"So, Mukami, have you ever felt...a little nervous about what we'll experience during *nyambura?*" Kanini asked as they headed out of the cool valley.

"What do you mean? Why would I feel nervous?"

"Well, there's just so much that's going to happen. I know I need to trust our elders—they'll take care of us. But, sometimes I worry. There'll be a lot of pain, Mukami..."

Her words sounded blunt and intrusive in the still afternoon, like Gatiria's often sounded. Mukami faced her, her countenance resolute. "I don't think about that, Kanini. It's like having a baby. There's pain, but you need to see past the pain, to something better that will come. It's not good to focus on the pain."

"I try not to, but sometimes I can't help it. When I asked Mama what it felt like, she said she couldn't remember. I wish I could get my head in such a state that I wouldn't feel it. I've heard some girls are able to do that."

"Maybe we will be able to do that, Kanini. We'll be dancing for hours before we go before the *mutaani*. They say the dancing can help take the pain away."

Kanini envied Mukami's ability to trust in what her elders had planned and accept her fate as a matter of course. She wished she could spend more time with her friend. But there was very little time left before *nyambura*.

The evening before the ceremony, when her chores were done, Kanini took a short walk. She wandered along the goat paths, greeting mamas and *cucus* as they trundled back from the river or headed home from market.

The sky was awash with warm color from the fading sun and the hills had sunk into shadow. Near the river, she stopped to gaze up at one of her favorite trees, an enormous baobab with peeling bark, sparsely covered with dry, papery leaves.

She was not surprised to see Gatiria herding the goats toward her along the bank; her sister had been out with the scrawny animals all afternoon.

"*Muga*, Gatiria," Kanini greeted her. Gatiria did not respond, but that was not unusual. Kanini looked out over the river, which was roiling and churning even faster than the week before. "Do you think it's a good omen if the rains come at the time of my circumcision?"

Gatiria shrugged as her gaze followed Kanini's. "Oh, I'm sure it is. Rain is usually a blessing. According to Mama, circumcision is a good omen in itself. You'll bring us a lot of luck now, Kanini."

Kanini tried to catch her sister's eye. Had Gatiria overheard her conversation with Mama a few weeks before? "Do you think I'm getting circumcised only to bring our family good luck?"

Gatiria glanced at her, then away, again shrugging her narrow shoulders. She flicked her stick at a tiny goat that had wandered off. The animal trotted back to the herd and nuzzled its mother.

"You seem to think I have a choice, Gatiria. Just wait till you're my age."

Once again, Gatiria said nothing, but an infuriating little smile remained on her face. Tears of exasperation sprang to Kanini's eyes. "You act as though our traditions have no meaning, as though nothing we believe in affects you—"

As though she had not heard, Gatiria started driving the goats up the bank. Kanini stood a minute, trying to regain her composure. Her fingers pulled automatically at the annoying scab near her mouth. It came off in one satisfying piece, but then the sore hurt as blood oozed from it. Her tongue bristled with the metallic taste as it trapped the sticky liquid.

Kanini waited until Gatiria was far ahead before she started for home, heart pounding resentfully. *Why did I even talk to her? I came out here intending to calm my nerves. And now how do I feel?*

When she arrived *mucii* she heard the merry voices of women in the main hut. Njeri had arrived on a late *matatu* and was laughing and talking with Mama. Carolina was attached tightly to her back in a *leso*. When Njeri saw Kanini, she moved towards her and gave her a big hug, enveloping her in arms that felt thinner than ever.

"So good to see my eldest niece!" she exclaimed. "You must be so excited for tomorrow!"

"Yes, Aunt," Kanini answered in deference. She touched her mouth to make sure the blood had stopped. When she looked up at Njeri's face, she was shocked to see how lean and pinched it looked, a host of little lines around her eyes and more gray at her temples than Mama had. Her smile still glowed with warmth, however.

Mama scooted Gatiria and Gitonga away to wash up for the meal. Baba entered, carrying a parcel wrapped in newspaper. "Roasted goat meat, for my first daughter only." He reached over to place it in Kanini's hands. When Gitonga threatened to intercept it, Baba playfully swatted him away. Kanini tried to muster a smile as she carried the package straight-backed to the *riko*, but her face didn't feel like playing tug-of-war with her mouth anymore.

Supper breezed by, deluding itself with light conversation. Kanini tried to focus on her elders' talk instead of the heavy feeling in her stomach, which made the goat meat an experience of tasteless gristle. After everyone was finished eating, she and Gatiria took their mats and blankets to Cucu's hut to sleep, so that Njeri and the baby would have more space.

Kanini was glad her sister was still in her silent mood. She lay awake a long time thinking about the days ahead. Having gone over it again and again in her mind, she had less trouble picturing the initiation ceremony than the lengthy stay in the hut afterward. She knew she would feel useless and bored, lying on a mat all that time, eating constantly, like a cow getting ready for the slaughter. She knew this was part of the custom, but it was hard to envision being idle for so long, considering how much time her body usually spent in motion.

And how would she feel once she finally emerged from the hut? Older? More mature or womanly? There would be no more playing games like a little girl. It would be time to focus all her energy on growing up, so that she could marry and have her own homestead someday. This had always been her dream, since what else was there, really?

She was sure Gatiria had no more idea than she had.

Kanini awoke when the sun was already fairly high. They had let her sleep late! Both Gatiria and Cucu had left the hut and a new dress lay on Cucu's mattress. It was much larger and prettier than anything Kanini had ever owned. The dress of a woman! With a little gasp of delight, she untied her *leso* and slipped into the dress. The stiff polyester scratched at her skin. She buttoned the metal buttons up the front and twirled, so that the patterned skirt billowed around her. The shoulders and waist were a little large and the fabric hung below her knees, but she was happy that she could therefore wear it for many seasons.

Emerging into the sunlight she saw Mama coming from the *riko* with a big pot of *uji*. She greeted Kanini with a smile then spooned the maize gruel into cups for Cucu, Gatiria and Gitonga. She filled Kanini's cup from a gourd of *ucuru*. As Kanini sipped the freshly fermented gruel, she noticed envious glances coming from her younger siblings. She didn't feel bad; they would get theirs later when she was feeling too sick to eat anything.

After breakfast, Njagi appeared from his hut and offered to take Kanini's cup. "Ngai, Kanini, you look grown up!" he said in the gallant way he put on for special occasions.

"Kanini *is* grown up!" exclaimed Baba, from behind. "She is thirteen now and will soon be a circumcised woman!"

"Will Kanini get married soon?" asked Gitonga.

Baba laughed. "Maybe in a few years."

Kanini felt her face burn with embarrassment. She ducked out of her family's way and took refuge back in Cucu's hut. She was glad she wouldn't be in the company of any males for a long while.

As the sun rose higher, Mama and Njeri escorted Kanini down to the river to bathe and shave her. They settled on the bank under the meager shade of the baobab tree. The branches Kanini had climbed and played on as recently as last year seemed to call out to her. She longed to scramble up into them and look out over her favorite view, across the wide acacia-studded plain and shadowy valleys to the little outcropping of buildings that made up their town. She wondered briefly if she might dare to sneak up into the tree in the coming year, without anyone noticing, then hurriedly banished the thought.

At least she could take comfort from the tree's shade. The sun already felt as hot as iron as Mama drew her down onto a *leso* Njeri had spread on the sandy soil. Mama drew a long strand of carved clay beads from the hand-woven *kiondo* she always carried. "You will wear these beads for the next thirty days, Kanini," Mama said as she placed the strand around Kanini's neck. "Then you'll take them off and keep them in a special place. They're a symbol of the unity within our clan, which must never be broken or cast aside. You are now to be a trusted member of this clan."

After washing her limbs, back and privates with soft soap and a loofah, Mama took extra care shampooing her un-plaited hair for the last time. So rarely did Kanini feel anyone's hands on her, that the sensation nearly put her into a trance. If she could only carry the memory of Mama's soothing touch to the ceremony, she knew she could handle the most excruciating pain.

Then Njeri took scissors and a razor from the *kiondo* and proceeded to cut Kanini's curls. She finished the operation by shaving her hair as close as she could without cutting her. Then she oiled Kanini's scalp and tied a fresh head square around it.

The final touch was the massage Mama and Njeri gave her. They oiled her skin so that when Kanini glanced down, her body looked like the lacquered wood carving of a woman she had once seen in Aunt Jacinta's house. Kanini couldn't remember having been fawned over like this since she was a toddler with malaria and they had feared for her life. The warm sun, the sound of the river rushing past and her mother and aunt's touch were so tranquilizing that just the thought of leaving caused her heart to begin racing again.

"I know that you've heard many times that you mustn't scream or cry out, Kanini," Mama was telling her.

"If I scream, there's the belief that I might kill any child I give birth to," Kanini whispered. She saw Mama lock eyes with Njeri.

"Well, that's an old superstition, Kanini," said Njeri. "But the women will respect you and our family more, if you don't scream or cry."

"Will they slaughter a goat if I don't?" asked Kanini.

"Maybe," smiled Mama. She glanced again at Njeri. Kanini knew that one reason Baba had given her goat meat the night before was because she would have no appetite to feast on this day. She breathed deeply, and foreboding once again descended into her gut.

They finally stood, collected the things and climbed up the bank. As they left the shadows behind, the mid-morning heat grabbed Kanini with a vengeance. She wished they had an umbrella to block the sun; she wanted to block out everything. The thud of drums had begun across the field. From a distance, the women on the compound pulsed like a wound. It seemed as if everyone were wearing orange or red, the colors of fire. And blood.

As Kanini, Mama and Njeri drew nearer, the women took on familiar identities and her bubbling heart eased to a simmer. There was Bahati's mother, Jacinta, as well as a number of Bwana's other wives, daughters and daughters-in-law. Kanini knew Bahati would be lying in her mother's hut, recovering from her circumcision the day before, and wondered how she fared. Mukami's mother had come, as well as a number of other neighbors, acquaintances and distant relatives. Women would continue to arrive as the sun rose to its zenith.

The only men were Baba and two of his cousins, Bwana Mkubwa's sons. They stood outside the thorn fence, arms folded, poking at the dirt with sticks, as though unsure of what to do. When Kanini asked Mama why they needed the sticks, she replied: "The dancing could get out of control. They may need the sticks to keep order." Kanini didn't understand but asked no more questions.

Instinctively, she looked around for her siblings, though she knew they would be elsewhere. Cucu had probably taken them to one of her niece's houses.

Most of the women were chattering and laughing together, though a few had started swaying to the rhythm of the drum. As Kanini, Mama and Njeri reached the open gate, a swarm surged with them into the compound. Women's fingers touched Kanini's covered head and dress, and there were supportive and mysterious comments.

"Kanini, it is so good to be here with you."

"You will be a changed girl this day, my daughter."

"We will dance together and you will enter a place you've never been before."

"I look forward to seeing you enter the blessed state of womanhood, child."

Their words caused her heart to swell and her head to pound. She knew that all the women of her community might respect and honor her on this day, but she did not feel worthy since she herself was so troubled. She felt like she knew too much. Why couldn't she have avoided girls like Kagere and Gatiria—girls who gave her an inkling of a different fate? There was nothing she could do now. Was there anything she could have done before? Her entire upbringing had funneled her to this destiny; she must either embrace it or regret it. To regret it would leave her with nothing.

A second drummer started up and more of the women began twirling their hips and shaking their arms. They shrieked with delight when Kanini backed away, but Mama pushed her into the crowd, saying, "Oh, no you don't. It's your turn now."

As Kanini's feet started to move, they fell into rhythm with the other dusty, calloused feet around her. Hers were just one pair of the many, all of which belonged to the women of her community, women who'd undergone the same rite she was now undergoing. Feeling bonded to them, she lifted her eyes from the pounding feet and smiled back at their grinning faces.

It wasn't long until an intense thirst overcame her. Her face was running with sweat and her bare feet ached. She bowed out of the crowd and went to search for a calabash of water. The cool liquid running down her throat felt like rain after a drought. Later she would wish she'd taken more; it would be a week until she really drank again.

She returned to the throng, took up the chant, and this time did not quit moving. A long time seemed to pass. The repetitive movement started to feel like her natural state and Kanini found that she grew less and less tired the longer she did it. She did not even feel thirsty anymore. The flowing colors, the beating drums, the trilling and shrieking laughter all whirled together in her head and made her mind ascend above everything. Had someone given her some *uki* or *pombe*? She felt dizzy, light-headed and numb within her body, though her mind felt finely attuned to the sights and sounds around her.

Mama appeared before her with a plate of food. Kanini waved it away, unable to eat. The smell brought her back to her body; made her feel as though she might tumble down. She realized that the crowd was opening up and forming a circle. Her first instinct was to back up and join them. Then she realized that hands were guiding her to the center, and that she needed to continue dancing, all alone this time. Feeling conspicuous, she slowed her movements and stared at the ground. She did not want to dance alone.

Relief washed over her when she sensed Mama's presence at her side. One hand under her elbow, she drew Kanini out of the circle and into the house. She faced her squarely in the dusky interior, her hands resting on Kanini's shoulders. "You will do well, Kanini. You are a strong, brave girl—my first-born daughter. I know you'll make me proud." Her mother's voice wavered, as though tears hid behind it. Another woman appeared and silently helped Mama remove Kanini's new dress, leaving her adorned in nothing but the strand of beads. She recognized this person. It was Bwana Mkubwa's youngest wife, Florence. She would be her caretaker during the weeks of healing.

Florence's touch was like feathers on her sweat-glazed skin. As she guided Kanini back outside into the blinding light, the crowd seemed to surge towards her, the colors and movement a frightening blur. She heard a gruff shout and glimpsed a waving stick. One of the men was trying to

hold back the crowd. In spite of a brief moment of shame, she could now
see the reason for his presence.

She felt hands putting pressure on her shoulders—Florence's hands.
They pushed her gently down onto the ground before an old woman seated
on the threshold; the vein-streaked legs closed in tightly around Kanini. A
glance at the face of the circumciser startled her; she had forgotten that it
would be painted in black and white ochre.

The crowd surrounded her on all sides. There was no escaping now. She
felt the soft flesh of her inner thighs being pried apart by the circumciser's
gnarled fingers. She already felt violated, though the razor had not yet
touched her. How quickly everything was happening; she wished she had
more time to prepare herself.

Kanini wanted to slap the woman's hand away, stagger to her feet and
run into the bush, to the comfort of her baobab tree. Would no one come
to her rescue?

She remained rooted to the ground. She tried not to wince as the
circumciser's fingers grasped the sliver of flesh in her most private area.
She couldn't tell the exact moment the razor's cool edge met this tissue.
After the first searing pain, a faint numbness tingled into place. She bit her
tongue and prayed that it was over.

The razor returned, cutting out more parts than she knew she had. The
pain surged, like an angry tide, but it was impossible to cry out. Everything
that was in her stomach rose to the surface. She wanted to vomit; she wanted
to die. Spasms wracked her.

The few seconds it took could have been hours. Her body was an
overflowing volcano; then it was a crater, hollowed out by fire, empty and
spent. Her legs continued to spasm. How would she stand? She still felt
assaulted by the gouging blade, though she knew it had ceased.

It was Florence who helped her stand on her shaky legs. The world
spun as she rose, threatening to crash down upon her. She squeezed her
eyes shut and swallowed back whatever was climbing up the back of her
throat. Florence grabbed her under the arms and helped her into the hut.
Her caregiver eased her down onto a mat, where she curled into a loose
ball. She could feel hot, sticky liquid flowing from between her legs. It felt
like her monthly blood, except much more. This terrified her. How much
blood had she already lost? How much might she still lose? The desire to
staunch and preserve her blood consumed her. If it all drained out, she
would die.

She began to panic. Her breath came in short gulps and she felt darkness start to close in. Her words came out squeaky and shrill. "Mama, Mama—"

"Kanini, it's all right," Florence's voice was low and soothing. She placed a strong hand on Kanini's shoulder. "You need to stay calm. Try breathing deeply." Kanini knew she was panting; she kept her eyes closed. Florence's voice continued, as though from far away. "Think about your breaths as you breathe them."

Kanini clung to the *mugwatani's* words, as though to a vine over a raging river. The river was swirling, spinning into a vortex where it would suck her in if she let go. She noticed the faces of women enmeshed in the wall of spinning water. Who were they? Women she knew, women from Tharaka, who had participated in *nyambura*. They had all known this agony, but none of them had warned her; none had come to her rescue. They were all there, even Mukami and Bahati. All except Gatiria.

She tried to focus on the images of the faces as she measured her breathing. She wondered if they had felt the same way after their ceremonies. Abandoned, betrayed even. How could she blame them for what they'd done to her? They were all victims themselves. Her heartbeat slowly became steadier.

Florence was hovering over her with something in her hand. As the wet cotton wool stung into place on her private area, Kanini snapped to. She knew this saltwater poultice would cleanse and disinfect the wound. Though more pain shot through her, she felt less panicky. She no longer felt like she would faint, although her head had started throbbing. The sensation of the headache was almost comforting in its familiarity.

Now Kanini felt Florence tuck an oily banana leaf between her legs to prevent them from sticking together. Her caretaker covered her with a heavy woolen blanket, whose weight would help control her trembling. She heard a slight shuffle as Florence left the hut.

Kanini lay for how long she did not know, on her side, her legs pasted together. The nausea had only lessened a tiny amount and the pain, more consistent now, continued to flame between her legs.

Florence returned to sit with her for a while; she mumbled comforting things and stroked her head. Kanini's consciousness seemed to wax and wane, but her caregiver's voice and touch were tangible evidence that she was still alive, that her mind was still working. During her more alert moments, she wondered what the women were doing outside. Was the party continuing without her, the initiate? At one point Florence brought her a plate of *ugali*, but the smell of it caused another wave of nausea.

She wanted to sleep to escape the pain, but the terrible throbbing and her woozy stomach would not let her remain long in that sweet state. She clung to the vision of the women in the spinning vortex and was able to doze off for a while. When she awoke, the light had faded at the window, as though evening had come. Florence came in with new cotton.

"How long does the bleeding last?" Kanini asked her feebly.

Florence smiled at her. With her hand, she smoothed the lines of tension on Kanini's forehead. "It should stop soon. Try to keep it as clean as possible. Don't ever touch it to the ground. When you have to urinate, tell me and I'll bring a calabash." Kanini did, in fact, have to go, but the thought of the heightened pain sickened her all over again. *I'll wait as long as I can*, she thought.

She wondered if she had cried out while she was being cut. When she asked Florence, her caregiver smiled her slow, reassuring smile. Kanini stared at her teeth—evenly marching kernels of fresh white maize. "You didn't let out a peep, Kanini. You were very brave."

A glimmer of pride warmed her heart. "That's because I was about to faint," she muttered.

"Right now, they're roasting a goat in your honor," Florence told her. "They'll be here for many more hours."

Kanini didn't know if the tears that burned were a result of pride or because she felt sorry for the goat. She personally knew how the animal must have felt during its final moments.

She listened for a long while to the voices outside and the intermittent beating of drums and jangling of bottle caps. Finally, hours after the hut had drifted into total darkness, the celebratory sounds faded away and stopped.

Chapter 8

The night seemed to last forever. The burning of her wound would not go away; indeed would not even lessen. If anything, it seemed to intensify and it was all she could do not to begin moaning. She tried to stifle any sound, since she didn't want to bother Florence; her caregiver was sleeping on the other side of the curtain.

After what seemed like a hundred nights, the gray light of morning appeared at the window, awakening her from a light dream-tormented sleep. She was mildly surprised to hear the pattering of rain on the roof. The sound lulled her. Then she heard a stirring behind the curtain and the fresh face of Florence appeared.

"Good morning, Kanini," she said in her quiet voice. "How did you sleep?"

"Not so well, but...I did sleep a little."

"Well, I'm sure you're hungry. Let me go see what your mama's fixing for you to eat."

"I would really like a drink of water," said Kanini, though she knew liquids were forbidden during the first week. This was to prevent her from urinating, which might cause infection. "But I'll take whatever there is."

She struggled to hoist herself up onto her elbows. The pain, which had seemed a little duller a few moments ago, raged again. With a groan, she lay back down. She was thankful for Florence's strong hand on her shoulder.

The young woman knelt to examine the wound. At first, Kanini felt ashamed to part her legs before this relative stranger. But she was aware that Mama had good reasons for choosing Florence to care for her. She needed to get used to being touched and tended by someone she hardly knew. Perhaps by the end of the month, they would be friends.

Florence disappeared and returned with an empty calabash as well as a *sufuria* with warm water, a rag and a bowl full of damp herb-infused leaves. Urinating proved to be an excruciating activity; Kanini clenched her teeth and squeezed her eyes shut as she squatted over the calabash. Then Florence gently washed her wound. The warm water was soothing, but the pressure of the rag tortured her; Kanini caught her tears with a handkerchief Florence gave her.

After patching her up with fresh cotton wool, Florence left to get her breakfast. Moments later she returned with a steaming plate of millet *ugali*, made with real cow's milk.

○

The next few days passed in a blur. Her family members began to come and go from the hut, and Mama, Baba and Gitonga went back to sleeping in their old places. Gatiria, she assumed, slept in Cucu's hut. Kanini stayed alone behind the curtain. She was not allowed to see or speak to anyone but Mama or Florence, who now went home every evening.

The first time Kanini saw Mama's face in the parting of the curtain, she burst into tears. Mama knelt to comfort her and stroke her head. She told her how well she had done during *nyambura* and how proud she was of her. Kanini could only lie there, trying to stifle her sobs.

Why did the sight of Mama depress her? Maybe it was that feeling of betrayal, which she continued to battle, in spite of the realization that all the women were victims, just like she was. Mama had made *nyambura* out to be such an honorable thing, when really it was just a test in enduring pain. She hadn't even gotten to enjoy the party. At least Njagi had gotten that much. It no longer comforted her that she was the last in the line of women who'd come before her, each having gone through the same rite. She felt no pride in the fact that she had joined the ranks of her ancestors. She only felt violated: something had been ripped from her, a part of her body that she would never get to understand the importance of.

The first week all she did was lie there with her thoughts, hour after hour, taking her meals as Florence brought them, and patiently enduring the doctoring of her wound. She became quite thirsty in the warm afternoons, so much so that she would often get a headache. Despite not drinking, she still needed to relieve herself at times. Since she could not go outside, she was obliged to use a hole dug in a corner of the hut. Then Florence would scoop out the waste material and carry it out.

As Kanini started feeling better, she became curious about what was going on outside. When had Njeri left? How was Cucu doing? How were Mukami and her sister faring after their *nyambura*? What about cousin Bahati? Where were her family members during the day? It sounded so quiet in the compound, she could hardly believe Njagi and Gatiria were both around.

Five days after the ceremony, Florence left early in the afternoon and didn't return until the next day. Her brow was creased with anxiety as she entered the hut bearing Kanini's breakfast. As Kanini dipped her spoon into the mashed plantains, she tried to coax the news from her caretaker.

"A few nights ago, when I first went home, I found out Bahati wasn't doing so well after her *nyambura*," began Florence. "You remember she had it done the day before you. From the day after the ceremony, she had a high fever and slept constantly. Her *mugwatani* did everything she could to bring the fever down. When Bahati woke up delirious, the caretaker began telling people how she must've been cursed by a spirit, or perhaps had already gone in the bush with a boy. A lot of negative rumors."

Kanini was stunned. After all her cousin had gone through! "Do people really believe those things can make you sick after *nyambura*?" Florence nodded, a grim look on her face. "Bwana Mkuu didn't believe any of it, of course, and went to fetch a nurse from the dispensary. The nurse said Bahati probably had malaria and gave her chloroquine. But two days later her situation was the same. Now her fever is still high and her wound is red and swollen."

"More than mine?" Kanini asked with concern.

"Oh yes. Yours looks much better. We're not sure what happened with Bahati. Everything's been done in the same way as with you. When the nurse came again yesterday, she brought some special ointment for the wound. She said if it didn't improve in a day or so we should take her to the hospital at Meru."

"The hospital!" Kanini breathed. She wondered whether the doctors at the hospital would send Bahati to prison. She had just been circumcised, which was against the law. How terrible for her poor cousin, who was possibly infected, to have to stay in a cold, filthy cell. She wondered what Bwana Mkubwa's family would do if such a thing happened. Even if her cousin did not get locked up, the fact that some people would assume that Bahati might not be a virgin could bring disgrace to Bwana's family.

The next day, Florence told Kanini that Bahati's wound had begun to ooze a thick yellow fluid. At this point, her father and uncles had carried her to Kajuki, where they got a vehicle to transport her up to Meru. "I hope she makes it there in time," said Florence, shaking her head. "I thought they should've brought her days ago, but they wanted to put it off as long as possible. Now, it may be too late."

Kanini lay on her mat in the morning light, feeling alternately sickened at the thought of her poor cousin, and vastly relieved that the same fate had not befallen her. She remembered the conversation she'd had with Gatiria the morning Njagi had been circumcised and thought, *what happened to Bahati will make Gatiria all the more determined not to be circumcised.* Would Mama and Baba still make her go through with it? Kanini couldn't even imagine attending her sister's ceremony. How could she attend? She would boycott it, to lend solidarity. There was no way she could stand behind Gatiria undergoing such unnecessary, and possibly life-threatening, pain and misery, especially after Kanini herself had now undergone it and had a thorough understanding of it. She felt like it was her personal responsibility to break the cycle; someone who had experienced it had to.

If she really intended to support Gatiria in her quest not to be circumcised, why stop at boycotting the ceremony? Why not do everything she could to help Gatiria get away, so that she wouldn't have to be initiated at all?

Her eyes were still wet with tears when Florence re-entered the hut with her breakfast.

"Are you all right, Kanini?" asked her caregiver.

"Yes, thank-you, Florence. I feel...I'm just really sorry about what Bahati's going through." She blinked her eyes, breathed deeply and sat up to accept the cup of thick, warm gruel.

Kanini felt grateful that she was healing rapidly and gaining weight as well. During the second week, Florence brought her delicacies like chicken, millet *ugali* and mashed green grams cooked with chunks of goat meat. She was finally able to wash the food down with cool water, which had never tasted so good. Thankfully, it did not hurt as much now to urinate.

By the third week, Kanini became restless, lying in bed all day. Her wound was now only inconsistently sore and she no longer had to put poultices on it. She got out her old school books and read through some of them again. Florence's stories of the outside world entertained her, though she brought no more news of Bahati's condition. One day Florence told Kanini that she had run into Mukami's mother at the market. Both her daughters were healing well, and Mukami sent greetings to Kanini, saying she couldn't wait to see her again. Kanini's heart was full. She tried to send good feelings through the airwaves up to Meru to Bahati, but she received no sign that they had arrived.

During the requisite month of healing, the families of the girls who had recently been initiated planned their *mpumiro* ceremony. Kanini knew of four others who would be attending: Mukami and her sister Njoki, whose family would host the party, a girl named Karimi, who'd been in their class at school and Kanini's distant cousin, Mary. When Kanini asked about

Bahati, Florence looked away and said she would not be able to come. She'd heard from Bwana Mkubwa that her condition was still not stable.

On the morning of *mpumiro*, Kanini awoke early, feeling refreshed and energetic. Florence gave her a thorough sponge bath, after which Kanini donned her new dress for the first time since taking it off during initiation. It fit her perfectly! She really had grown bigger during the month of inactivity and constant eating. She felt the seam at her waist, where the fabric had been loose before. Even her breasts had grown, easily filling up the bodice of the dress. Now no one would have any doubt that she had matured. She wished she could see herself in a full-length mirror. Her mind flitted briefly to Kagere, whom she would probably never see again. She wondered what her old friend was doing now.

Florence greased her cap of hair and oiled the dry skin on her feet and hands. Kanini was astonished to see that all her bites, scratches and other sores had completely healed. At no time during the past month had she felt the urge to scratch open a single one of them.

When she was ready, her caregiver pushed open the bamboo door and called all Kanini's family members around to greet her. This would be the first time she'd left the hut since entering it a month before. Feeling both shy and excited at the prospect of seeing her family again and having them see her, Kanini bowed her head as she stepped through the doorway.

Gitonga was the first to say anything. "Look how grown-up Kanini looks!" he cried, clapping his hands. Baba and Njagi laughed and approached her, in order to shake her hands and clap her on the back and shoulders.

Then Cucu drew near and squeezed Kanini's shoulders between her thin, gnarled hands. When she spoke, her voice was muffled. "My oldest granddaughter! You are one of us now." Her eyes were glassy pinpricks amidst the wrinkles that mingled with the ancient scars on her face. This was one tradition that had mostly come to an end, Kanini thought with relief—that of ritual scarring, which Cucu, Baba and Mama had all had to endure. It was one thing to bleed between one's legs for a month. She couldn't imagine staunching the blood that spilled from gashes cut into her face.

From behind Mama, Gatiria smiled and without a word, stuck a shilling into Kanini's palm. Kanini reached out and grasped Gatiria's hand. Mischief seemed to dance in her sister's eyes. Gatiria was still the same, while Kanini felt as though she had stepped into a whole different world, a different body even, and aged immeasurably.

The entire family surrounded her; they gave her coins, shook her hands and spoke words that were animated and supportive. Only Gatiria stood a little apart, and Kanini wondered what she was thinking. She couldn't ask, since she was not allowed to speak until the main portion of the ceremony was over.

Gatiria turned and saw Kanini's eyes on her. "Isn't it time to get ready to go to Mukami's?" she asked.

Kanini smiled and looked around, from Gatiria to Cucu, from Mama to Baba, Njagi and Gitonga and finally to Florence. Everyone nodded and smiled in agreement.

When they arrived at the neighbors' compound, they found that Mukami and her sister had still not emerged from their hut. While waiting, the assembled guests greeted the rest of the initiates and gave them coins and cups of *ucuru*. The fermented liquid slid down Kanini's throat easily. She drank the entire cup and was surprised when it was taken from her and immediately refilled. She noticed her siblings sipping their first cupfuls more slowly.

By midday, all of the guests had arrived. Mukami and Njoki were escorted from their hut by their *mugwatani*, an aunt of theirs. Both were dressed in new dresses and Kanini was amazed to see her friend looking even more beautiful than before. Her face was still softly curved, her skin supple and flawless, while her slender body had filled out to reveal a more womanly figure. Kanini went forward through the throng of visitors to greet her with a hug. Mukami's eyes lit up when she saw her.

"Let's talk later," she whispered and Kanini nodded.

Now that the girls had been initiated, there would be no more running about, talking loudly and doing as they pleased. No more acting like Gatiria, Kanini thought wryly. Girls who had been initiated one or two years before would take them in hand and give them lessons on how to behave. Kanini and Mukami would meet these girls the first time during the *mpumiro*. Then they would get together with them as often as possible for a year, until they were knowledgeable and mature enough to be considered adult women. Women ready for marriage, Kanini thought with both apprehension and a little thrill.

During the feast, Kanini sat with the four other initiates, talking in low tones and chewing politely. The girls' eyes were cast down most of the time; at one point Kanini raised hers and noticed many of her elders gazing upon them in open admiration. Embarrassed, she immediately lowered her eyes again and finished her meal.

"Does anyone know how Bahati's doing?" asked Mary in a muffled tone.

It seemed as if no one knew her cousin's fate. Mukami was looking elsewhere. "I think we should probably not talk about it," Kanini told them as she set her spoon in her empty dish. "It might be a—it might not be a good omen."

By late afternoon, Kanini was exhausted, so unused to all the activity was she. She was glad when the families started gathering their children together and heading off. In the pool of lamplight that spilled from Mukami's doorway, Kanini said farewell to her friend.

"I feel blessed that we're both healthy and whole after our circumcisions, Mukami. Not everyone was as lucky as we were."

"You mean Bahati?" asked her friend.

"You've heard about her?"

Mukami nodded. "Yes, my caretaker told me. It's very sad."

"Well, she may still recover. She's at hospital."

Mukami looked away and did not give her opinion. Kanini grasped her friend's hand one more time in both her own and whispered, "There's so much to talk about, Mukami. We'll have to get together soon."

She hurried off, but turned back to see Mukami still in the doorway, waving good-bye.

Kanwa and Kajuki
1990

Chapter 1

It was mid-afternoon on a boldly clear and hot January day. Kanini straightened from her bent-over position and pulled off her head square, then used it to wipe the sweat that ran freely down her face and neck. A starling darted past her, its iridescent head flashing purple in the light.

She sighed at the pathetic pile of legumes she'd harvested, picked up the baskets and started trudging *mucii*. The heat floated around her in watery layers; she could have been walking along an ocean floor. Due to the onslaught of erosion and drought, the landscape was now more barren than ever. Definitely worse than the time when she had undergone circumcision, nearly four years ago.

She arrived at the compound and forced open the gate of thorns. In the shade of the main house, Mama was grinding millet on the grinding stone. Mutwiri, the new baby, whimpered as his head wobbled about on her back.

"I got some green grams and peas, Mama," Kanini said as she emptied her baskets into the storage bins. "I think there's more out there; we'll just have to go through the plants more carefully tomorrow." She bent to take Mutwiri off Mama's back. He was a fussy baby, and Mama couldn't put him down for even a few minutes without him crying inconsolably.

Kanini had grown little since circumcision. She was still shorter than Mama, but was now stronger. The well-defined muscles in her arms and legs attracted interested glances from men in the village. She could easily carry over half her weight in firewood or water and walk with the load for many kilometers.

For a few minutes, Mutwiri gurgled and flailed his fists around as Kanini walked him around the compound. She brought him into the main house and searched around for a treat. No fresh milk in the bottle on the shelf and no bananas.

"Mama, are you going to milk the goat? Or should I fix him something else?" Kanini called.

"I bought some Cerelac at the market; we'll give him that," said Mama as she straightened and stretched. She continued, almost as if to herself. "I hate to buy that *mzungu* porridge, but it has more nutrition than *uji* and since my milk dried up, what else can we do?"

Njagi came in, herding Gitonga in front of him, along with the few goats they still owned. "*Mugeni!*" her older brother greeted them cheerfully. Njagi was now nineteen and stood taller than both parents. A fine combination of their traits, he had Mama's prominent cheekbones, high forehead and lanky limbs and Baba's strong build.

Gitonga, at nine, was still small and bony. A few years before, his hair had turned pale and his stomach had become overly distended, the navel protruding like a knob. Protein deficiency was so common in Tharaka that the nurse had barely given him a glance when Mama brought him into the clinic. The advice to supplement Gitonga's diet with more meat was like the previous advice to buy mosquito nets for everyone in the family. Njagi had been the one to come to the rescue: he learned how to fish and now joined other young men at the river on a regular basis. Although Cucu wouldn't touch this new addition to the diet—she claimed it was like eating snakes—everyone else in the family learned to relish the fish, and Gitonga's kwashiorkor eventually disappeared.

"*Muga mono*, Njagi," said Mama. "Did you get any jobs today?"

"Yes, Mama. A man asked me to write three letters and gave me five shillings each. It wasn't much, but it was as much as he had." Njagi scooped some water into a basin and washed his hands and face. The grin on his face reminded Kanini of the one he'd worn after Bwana Mkubwa had given him school fees the week following his *mpumiro* ceremony. That was a year and a half before he'd been obliged to completely drop out of school due to the expense, at the end of Form Two.

Gatiria was the last of the children to arrive. She came from the river, hauling a full *mtungi*, and set it down before the *riko* with a grunt. Gatiria had grown quite a bit. She was taller than Kanini, slim and lanky, her face plain and thoughtful except for when she was engaged in a discussion or argument. Then it blazed with vitality.

"This *mtungi* seems to get heavier everyday," she complained.

"That's strange, since you should be growing stronger everyday," Njagi observed.

"What do you know about physical labor?" snapped Gatiria. "All you do is wander around the market, talking to friends and writing a letter or two. I will never understand why this strenuous work is reserved for women, when men claim they are so much stronger than we are."

"I will never understand why you are always questioning your station in life, little sister," mocked Njagi.

Kanini was happy to leave the sound of their squabbling outside. In the *riko*, she removed the *sufuria* of boiling water from the mud stove and poured a small amount into the Cerelac powder that she had carefully measured into a bowl. After mixing it, she spooned some of the mash into another dish and spread it around so that it would cool quickly, the sooner to feed her baby brother.

She turned around to find Gatiria looking over her shoulder. "I can't believe Mama bought that awful cereal! It costs so much and only profits some *mzungu* company. What happens when we can't afford it anymore and Mutwiri has become used to eating it?"

"We'll worry about that then," said Kanini, lowering her tone. "It sounds like you're still obsessing about...what we talked about the other day."

"Of course I am, Kanini," her sister said, not bothering to lower her voice.

Gatiria had attended one more year of primary school than her siblings. The Kenyan education system had recently changed, and pupils now attended eight years of primary followed by four years of secondary. Gatiria had just finished her eighth and final year of primary and would now be initiated into womanhood. The girls knew Mama was planning Gatiria's coming-of-age ceremony.

Just a few mornings before, they had entered into the familiar discussion while going to collect water.

"How can Mama truly believe that droughts are caused by girls not getting circumcised, Kanini? It's all superstitious nonsense, and you know it!"

"It does offend me that I went through the ordeal and the droughts have been worse than ever," Kanini concurred in a whimsical tone. "Maybe Ngai is just angry since so many others have stopped following in His path. It's too bad he couldn't just make it rain on our *munda*—"

"Why does everyone think His path includes the mutilation of women?" Gatiria was not in a jocular mood. "It sounds like someone made that up—probably a *man*—in order to keep the women under control."

"What about the theory that you'll be born again into the clan and become part of the unity of our tribe after you're circumcised?" Kanini asked, pulling a thorn from the rubber sole of her slipper.

"It's just more propaganda, Kanini, and I don't buy it. I believe in what my own mind tells me and nothing else. What it tells me now is to do everything I can to get out of this outdated tradition!"

"I've known your opinions on circumcision for years now, Gatiria," Kanini said evenly. They had reached the river and waded into the sluggish water to where a slow current flowed. "What we should start talking about now is a plan for you to get out of it."

Gatiria stopped short and turned to face her. "Are you saying you'll help me, Kanini?"

Kanini shrugged and continued filling her *mtungi*. "Someone's got to protect you from what happened to Bahati. The procedure is a dangerous one...No one around here wants to see it for what it is."

Gatiria's eyes fell to the water swirling around her bare legs. She took a deep breath. "After she died, I kept thinking our elders would change their minds about making us all go through it. I mean, how can they keep such a tradition going when girls are becoming infected and dying?"

"I wondered for a while if Mama and Baba would still be forcing it on you if it'd been *me* who'd died..."

"Did you ever find out whether Bwana Mkubwa changed his mind about it?" Gatiria submerged her *mtungi* in the water.

"He doesn't have any more young daughters or granddaughters, so...I'm not sure if he's changed his mind or not."

Gatiria had finished filling her jug, her lips pursed together.

Everyone except Baba, who was not around, took supper together outside in the cool of the evening, and afterwards they sat around the fire Njagi had built. Mama was sitting in one of their three chairs, rocking the baby to sleep. Cucu sat idily—her eyes were so bad these days she could not even make her sisal baskets anymore—while the children busied themselves mending torn clothing, shelling peas or fixing tools. The soft breeze swung the lantern from a branch, and the orange light flickered around them. Baba was usually not present for these evening gatherings; he often went to "beat water"—*kupiga maji*—which meant seeking and imbibing in alcoholic refreshment, an activity reserved exclusively for men.

"So, Second Daughter," Mama began, her eyes on the baby in her arms. "I'm sure you've been giving some thought to your special time coming up."

Without missing a beat, Gatiria answered, her voice surprisingly even. "I have been thinking about it...About how I don't want to go through with it." Her eyes did not leave the piece of fabric she was sewing.

A numbing silence fell around them. It was hard to believe this was the first time the family had heard her true feelings on the subject, though Kanini was sure Mama had had some inklings. This outright admission was blunt, even for Gatiria. *Maybe our conversation earlier this week emboldened her,* Kanini thought. Njagi snorted and then guffawed, while Cucu started on a rant that no one could understand, her speech was so garbled and scratchy these days. Kanini continued staring down at the button she was stitching, knowing what would happen if Baba were in the house and wondering what Mama would do without him there.

"How insolent you are, Gatiria!" breathed Mama. Mutwiri stirred in his sleep. "Another parent would whip you, do you understand? How can you sit there and tell me, your mother, what you'll have done and what you won't?"

"I mean no disrespect, Mama," Gatiria said, all defiance gone from her voice. She stared into the fire. "I've thought about this a long time. Kanini knows how I feel. I've never wanted to go through with this ceremony, not even when I was little and hardly knew anything about it."

"You mean no disrespect! But you *are* disrespecting me! It's not for you to decide what will happen to you. You are the daughter and Baba and I are your parents, and you'll do what we tell you to do." Mama's words hung suspended in the air for a moment or two. Then, without a word, Gatiria rose, walked to the main hut and disappeared inside, pulling the thick wooden door shut behind her.

Mama cast her eyes around the firelit circle. They landed on Kanini. "So, she's talked to you about this notion of hers, not to be circumcised?"

"Yes, Mama," mumbled Kanini.

"And why didn't you come and tell me?"

"I didn't think it was my concern...I guess I...I thought she'd tell you on her own. I didn't know what to do." Kanini looked at Mama helplessly, still pinching the needle between her fingers.

"Well, it certainly isn't like her not to speak her mind; she's always told me everything before." Mama's voice had grown calmer and Mutwiri's eyelids stopped fluttering. "But when it comes to *nyambura*...Now it's so late. The time for her ceremony is less than three months away. I've already discussed some dates with the *mutaani*."

Njagi spoke up in Gatiria's defense, which wasn't like him. "I'm not sure forcing Gatiria to go through with *nyambura* would be a good idea. Especially since she seems so set against it."

Mama turned to face him. "Has she spoken about this to you too?"

Njagi shook his head and looked down, a strand of rope dangling from his hands. "No, but I could tell how she felt about it. She was never excited like other girls are. She never wanted to make any plans for it or talk openly about it."

Kanini stared at her brother. It had never crossed her mind that Njagi would have sensed where Gatiria's head was concerning *nyambura*.

"Mama," Kanini said quietly. "Gatiria first told me how she felt back when I was going for mine."

Mama looked grave. When Mutwiri began waving his fists she rocked him again, but so roughly that the baby began to cry. Kanini got up to get the leftover cereal for him and Mama attempted to feed him. He spat it out and continued with his fretting, while the rest sat in somber contemplation.

Mama started on a new track. "Haven't you been able to convince your sister that circumcision is a fine custom, one that must be continued if we are to have any hope for the future? What have you told her, Kanini?"

"I tried to talk about those things with her, but she said she didn't want to hear them. She said she's heard all that and it didn't make any sense to her."

"Didn't make any sense! Where does she get these ideas?" Mama jiggled and patted Mutwiri on the back. "Maybe it's not a good idea to educate our children," she mused. "They start thinking like the *wazungu*, who've basically taken over our beliefs with this education system of theirs. Before you know it, our children believe everything they say and want to do what they do." She took a deep breath. "We'll see what Baba says when he gets home."

Kanini and Gatiria prepared for bed in silence. They lay awake a long while, finally hearing Baba's step at the door. He entered the hut, his talk loud and slurred, and Kanini heard Mama shush him. Kanini knew Mama would wait until later to bring up what had been discussed. Baba returned home more and more often in an inebriated state, and their mother had begun to keep pertinent information from him until he sobered up the next day.

Chapter 2

One afternoon, more than a month later, Kanini started off for the market to buy some Kimbo and onions. She carried Mutwiri along, hoping there would be some *gasukari* up there for him to nibble. She would have just enough money left after her other purchases to buy the tiny sweet bananas.

She made her way along the dusty track, returning greetings to the *wazee*, mamas and the children she knew. "*Muga*, Kanini," young and old greeted her from their perches or doorways. As usual, few seemed to be going anywhere or doing anything. Only a woman or two bustled about the market while a few vendors sat under the thatched roofs of cheaply built lean-tos, their piles of mangoes or onions spread out around them on flattened sacks.

Kanini always went to her favorite shop, the one Florence owned. They were now good friends, and Florence often gave Kanini something free or lowered a price if she was short a few shillings. After reaching the shop, Kanini peered into the cool gloom to see if her relative was there. The muffled cry of a baby told her she was.

"*Muga*, Florence," she said. Florence's teeth flashed white in the dark of the shop as she re-buttoned her dress then tied her little one on her back with a *leso*. Having recently borne her third child, Florence looked haggard. Dark smudges encircled her eyes and despite not having the facial cuts of their older clan members, other lines had appeared on her face. Her eyes still shone whenever Kanini paid a visit, however.

"*Muga mono*, Kanini. I have a letter for you. From up…Let's see, here it is. From Njeri, I think." Kanini accepted the small envelope, her heart beating heavily. She was relieved to see Njeri's neat, faint script, which told her she was still well enough to write.

Life had been very difficult for Njeri ever since Ezekial had forced her to marry him. Following the marriage, the stress of her new home weakened her and her health had declined a great deal. She had carried another baby only seven months before it was born dead. In recent months, a severe case of malaria had caused her to lose another few kilos and most of her old optimism.

"Would your mother mind if you opened it now?" asked Florence.

Kanini tore open the envelope, hungrily scanned the letter and paraphrased the news aloud. "She says she's doing very poorly. She can no longer get out of bed to do any of the chores and her husband's first wife—Endelina, the one who orders Njeri around so much—won't help her with anything. The children are back with Njeri's mother-in-law, all but the youngest, who's never been well. She's asking...she is asking whether Mama could spare one of us—Gatiria or me—to go and help them up there. Otherwise, she doesn't know how she'll deal with it all—" Kanini's heart started pounding. "One of us to go and help them! Oh, that might be the perfect—"

"The perfect what, Kanini?" asked Florence.

"Oh...The perfect chance to find out how she's really doing."

Florence tsk-ed her tongue. "Njeri hasn't been healthy since little Carolina was born, has she?"

"No, it seems like that one took the last strength she had. Mama was going to go up and help her out with the new baby, but before we could even make preparations it came early and...died."

Mutwiri had started fussing, so Kanini began bouncing up and down. Florence handed him a lump of *ugali* from a pot in the corner of the *duka* and he stopped the noise, mouthing the morsel with interest.

"Carolina came early too, didn't she?"

Kanini nodded. "Njeri was probably not healthy enough to have another baby."

Florence nodded. "At least your mother's baby is healthy." Florence smiled as Mutwiri dropped the *ugali* in the dirt. She gave him her little finger, which he immediately put in his mouth. "He must be cutting teeth."

"Njeri's baby would've been just a few months older than Mutwiri," Kanini said wistfully. "If he'd lived."

Florence jiggled her son on her back as well. Kanini knew Florence's children were always plump and healthy. "Well, if your mother can spare you, it seems you'd be the obvious one to go up and help your aunt, Kanini. Gatiria will be going for *nyambura* soon, won't she?"

Kanini nodded again. She hurried home, thinking, *What an adventure, as well as a worthy endeavor. To stay with Aunt Njeri and nurse her through her illness. I wish I could take the trip and help her out. But Gatiria has to go. It might be her only chance.* She felt an urgency she'd never felt before; a drive to get to Gatiria before Mama made her own plans. As she shuffled through the dust, one hand on Mutwiri to keep him from falling off her back, it dawned on her that she might never see Aunt Njeri again.

Mama was milking the goat when she arrived; Gatiria was nowhere in sight. "Mama, we got a letter from Njeri," Kanini told her. "It says—"

Mama's snatched the letter from Kanini. Her mouth pinched into a grim line as she began to read. After setting the letter down, she spent a few moments slowly picking up some things and untying Mutwiri from Kanini's back. When she spoke, her voice was muted. "I should probably go and tend to her. She may be dying."

"Njeri's strong; she won't die, Mama. Maybe if one of us could go up and help her with things…"

"When was the letter written?" asked Mama. "It may already be too late."

The letter had been written five days before. Mama hesitated only a minute, a deep wrinkle piercing her brow. Then she was in motion, untying her dirty head square, as she headed into the main hut. She shouted for Kanini to bring her a basin of water. As Kanini sloshed water out of a jug, Gatiria entered the compound, more water on her back.

"Don't use up all the water before the chores are done," she admonished.

"Hush! It's for Mama. She's going up to Njeri. We got a letter—"

"Is that Gatiria?" Mama called. "Come in here, Gatiria!"

Gatiria entered the hut carrying the basin Kanini handed her. Mutwiri lay in the shade, flailing his fists and crying. Kanini squatted by him, her thoughts on Mama's possible intentions. Several minutes passed. Gitonga came through the gate and knelt by the baby, dangling something before him. Kanini hurried inside the house.

"Kanini," Mama said, zipping up a stuffed vinyl carryall. "Gatiria and I are taking the next vehicle up the mountain. We're going to Njeri's. I want you to take care of things down here for me. You're my big girl; I know you can handle it." She glanced around the hut. Her eyes finally alighted on Kanini, the crease between them having deepened. "We'll only be gone a few days. I want to see my sister and find out exactly what's happening up there."

Kanini took a deep breath and smiled at her mother. "I'm glad you're going up, Mama. I'll take care of everything, and I'll let Baba know."

A frown blemished Mama's face. "Don't mind whatever Baba says," she said. "I have to go. Tell him that."

They were off into the late afternoon, fresh head squares fluttering from their heads, their vinyl bags bouncing against their hips. Kanini was surprised to notice, as they disappeared into the hazy horizon, that they were the same height.

Two strands, one of disappointment and one of relief twisted together inside her. Kanini bit her lip as she checked on Mutwiri, who had fallen asleep under the tree. She debated moving him inside—the flies were already swirling around his face—but she knew the movement would wake him. Where had Gitonga gone? He could sit there for twenty minutes and swat flies away. She went to call her brother, who was probably constructing something or other. That boy was always creating little toys or tools. After she found him, she headed to the *riko* to start supper.

Already, Kanini's stomach was growling. She wondered how Mama and Gatiria would make it on the hour-long *matatu* ride followed by the two-hour walk without any food. Hopefully they'd brought a few coins along for *mandazzi*, the fried blobs of dough you could buy at *chai* shops. As she chopped onions, tears formed. Tears from the onions, but also tears of sympathy for her aunt who'd been living in such an abusive situation for so many years. It was terrible that her family had never prioritized going for a visit in all that time. After the death of Njeri's baby boy, Mama had debated making the journey anyway, but decided she could not justify the expense or the time away.

What would become of Njeri's children if she died? Her mother-in-law was probably too old to care for them, and Ezekial, though he was obligated as the uncle and Njeri's husband, would never be a fit parent. His first wife had finally given birth to a healthy baby of her own, and when he was home, he spent all his time fawning over this son.

She also wondered about Gatiria. Would she slip away somewhere while she was in the Chuka area? She couldn't just run off while she was staying with Njeri, especially with Mama there. Kanini wished she'd discussed more possibilities with her sister; they'd made no plan for her escape, since they'd still been waiting for an opportunity to present itself. Now, almost magically, one had. Although taking advantage of the trip to help Njeri was not the noblest idea, her sister did not have many choices in escaping *nyambura*; she had to seize on whatever came her way.

During supper, little was said as Cucu, Njagi, Gitonga and Kanini sat around the compound. Kanini fed Mutwiri, the two boys talked quietly and Cucu sat in silence and stared straight ahead with her cataract-washed eyes. She mouthed the fibrous peas between her gums, spitting out whatever she couldn't chew onto the hard dry ground. Finally she set down her bowl and took a lump of *ugali* from the plate on the table. She dipped the spongy mass into her glass of water, then pulled it out and ate it, leaving soggy bits in its wake.

It was almost bedtime when Baba returned. He entered the hut boisterously and then circled the room, slamming pot lids and dropping utensils on the ground.

"What's for supper? Where's your mother, Gitonga?" Kanini heard Baba's voice from behind the curtain. She was kneeling on her parents' mat, removing Mutwiri's wet nappy.

"She and Gatiria went to visit Aunt Njeri, Baba," Gitonga answered. "Kanini got a letter today at the market—"

"What? They've gone up to Kanwa? Why didn't they wait and discuss it with me? We don't have money for trips like that." Kanini could hear the sound of a fist hitting the table. "And now they'll be gone who knows how many days? Who'll do the work around this house?"

"I will, Baba," said Kanini in a low voice, entering the room with Mutwiri on her hip.

"Mama's worried she might die," Gitonga spoke up. Her younger brother stood with his hands sunk in his ragged pockets.

"Njeri asked for Gatiria or me to go alone to help her out, but Mama worried that if she didn't go herself, she might never see her again." Kanini looked her father straight in the eye. She hoped his brain was sober enough to understand.

It was quiet as Baba stopped pacing and stared off, his eyes on neither Kanini nor Gitonga. When he spoke, his words were calmer, his voice dull and steady. "This is the sister who was married by a man who has enough money to support two wives, as well as many children, and take trips to Embu and Nairobi whenever he feels like it. He has a coffee plantation, plenty of large cows and a good business in Chuka. How can this man not spend a little money—or at least some time—on the woman he inherited from his brother, a woman he is legally married to? This is what I don't understand."

So often, in his drunken rages, Baba blamed everyone but himself for their financial troubles and inability to help relatives in need. He could discuss in detail the situations of men more successful than he was, making Kanini wonder if he was envious of them. She was often as contemptuous of his useless envy as she was his costly drinking habit.

But every once in a while, such as right now, Kanini could understand her father's perspective.

"Maybe Ezekiel is gone so often he doesn't even know how Njeri is," mused Kanini, as she sat down to rock the baby.

"That wouldn't surprise me," Baba said. He had begun helping himself to the food that was hard and cold. "Ezekiel isn't focused enough on his own home. Then your mother goes up there, thinking that she can actually do something to help, when it's really none of her concern."

"I don't think she really thought she could do much," Kanini dared to contradict Baba. "I think she just wanted to see Njeri again, since it's been so long and she's doing so poorly."

Baba took a breath as though to say something, but seemed to think better of it. He sat down heavily and began spooning food into his mouth. Kanini stared at him a while, but he was quiet for so long that she finally got up to take Mutwiri to bed.

Suddenly, Baba's voice boomed forth. "This financial situation is getting so bad we're going to have to do something I didn't want to do for a while. But it's time now; it's nearly time."

"Time for what, Baba?" asked Gitonga, looking up from a schoolbook. Kanini turned to face her father, her heartbeat picking up its pace at the urgency of his tone.

"Time for Kanini to get married."

Kanini nearly dropped the baby.

Get married! She'd thought they wouldn't marry her off till she was at least nineteen or twenty. She was only seventeen. If she started having babies now, she'd be an old woman before she was thirty, her skin sagging and her hair graying. She thought of Florence, who was not more than twenty-five and already had so many.

Baba looked up from his food, raised his eyebrows at her, and then returned his attention to his plate. He was liable to say anything when intoxicated, Kanini knew, especially after the sort of discussion they'd just had. They weren't that desperate for money that they would force her to marry this soon. Were they?

"So, start thinking about it, Kanini," Baba continued. "I've been talking to some men in the market who have eligible sons. Don't worry, I won't choose one who wouldn't take care of you, who'd throw all his money away on drink." He chuckled. "I've been waiting to talk to a certain man, not from around here, who Bwana Mkubwa knows, a man who owns a lot of cows and goats. He has a son in his early twenties. An educated son who finished Form Four. I haven't met the man yet, but he should be coming this way soon."

Chapter 3

Late in the morning, three days after Mama and Gatiria left, Kanini was preparing to milk the nanny goat once again. She'd finally gotten the little beast to accept her and was able to get a cup of milk out of her a few times a day. A shout from Gitonga, followed by Mutwiri's gurgling, caused her to look around. Mama was walking towards them, her slim form shimmering in the waves of heat that rose off the ground.

Kanini waited as Gitonga ran to greet her and escorted her back to the compound. Mama scooped up Mutwiri from the *leso* and cuddled him. Then she caught Kanini's eye and smiled.

"Njeri is doing all right," she said as she unwrapped her bundles inside the house. "She needs a lot of care, and so does Carolina. They seem to have the same sickness, but it isn't malaria, or at least not anymore. It's something that weakens a body and causes it to get all sorts of strange symptoms. Both Njeri and Carolina have boils on their skin, like infected mosquito bites. Njeri also gets diarrhea now and then."

"Where's Gatiria?" asked Kanini.

"I left her with Njeri. She's the best one to stay with her right now. Caring for my sister will keep her mind off trying to get out of being circumcised." Mama dropped down into a chair and fanned her face with her hand. Kanini poured her a glass of drinking water, cloudy with silt. "Perhaps Njeri will even be able to influence her; I know Gatiria respects her. Meanwhile, I can plan her *nyambura*."

"Aren't you worried that Gatiria might get Njeri's disease?" Kanini asked. She hoped Njeri might join forces with Gatiria, rather than influence her in the other direction.

Mama's forehead crinkled with concern. "I have thought of that. Njeri must have someone to care for her, though, and there's no one else. Besides, Gatiria is strong. If anyone can withstand this sickness, she'll be able to."

"How was Gatiria's attitude toward caring for Njeri and Carolina?" asked Kanini, taking a sip from her own glass.

"She seemed fine after we stayed with them a few days. When we first arrived, Gatiria asked me why Njeri couldn't go back to her old home and live with her mother-in-law." Mama shook her head and tsk-ed her disapproval.

"Gatiria needs to understand that Njeri's old home isn't her home anymore, now that Mugendi's dead," mused Kanini, though she too wished Njeri could move back.

"You know Gatiria; she's so stubborn—it's not that she can't understand certain things; she just refuses. She's so quick to recognize injustice."

"How was the atmosphere where you were staying, at Ezekiel's place?"

"Very bad. His other wife screams through the compound whenever she feels like it. Her focus is all on her baby, and in fact, she really has no other work since her sister lives with them and takes care of most of it." Mama dipped her handkerchief into her glass of water and moistened her face with it. "Njeri was caring for the *munda*, but since she became so sick, very little was harvested. I wish we'd known she was in such a state! We could have gone up to help her harvest her crops before they withered in the field."

"But then Baba would've become angry since we would've neglected our own *munda*," sighed Kanini.

Mama looked at her and then away again. "We have many healthy people in our family, Kanini. Both harvests could have been taken care of, if we'd only known." She sighed, and Kanini could see anguish clouding her eyes.

Kanini wanted to ask more. What would happen if Njeri did not get better and was no longer able to care for her children? She dared not mention such a devastating circumstance, at least not now.

Three weeks later, a letter arrived from Gatiria. She wrote in their mother tongue, *Kitharaka.*

Kanwa Market
2 March 1990

Dear Family Members,

Mugeni? I hope this letter finds you in good health, as you were when I left our place. And Mama, how was your trip home?

My time here with Njeri and Carolina has been difficult, but we are carrying on well. Njeri is as kind as ever, though she loses strength by the day. I need to help her with almost everything now—using the toilet, washing, feeding herself. Carolina also needs help in most things, though she doesn't seem as badly off as her mother.

We try to avoid Endelina, if we can help it. I have only seen Ezekiel two times, and only once up close. He doesn't seem to care at all about Njeri, and I wonder why he married her. At least he always has money, which is good, since I need to go to the market for nearly everything here.

At Kanwa a few days ago, I met a *mzungu*. Her English was hard to understand, but finally I found out that she's an Italian nun and lives at the mission near Chuka. I felt sorry for her, since the sun seemed to be bothering her a lot. She was friendly and seemed impressed with my English. She told me that maybe sometime I could come and visit the mission.

I will stay and help Aunt Njeri for as long as I can. If she gets much worse, I'll take the next *matatu* to fetch you, Mama, or at least send you a letter. I'm worried about her, but am doing the best I can.

Send greetings to any of my classmates you see and everyone in town. I look forward to seeing you all soon!

Sincerely,

Lucy Gatiria

Kanini felt her heart beat faster as she finished reading the letter aloud. A *mzungu*! At a mission! She could visualize the conflict that would torment Gatiria regarding a possible escape. She'd deliberate calling on these Christians for help—since it was possible they could provide her with some sort of refuge—then chide herself for even considering it. Gatiria had always thought of whites as the enemy: the moneyed elite, who tempted women away from nursing their own babies with their expensive milk formulas; the tourists, who dictated how Kenya should use its land; the self-righteous buyers of cash crops, who tempted the locals to plant tea and coffee when they should plant traditional crops to stave off famine; and the Christians, who promoted worshiping a god that meant nothing to many Africans. How could she ever justify running away from her own people in order to take shelter with them?

On the other hand, wouldn't they have a clinic or hospital there? Maybe Gatiria had suggested to the nun that Njeri be checked out. That would be the responsible thing to do. Kanini felt a burning desire to respond to her sister's letter. After her chores were done that evening, she scrounged up a foolscap and a pen, lit the lamp and started her letter. She wrote in English, in case Gatiria needed to show the letter to the *wazungu* and to keep certain information secret from their elders.

Kajuki Market
11 March, 1990

Dear Gatiria,

We thank-you for your kind missive, which we received today. I hope the atmospheric pressure up where you are is treating you well. On our side, we are doing well down in Tharaka.

I am happy to hear that Njeri is doing okay, however still worried that she is not cured. Might be that *mzungu* lady could be helping our aunt over at the mission. Is there not a health center there? Perhaps they would be knowing what to do concerning Njeri's extreme condition. Did you ask her? Please do it next time that you see her.

As for any other plans, I hope you keep me informed. Maybe I will be going up there to take your place, you know when. Then you can tell me what you intend to do. Until then, pass our regards to Aunt and the cousins. Also Mugendi's mother if you see her.

With sincere regards,

Angela Kanini

The next day she breezily walked the letter to market and gave it to Florence for safe keeping until the next *matatu* came. Later on, as Mama and Kanini were on their way home from gathering firewood, Kanini asked her about the plan for Gatiria's return.

"The date for her circumcision is the twentieth of April," said Mama, as she shifted the trumpline on her forehead. "Njeri has instructions to put Gatiria on a vehicle by the fifteenth. That's about a month away."

"Who will care for Njeri once Gatiria is back here?" asked Kanini quietly. Her own trumpline was digging into her flesh and her back ached.

"I've been thinking about that. Maybe I'll send you up there. The only problem is all the work I would be left doing here at the house. With Gatiria healing and Njagi out everyday, most of it would fall on me—Kanini, let's stop for a minute." Mama set down her load with a sigh. Kanini stopped, but did not remove her load.

"Gitonga has been so helpful lately," Kanini said. "I could teach him some more about cooking and grinding. He already fetches water and firewood and herds the goats. Maybe he could even be taught to milk!" The ideas rushed from her brain out her mouth.

Mama's smile appeared slowly. "Well, I would love for you to be able to stay with your aunt a while. Let's hope it can happen, Kanini." With that, she heaved the heavy load of wood back onto her back. A surge of energy propelled Kanini homeward. Not only was she excited about being a part of her sister's adventure, despite the rebellious nature of it, but she felt a lightness blossom in her heart for her own. Something to look forward to! A new place to go and new people to meet. She might never get to do such a thing again if she were going to be married so soon. Maybe she could even be the one to get Njeri the medical attention she needed. She was, after all, the older daughter and had more wisdom and experience. She would be the appropriate one to stay with her aunt. This would be obvious to everyone as soon as Kanini could go there herself and prove it.

Chapter 4

The month passed slowly for Kanini. She helped Mama with the planting, while Gitonga spent the days herding goats. Everyday she checked at the market to see if another letter had arrived from Gatiria, but nothing had.

The plan was for Kanini to leave Kajuki on the fourteenth of April and arrive at Njeri's place that evening; whereupon, Gatiria would take off the next morning to return home. As the day neared, she found herself obsessing over what clothes to bring and what food to carry from the *munda* to surprise Njeri. In the end, she packed a small vinyl bag with an extra dress, a bag of ground millet meal, and a new head square that Mama tucked in at the last minute.

The evening before her departure, Kanini went down to the river to get water. She noticed black thunderheads piled up on the mountain, and for the first time in her life, prayed that it wouldn't rain.

She awoke the next morning to the sound of a steady downpour on the thatched roof. The sound that usually gave her comfort aggravated her today. She knew the vehicles would not be able to get up the mountain through the mud, and there would be no transport until the roads dried again. As disappointed as she was to put off her trip another day, she knew that Gatiria would also be obliged to wait a day to return.

As she ate her *uji*, her thoughts were far away and she hardly heard Mama speak to her. "Kanini, did you hear me? I said maybe if the rain stops by noon, you might be able to get a vehicle after lunch."

"I'll go check at the market," said Kanini without much hope.

As Kanini suspected, there wasn't a vehicle to be had. The rain ended late in the morning, but it was obviously still coming down on Kirinyaga. No *matatu* would head their direction. She spent an hour milling about the market and finally came home, a bunch of *gasukari* in her bag for Mutwiri.

That night the sky was clear and a fresh breeze blew across the greening hills. Despite the cooler weather, Kanini couldn't sleep. Too many thoughts of the journey crowded into her head. She couldn't stop wondering what Gatiria was up to: where she was planning to go and how or if she would call upon Kanini to assist her.

Kanini arose in the morning feeling light-headed. She lit the fire and put water on for *chai*; then got her things ready and tidied up her sleeping area. Mama met her in the *riko* and they sipped tea together.

"I'm certain Njeri won't send Gatiria back today," Mama mused. "It'll be too muddy up there and really, there's no rush for her to return. Her ceremony is still five days away. I want you to promise me you'll escort her to the *matatu* stand in Kanwa tomorrow, Kanini, and make sure she gets on a vehicle coming to Kajuki. You can even tell the driver not to let her off until she gets here."

"Are you worried she won't make it home on her own?"

"Yes I am, Kanini. She seemed so determined not to be circumcised. She's impulsive. I'm not sure what she might do. I just need to make sure she makes it back here."

It dawned on her that Mama might not be too surprised when she heard about Gatiria's escape. Did Mama regret taking Gatiria up the mountain in the first place? The concern in her voice wrung Kanini's heart. How she wanted to make Mama happy! She always had in the past. By helping her sister escape, Kanini would be acting as a traitor to Mama. A sick feeling crept through her insides. How could she be an accomplice in her sister's disobedience, basically throwing back in Mama and Baba's faces something they so valued?

On the other hand, what else could she do? Escorting Gatiria to the *matatu* that would return her to Kajuki, even if her sister were to obediently follow her, would make Kanini feel like a traitor to both her sister and her own beliefs. If circumcision were to kill Gatiria, wouldn't Mama feel like *she* had betrayed her younger daughter? Or was Mama just so faithful to the custom that she would only feel like a traitor if she did not force her children to undergo it?

With resolve overcoming her turbulent stomach, Kanini said good-bye to her sleepy-eyed brothers and hugged Mama before heading off to the market to await a vehicle. Luckily, a lorry happened to be heading up and she was able to hop aboard after only a short wait.

She loved riding in lorries. Her seat afforded her a terrific view of the changes in terrain as the road climbed in elevation. The gray acacias and red dirt gave way to the glossy green of the tall eucalyptus trees and round mango trees growing in the dark loamy earth. As she expected, the road became quite muddy as they neared Kanwa, but the lorry's huge wheels maneuvered through with ease.

After an hour's ride, she jumped from the vehicle, poked around the market to pick up some fresh oranges and a pineapple, and then headed onto the trail that led to her aunt's. Now that her adventure had begun, her step was light and her heart sang with the thrill of finally being away from the doubts and drudgery of *mucii* for an indefinite period of time.

As she walked, she looked out over the square huts clustered tightly together, their corrugated tin roofs glinting in the bright sun. Banana trees drooped fan-like leaves over the *bomas*, the bamboo structures where the cows were kept. There they stood all day in their own manure, chewing the tall rapier grass that their owners hauled in for them; they were rarely taken out and grazed. The *mundas* here were much closer together than down in Tharaka, as the land was more fertile and therefore every inch required cultivation.

Not knowing the entire route to Njeri's, she stopped at a small *chai* shop to ask directions. An older woman greeted Kanini at the doorway, her gnarled hands raised in welcome. "*Nimwega! Wathieko?*"

"*Ndathie mucii Aniceta,*" Kanini responded. "I'm not sure which way to go."

The woman nodded her head and indicated that Kanini follow her. "I'm going that way myself," she said. Kanini noted the difference in her dialect of the Meru language.

As they headed off, Kanini asked her if she knew Njeri, Ezekial's second wife.

The woman hesitated a minute as she squinted at Kanini, her eyes mere slits in her wizened face. "Njeri...? Young Mugendi's wife? She...she died last month."

Kanini stopped in her tracks and stared at the woman. The words echoed thickly in her head. "Njeri...? But...that's not possible. Someone would have contacted us—" She stepped into the shade of a tree and steadied herself against the trunk.

"Njeri became very weak," the woman went on. "One morning she just didn't wake up. Aniceta arranged her funeral and brought the children. Many neighbors and friends went to pay their respects, my family included."

Kanini squeezed her eyes shut. She didn't know what to think. Poor Njeri! It must have all happened so suddenly, with no time to contact Mama. And what had happened to Gatiria? At the very least, she could have written them a letter. Or did Gatiria selfishly run off as soon as Njeri's body was in the ground?

She opened her eyes to see the woman gazing at her with concern. "Is my sister, Gatiria, still around, do you know?" she asked.

"I don't know about that, but Aniceta will."

Kanini got up heavily and followed the woman the rest of the way to Njeri's mother-in-law's. The landscape blurred into a wash of greens and yellows. A terrible ringing started up in her head and the sick feeling returned to her stomach.

"*Hoti*, Aniceta!" shouted the neighbor as they approached the decrepit hut. Kanini noticed gaping holes in the mud and patches on the roof where the tin was loose and flapping. Kanini was astounded that this was where Ezekial's mother had been living all this time. The place looked like it was falling apart!

Seven year-old Silvia appeared at the door, her shy doe eyes taking in the visitors. Kanini had not seen her cousin in years and noted that she had grown into a lanky, healthy-looking little girl. "*Karibu*," the child welcomed them.

"Where is your *cucu*, Silvia?" Kanini asked.

Silvia glanced around, as though unwilling to give information to a stranger. Then Kanini's escort reached out her hand and Silvia smiled, recognizing the woman. "She's...she's in the *munda*, weeding the maize."

"I'm Kanini, Gatiria's sister. I'm one of your cousins. Do you remember me?"

Silvia nodded slowly, then left the hut and led Kanini around to the garden in back. Kanini turned to say thank-you to the helpful neighbor, but the woman had disappeared.

Silvia called out to her grandmother, whose crooked form straightened amidst the tiny maize plants. As the old woman wended her way toward them, she wiped the sweat from her forehead with a handkerchief. Her dress was a scrap of colorless polyester that looked to be at least twenty years old. A ragged straw hat shaded her eyes. Sylvia introduced Kanini to her *cucu*, and they shook hands.

"Let's go to the house, Kanini," Aniceta's voice had the sound of gravel tumbling off a shovel. "I'm sure you're thirsty." She led the way, hobbling slowly around chunks of earth and unruly undergrowth. Kanini wondered if she had rickets in her legs, or perhaps knee problems.

"*Bibi* Aniceta, I just heard the news about Njeri. I don't know what to think—" Kanini's words fell over themselves as she followed her elder inside the hut. Aniceta nodded at a chair and sat down on the other side of a sturdy wooden table. Kanini noticed the same milky sheen clouding her eyes as clouded Cucu's. She wondered if her son ever gave her money to be treated at the hospital.

"You only just heard the news? How can that be? We sent Gatiria home more than a week ago."

Kanini squinted at Aniceta. "Gatiria hasn't been home, Aniceta. We haven't seen her."

Aniceta looked over to the doorway as her grandson, Zacharia, entered. She pointed to a *mtungi* of water and an empty *sufuria*. Zacharia collected them and went back out.

Aniceta's eyes returned to Kanini's face. "Well, she's not here."

Kanini forced herself to take a deep breath over the agitated beating of her heart. "Could you tell me everything from when Mama left, Aniceta? I would really like to know."

Aniceta sat back in her chair and folded her hands. "Njeri died maybe two or three weeks ago now. We'd thought she was improving a little. But it was just a last bit of strength before the end." The old woman suddenly began fumbling around under the table until her hands alighted on a *kiondo* with knitting needles sticking out of it. She dragged it up to the table and absently begin clicking away.

She was silent for so long that Kanini wondered if she remembered the story she was relating. "What were her—?"

"So, let's see, where was I? Oh yes, Njeri. She had become so weak and was having diarrhea all the time. Then she began coughing up blood. Her mind had also become muddled. Sometimes she didn't know what was going on." Aniceta shook her head sadly, her eyes on her gnarled hands. "Gatiria was there, caring for her everyday. Doing a very good job. Every time I went over with the children, she would greet us with a smile. The house was clean, the clothes all washed…Very good work she was doing…"

Another lengthy silence passed. Kanini could hear her cousin outside the door rinsing cups for *chai*, as well as the boisterous voices of men walking by on the road.

"Then one day, Njeri just didn't wake up. It was like her heart had given up the fight. I wanted all of you to attend the funeral, but so much was happening, there wasn't time…Carolina started failing, maybe because of Njeri's death, I'm not sure. She had a chest infection and was coughing… By the end, she could hardly breathe."

Zacharia entered with a teapot and two dripping glasses. He set them down on the table and poured two cups of *chai*. Aniceta waited until he had set the sugar dish on the table and helped herself to two spoonfuls. Then she continued her tale.

"Gatiria had gotten some medicine for her at the mission clinic—by that time she and Carolina were staying here with us—but it didn't seem to help. A week after Njeri's death, Carolina died in Gatiria's arms." Aniceta had set the knitting down and turned to gaze out the small open window. "All the life seemed to go out of her as well; it's like she took the blame for their deaths. When I told her 'Ni kwenda kwa Ngai', she left the house without saying a word."

Kanini nodded in sympathy. "She doesn't believe that things are just Ngai's will."

Aniceta tsk-ed her tongue. "I guess not...After Njeri's death, Gatiria said she sent you a letter telling you what happened. I didn't think it would get there in time for you to come up, so we made the necessary arrangements without you." Aniceta took a long draw of tea. She smacked her lips in satisfaction. She picked up her knitting again, but then set it back down. "The day after Carolina's funeral, Gatiria said she needed to get back home to you all. I gave her transport money and she packed her bag and left."

"Did she go by herself?" asked Kanini

"Yes; there was no one around to escort her. I walked with her part of the way to Kanwa. That was the last I saw of her."

Kanini sipped her *chai*. She toyed with the teaspoon that lay on a dish beside the teapot, weighing her words. "Just before I left home, Mama told me to be especially careful to escort Gatiria to the *matatu* and make sure she got on one going to Kajuki. She was worried that maybe...maybe Gatiria wouldn't make it home because...because she was going back to be circumcised. And Gatiria didn't want to be circumcised."

Aniceta gave a sharp bark. "I heard about all that from Njeri. Gatiria didn't know what she was talking about. Njeri said she talked to Gatiria quite a lot about *nyambura*...got her to understand why it's so important... and Gatiria listened. Njeri was fairly sure she'd gotten through to her."

"Then, what do you think happened?" asked Kanini.

"Maybe something awful happened, like thieves or an accident. If a lorry hit her *matatu*, the crash might have killed everyone. Have you thought of that?" Aniceta's washed out eyes settled on Kanini's face.

Kanini nodded humbly, though she doubted whether a *matatu* crash could've happened on the Kajuki road without everyone in town finding out about it. Aniceta offered her a slice of bread and she accepted it absently. She chewed the bread without tasting it.

"Do you think Ezekiel would know anything about Gatiria?" Kanini wondered aloud. "Has anyone talked to him lately?"

"Ezekiel went to Nairobi a few weeks ago and hasn't returned yet. He doesn't even know that Njeri died."

Kanini let that sink in with another draught of *chai*. "What about Endelina? How did she feel about Gatiria living with them there?"

Zacharia sat down in a chair across the room and stirred his glass of tea. "I don't know how Endelina felt about Gatiria, but I know that she was jealous of Njeri. She never helped her with anything and always made her do more than her share." The older woman took a large bite of bread and chewed. A shower of crumbs sprayed from her mouth.

"I was always proud of Zacharia and Silvia," Aniceta went on after swallowing. She glanced over at her grandson, who looked at his feet. "Whenever they were over at Ezekiel's place, they helped Njeri with whatever needed doing. They were especially good with Carolina."

"I'm thinking that if I can stay with you, I'll see if I can find Gatiria," Kanini stated. "I'm pretty sure she's still around this area. Would that be all right, Aniceta?"

Aniceta's eyelids peeled back; her eyes were riveted on Kanini. "Wherever she is, you're welcome to stay here with us." Aniceta smiled for the first time, revealing fragmented and discolored teeth. "If you find that sister of yours, I'll personally escort her back to Kajuki and see to it that she gets circumcised! Young people these days..." Her voice trailed off with a series of tsk-tsks.

As the old woman sat back in her chair, a strand of knitting caught on her sleeve and the whole thing toppled off the table. Kanini lunged for it and placed it back in her hands. Such a misguided, yet pathetic old *cucu*! The intense sympathy Kanini felt for her aunt's mother-in-law far outweighed any other emotion.

Chapter 5

The next day, Kanini made the short trek to the home Njeri had shared with Ezekiel. Though she knew Gatiria would be nowhere near there, she wanted to check the place out and glean what she could, since it would give her some context for their later conversations.

"*Hoti!*" Kanini called as she neared the compound. A mangy dog ran out at her, barking and snapping. She hissed at it and raised her hand, and it retreated to the shade of one of the huts. The place seemed deserted and unkempt. The cows' *boma* was full to overflowing with manure, and the area around the huts had not been swept in days. Chickens squawked and dodged among stalks of sugar cane that leaned against the main house, a house made of stone. Torn plastic bags blew about, catching on weeds and rocks. A curl of smoke wound its way out from between the slats of the *riko*, and Kanini heard a dull scuffling sound from within.

"*Karibu!*" came a voice. A girl about Kanini's own age appeared at the door to the kitchen, drying her hands on her faded dress. Her plaits were wispy and uncovered, though her face looked freshly washed. Kanini walked towards her, hand outstretched, and introduced herself.

"I'm Kanini, Gatiria's sister," she said as she received the girl's hand in response.

"I'm Jescah, Endelina's sister. *Karibu chai.*" Kanini followed Jescah to one side of the *riko* where she saw two stones and a chair in the shade of a scraggly jacaranda tree. Kanini sat on one of the stones as Jescah disappeared back into the *riko*. When she returned some minutes later, she carried a teapot and two cups. Having not yet taken anything that morning, Kanini's mouth watered at the sight of the rich, milky *chai* streaming into the cups.

"*Nikwega mono*," Kanini said. Jescah settled herself onto the other stone, tucking her skirt between her thin legs. She took a long drink.

"So, you're visiting from Tharaka, Kanini?" Jescah spoke in a completely different dialect of the Meru tongue.

"Yes. I came to take Gatiria's place helping our Aunt Njeri."

"You came to take Gatiria's place, eh? Hmmm..." Jescah absently dug her rubber slipper into a mound of dust. "Your aunt was a kind-hearted woman."

Kanini nodded, trying to get past the ache that returned every time she thought about Njeri. With a deep breath, she said, "Now we're wondering where Gatiria went."

"You're wondering where she went? I thought she'd be home by now!"

"That's what Aniceta thought. But—tell me, Jescah, how were things when Gatiria was here? Did you see her much? Her and Njeri?"

"Did I see them much? I saw them everyday. Though Gatiria usually avoided me—" Jescah said. "Endelina didn't like me talking to her, and Gatiria was always busy. She also seemed sort of...preoccupied. So we'd usually just greet each other and that was all."

"Did you have any idea why Gatiria seemed preoccupied?"

"Why was Gatiria preoccupied? Well, I thought it was because of her responsibilities here. She was taking care of two sick people and she's only fourteen. I wanted to help, but my sister told me not to." Jescah toyed with the hem of her dress, never taking her eyes off the fabric between her fingers. "I really admired her for what she was doing, in fact."

A tendril of envy wormed its way through Kanini. Leave it to Gatiria to end up the heroine and get out of circumcision to boot. "Do you know when Endelina will be back?" Kanini asked with restraint.

"She'll be back soon. I'm supposed to be cooking lunch." Jescah got up and went back to the *riko* to tend to the food boiling on the fire. Time passed. Kanini began to wonder what she would do if Endelina returned. Her intuition told her Jescah might not be so friendly or open once her older sister came home.

The shade had moved enough for Kanini to seat herself on the other stone by the time Jescah reappeared with two plates piled high with aromatic food. It was *irio*, a Kikuyu dish made of mashed potatoes mixed with maize, beans and finely chopped green vegetables. "Let's eat together now," said Jescah. "Endelina can have hers when she gets here."

While they ate, they talked about their backgrounds. Jescah came from the Chogoria area, which was closer to Kirinyaga even than Chuka, and therefore much cooler. Like Kanini, she had also been forced to terminate her studies after Standard Seven, and her father was presently searching for a husband for her. After establishing all they had in common, Kanini took a deep breath and asked Jescah if she had undergone the circumcision rite.

"*Allah!* Have *I* gone through circumcision? Me? No, of course not! That's only for boys!" Jescah seemed genuinely surprised.

"Haven't you ever heard of girls being circumcised?"

"I've heard of it, but that custom was outlawed long ago. No one does it anymore. Not much anyway. Those who are circumcised and go to Chogoria hospital—hunh!" Jescah wrinkled her nose. "They're treated badly by the doctors. Women are told if their babies cannot come out properly, it's their own fault!"

Kanini winced. Holding her voice steady, she said, "I got circumcised, Jescah. Most every girl is circumcised down in Tharaka where I come from."

There was a moment of silence. "So...*you* got circumcised! I didn't know that girls were still having it done! I thought our mothers or even grandmothers were the last ones...I know girls aren't circumcised around this area, are they?"

Kanini could only shake her head and stare at the ground.

Jescah continued, deep in thought, "I know Aniceta supports *nyambura*... Aniceta is so old, though. I'm sure most *cucus* wish their daughters and granddaughters would still perform the ceremony. But we refuse, and they're not strong enough to force us anymore. So now, no one even talks about it, at least not in my place." Jescah flicked the skin of a bean from her plate and took another bite.

Kanini found it odd that no one would talk about a rite that for so long had played such a significant role for the Meru people. "What do the men say?" she asked Jescah. "About your women not being circumcised, I mean."

Jescah chewed her food thoughtfully. "Well, the men want to be respected by the *wazungu*, you know. White people say that circumcision for girls is barbaric and uncivilized and should be outlawed, so—"

"So, men up here really don't mind that their women aren't circumcised?"

"Yes...that's true." Jescah had picked up their plates and was carrying them to the back of the *riko* where there was a basin of wash water. Kanini followed her. They washed their plates together in silence. Kanini was about to ask something else when she heard the front gate creak open.

Jescah looked quickly at Kanini and then darted back into the *riko* with the dripping plates. Kanini meandered back to the center of the compound to find a large woman with a toddler tied to her back, leaning an umbrella against the stone house.

Kanini had expected Endelina to be thin and weak after hearing Njeri's stories from long ago. The flabby bulk of the woman startled her. She also looked far older than Kanini had imagined.

"I'm Kanini, Gatiria's sister." Kanini approached the woman with her hand outstretched. Endelina glared at her and busied herself untying her child. She did not shake Kanini's hand.

"Jescah, is there any *chai?*" she called.

"Yes, Endelina," came Jescah's voice from the kitchen. Endelina sat down on the chair in the shade and set her son on her lap. The little boy was dressed in a fine suit of clothes and leather shoes. Shoes for a small child was an unheard-of luxury. Kanini tore her eyes away and stepped to the door of the *riko*.

"*Nikwega mono*, Jescah!" Kanini called out to the girl. "It was nice meeting you." Jescah's eyes glowed white in the gloom, but her teeth did not. The scrawny dog saw Kanini out the gate.

Heading back to Aniceta's, Kanini thought about Jescah and her plight. To be forced to serve such a sister! Even with Ezekial's money supporting them. Kanini couldn't imagine such a thing. Better to run your own home, even if it meant being married to a man you hardly knew.

The next morning, Kanini set off early for the mission, following Aniceta's directions. This was where she might have started her search, if she hadn't been so curious to see Ezekial's place. She walked back to the town of Kanwa, then turned west towards Chuka and followed the road a while. She came to a shortcut, which took her a few kilometers into lush farmland. The verdant hills dotted with coffee bushes led her eyes to a pillow of clouds that obscured Kirinyaga, as they so often did during the rainy season. Already this area had received so much moisture that the new maize crop was almost knee-high. Kanini felt a pang of envy. To think of being able to grow fresh vegetables like collards, cabbages and carrots even! She had only tasted these things when someone went to Ishiara market and paid money for them. Her family had never been able to grow any more fresh vegetables in their garden than the leaves they plucked off the *nthoroko* plants.

She rounded a bend and sighted the mission buildings spread before her like a small city. As she got closer, a two-story building stamped with a red cross and a long building with many rooms loomed before her. The latter looked to be a secondary school, complete with verandas and shaded walks, some built amidst terraced gardens. Brilliant pink bougainvillea overhung the walls, and tall trees shaded the patches of grass that grew among the concrete. They looked so inviting, Kanini wondered how anyone could resist plopping down and stretching out on the soft ground covering. *This must be a private school where children who've done well on their KCPE exams attend*, she thought. She glanced around for a sign of people. All she could see were a few workers across the school compound, removing something from a shed.

Where should she go to find someone to talk to? The school was obviously not in session and she could discern no office. She glanced back at the building she assumed was a health center. It must be open for those in need of medicine and treatment. Tentatively, she headed toward the door and knocked. There was no answer, but it was unlocked, so she opened it and went in.

As her eyes adjusted to the dim light, she noticed a woman sitting at a desk wearing a crisp white nurse's uniform. She looked up when Kanini entered. "May I help you with something?"

"Yes, please," said Kanini, her words rushing out in a stream. "I'm looking for my sister, Lucy Gatiria. Have you seen or...heard anything of her?" Deep in her pocket, her hand clutched her handkerchief. She had always found it difficult to ask for information on personal matters from people she had no connection to. This pinch-faced woman looked like she might have a hard time establishing connections with anyone.

"I'm not sure I can help you. What's your sister's name again?" asked the nurse, scowling. She scanned an open ledger book.

"Lucy Gatiria. She's about fourteen years old."

"Why do you think we might know anything about her?" The nurse did not raise her eyes from the page.

"Well, she met one of the *wazungu*—I mean, missionary workers, um... nuns—who works here, when she was at Kanwa market. Then...I think she came here to get medicine. After our aunt and cousin died, she was supposed to go home—we live down in Tharaka—but she never arrived. So I wondered if...maybe she came back here." Kanini paused as the woman looked up at her, the suspicious frown still on her face. "...Or maybe someone here might know where she is."

The nurse rose from her chair. "Well, let me go and....Which nun did she meet, do you know?"

"My sister said she was Italian. She was...older, with glasses."

"Maybe Sister Margharita. Let me see." The nurse got up and left the room.

When the nurse returned a few minutes later, a short pink woman with glasses and gray hair accompanied her. A long white head square hung down over her shoulders and she wore a sharp blue and white dress, stockings and clean white shoes. She walked directly up to Kanini and held out her hand.

"Good morning, young lady," she said in an accent of English Kanini had never heard before. At first Kanini thought she might be speaking a different *mzungu* language. "I know of your sister Gatiria. She's a very good girl."

Kanini was startled at how forthright this woman was. She had never seen a white person and had to force herself not to stare. The woman's skin was papery and thin, and Kanini was stunned to see purple and green veins criss-crossing her neck and arms. Transparent skin! Her eyes were even more startling. They were blue, not the pale color of Cucu's and Aniceta's, but a pure blue, like the sky on a sunny day.

After shaking the outstretched hand, Kanini asked in her best English, "Are you knowing where my sister is now?"

"Yes, we do know where she is." The *mzungu* cast her eyes over at the nurse. "She's here at the mission...with us."

"Here! You said she is here?" Kanini exclaimed. So her instincts had led her to the right place after all.

"That's right. We're keeping her here so that she will not have to return home for her circumcision ceremony." The nun's tone was smug, causing a wind of misgiving to blow through Kanini. She'd been hoping for Gatiria to escape the fate of *nyambura*. She'd been willing to support her, cover up for her and even lie to protect her from the awful rite. Yet, here was this *mzungu* declaring that she and her fellows would keep Gatiria so that she would not have to return home. As though it were *their* idea!

"But...but how is...how does Gatiria feel about that?" she asked, trying to sound meek.

The nun snorted. "It doesn't matter how she feels about it, young lady. She is a minor...a child, who cannot yet make her own decisions. And female circumcision is illegal in Kenya." Now her tone was starkly patronizing. "What your people practice down in Tharaka the government of Kenya is trying to stamp out. Do you understand? Therefore, we have every right to hold your sister here until there is—how do you say? No threat for her to be circumcised."

Kanini breathed deeply. Staying here would be the perfect solution for Gatiria. She had known it would be. It was just strange to Kanini that this nun seemed to have taken possession of everything. But maybe Gatiria didn't see it this way.

"So, how long can she be able to stay here?" Kanini asked.

"As long as there is the threat of circumcision, we will keep her. Perhaps, if your parents come to discuss a different plan, we would release her, but until then..." The nun's voice trailed off, but her direct gaze never left Kanini's face.

Kanini was sure her parents would never come to discuss anything with these people. A far more likely scenario, she thought sadly, would be their renouncing Gatiria as their daughter. What would become of her, they would wonder? An uncircumcised girl trying to get married in Tharaka? She just would not fit in. They would never be able to reconcile this.

"Can I be able to speak with Gatiria?" Kanini asked as humbly as she could.

Once again, the *mzungu* looked at the nurse. Kanini got the distinct feeling that neither trusted her. "I can let you do that. As long as you meet with her here in the reception area, with Rose. I will go find her."

Chapter 6

Kanini sat on a stiff vinyl couch and took in her surroundings. The room had gray concrete walls, the ceiling was high and an electric fan whirred from above, creating a slight, pleasant breeze. There was very little light coming in the window and Kanini found she could hardly see the face of Rose from across the room. Was the woman looking at her? Or down at her work? Kanini could not tell.

There were no patients waiting as one might expect to see at a clinic. Kanini wondered if anyone would come in needing medical attention. The dispensary at Kajuki always seemed to be overflowing with women and their children or old men with rickets; this place looked hollow and sterile by comparison.

Gatiria entered the room. She looked quite different than she had when she walked away from their *munda* less than two months ago. Gone were her ragged dress and spikey pigtails. Now she wore a green skirt and a starched white blouse and her hair was plaited and greased neatly. On her feet she wore bright white canvas shoes.

When she saw Kanini, her eyes lit up. Kanini blinked back tears as she met her sister halfway across the floor. She squeezed one of her hands in both of hers.

"*Muga*, Gatiria. How are you?"

Gatiria returned Kanini's smile. "I'm fine, Kanini. I figured you'd find me here."

"You knew I'd be coming up one of these days, didn't you?" Kanini asked. She paused, not wanting her sister's smile to fade. "But why didn't you inform us about Njeri?

Gatiria's eyes fell to the floor. "I feel so bad, Kanini...I lied to Aniceta. I told her I wrote to you all and that the reason you didn't come up for the funeral was because you didn't receive the letter in time."

Thoughts popped through Kanini's head like sparks from a fire. "So, you never wrote a letter?"

"You didn't receive one, did you? I couldn't have you all coming up if I was to make my escape." Now when Gatiria looked at Kanini, her eyes were moist as well.

A rush of understanding seized Kanini. "Oh, Gatiria, Mama will be so hurt—"

"I know, Kanini, but what else could I do?" Gatiria's tears spilled over now, and Kanini felt her own burning under her lids. "All I could think about was protecting myself and getting away...I'm a bad daughter, Kanini." Not an ounce of sarcasm tinged her words. Kanini pulled her over to the couch and they sat down together.

Kanini took a deep breath; she was trying as hard as she could to see things from her sister's perspective. "Well, then, you're the bad daughter and I'm the good daughter. But at least you've followed your heart and won't be forced into *nyambura*...You're right. If Mama had come up for Njeri's funeral, you couldn't have escaped. And you're still alive. While Njeri was already gone." She paused to fish out her wrinkled handkerchief and blow her nose.

"Are you saying that you're not angry that you didn't attend the funeral?" asked Gatiria.

"How can I be, really? You did what we were aiming for all along. You ran away from *nyambura*..." Kanini glanced at her sister, from under wet eyelashes. "I do feel shocked when I think about you putting yourself before everyone else—"

"Then you should *tell* me you're shocked! Don't always try to be the good daughter and please everyone all the time. You *never* put yourself before others!" Kanini stared at Gatiria, startled into silence. "I felt...I felt sorry for you when you were going through *nyambura*," Gatiria stumbled over her words, "...because you were so scared and nervous. I wish I could've helped *you* get out of it!" She sighed.

"I never even thought about running away," Kanini said. "Maybe if I'd still been friends with Kagere. But she rejected me, made me feel old-fashioned and ignorant. In some way I probably wanted to prove that our people were right and hers were wrong. But in the end, it looks like her people were right after all."

"I wish it didn't have to be a right or wrong thing." Kanini was surprised at how low Gatiria's voice was. "It ends up making our people look ignorant and backward and the people up here, the ones who've been more influenced by the *wazungu*, look wise and progressive. They always think of themselves as better than us." Gatiria took a deep breath. Kanini wondered if Gatiria had been forced to humble or ingratiate herself in order to win the mission folks over. How difficult for her sister to conform, even if it was just a means to an end.

"It's just that, for me, I knew I could never have *nyambura* done," Gatiria went on. "I had to do this crazy thing–running here to join the *wazungu*–since I knew they were the only ones who could protect me from it."

Kanini had twisted her handkerchief into a rope. "So, what are you doing here with them? How are you living?"

"I've offered to do whatever work they need me to do. I chop vegetables, help cook, clean up after meals, clean around the compound, help in the clinic–" Her sister stopped for breath. "There's so much work to do, and a lot of the other workers here are lazy. Despite making good wages! It's a whole different life up here, Kanini."

"Is that a secondary school I saw?" Kanini asked, pointing her chin towards the door.

"Yes, and Kanini, that's the best part." An undercurrent of excitement ran through Gatiria's voice. "Brother Severino, the man in charge of the school, said that if I work for the mission, I can attend secondary for free. I gave him my KCPE score sheet and he was impressed. So, everyday, starting next month, I'll go to school seven hours, then work two or three hours and then study after supper with the other students. On weekends, I'll work six or seven hours a day and study as well. I'll be very busy, but it'll be worth it."

So, Gatiria's running away had garnered her a free secondary education! Kanini was floored. She closed her eyes and focused on her breathing, as Florence had taught her after circumcision. Then she touched Gatiria's shoulder and said evenly, "Ngai, Gatiria, I'm impressed. And happy for you. I wish the same could happen for me."

"Well, it's not too late," Gatiria told her. "There are Form Ones here who are sixteen and seventeen. They have sponsors, from Europe and the United States. They come here without paying anything and don't even have to work! You could apply for a sponsor. We could talk to Brother Severino!"

Kanini was glad to see Gatiria's genuine enthusiasm. But deep down she knew she could never join forces with the *wazungu* in this way. It would be hard enough on Mama and Baba when they found out about Gatiria. Losing two daughters to the white missionaries would be too much for them. And how would Mama handle all the work alone?

"Thank-you, Gatiria, but I could never do it. It would hurt Mama and Baba too much for both of us to leave."

Gatiria folded her arms across her chest. "But if you stay down in Tharaka, you'll be leaving anyway! You'll probably get married within the next year or so, won't you?"

Kanini's heart leapt then fell as she thought of her future. "Yes, but my marriage will bring cows and goats, or maybe money to help the family. If I'm here studying, what will they get? Nothing."

Gatiria groaned. "Kanini, when are you ever going to think about your own prospects? How is your life going to be? Married to an *mtharaka* who goes off drinking, leaving you with children to care for and all the work of the *munda*–" Gatiria's grimace was steeped in both pity and contempt. "That won't be my life. I'll get an education and a job to support myself. If I get with a man it'll only be after I'm able to live independently first."

"So you'll never have to depend on a man?" asked Kanini wryly. "Why get with one at all then?"

Gatiria shrugged. "Oh, just because–maybe I'll want a few children someday. But I'll never have more than two or three, and only after I have enough money to care for them properly."

Kanini felt the old annoyance rise up in her. There went Gatiria, spouting off what she couldn't possibly be able to predict. As though she could control her own destiny. "And just how do you think you'll keep from having more babies than two or three?"

"I'll use family planning. The Catholics don't talk about it. But I know it's used. Njeri told me about it. She said that if she got well, she'd use it so as not to get more children from Ezekiel." Gatiria's eyes sparkled, as if she alone held the key to this secret information. "It's a modern invention. But it's a good one, Kanini. Just think, no more babies after you've had so many! Not like Mama who gets another one every few years, even though she's old enough to be a *cucu*!"

Countless thoughts spun through Kanini's brain. She wanted to stay and talk longer with her sister. She wanted to roam around the compound under the vines of bougainvillea and onto the shaded terraces. But she needed to head home, back to Tharaka, where she would tell Mama and Baba the sorry news. She felt a rush of anxiety at the thought of returning without her sister. Despite being glad that Gatiria had escaped the fate of circumcision, Kanini would miss her terribly. A hard knot congealed in her gut. She took a deep breath and blinked back the lingering tears.

"Well, Gatiria, I suppose I need to go."

Gatiria looked over at the desk, where Rose still sat. "Yes, Kanini, I know."

"Maybe Njagi could take advantage of the sponsors and come here to finish secondary."

"No, Kanini." A faint smile curled Gatiria's lip. "This school is Chuka Girls'. It's a school for girls only."

Kanini nodded, wondering how she had missed that. "Will you give me the address so that I can write to you?"

Gatiria got up and politely asked Rose for paper and a pen.

"So, tell me what I should report to Mama and Baba," Kanini said, after tucking the paper into her pocket.

"Tell them I'm very sorry for upsetting them, but I did the only thing I could. Also...try to smooth over what happened with Njeri. I did as much as I could for her...and Carolina. I just—" Gatiria's hands flew to her mouth, and she squeezed her eyes shut, cutting off the flow of tears. She took a deep breath and continued. "If they want to come here and visit me, they can. But I won't go back there. Not for a year, at least." She sniffed loudly as a large tear eased its way down her cheek. Kanini wondered, as she always did, if her sister even had a handkerchief to begin her new life. She wished she'd thought to bring a fresh one to give her.

"So, you won't go down for school holidays?"

"How can I, Kanini? I'm planning to talk to Aniceta to see if maybe I can go there...Please write me about what Mama and Baba say, all right? If they forgive me, I'll hurry down to spend holidays there. I would really like that."

"Maybe I'll return here to visit you sometime myself, if I can be spared," said Kanini. "Njagi could give me transport money."

"I'd love to have you here, Kanini. I know the nuns and Brother Severino wouldn't mind. Just write and inform me." Gatiria grasped Kanini's hands and looked into her eyes. "Thank-you so much for coming, Kanini. I feel so much better than I did before. You're like an ambassador. Able to see both sides. I wish I could be more like you."

The edges of Gatiria's bright face blurred as Kanini hugged her sister. She felt the thin arms squeeze her back with genuine warmth. She'd never felt so close to Gatiria, even though they had never been as far removed from each other as they would be now.

Kanini left the clinic and walked out into the blinding sunlight. A young woman was approaching. She carried a bag woven of plastic strips covered with a crocheted cover; a baby was swaddled to her back. "*Muga*," Kanini greeted her in *Kitharaka*.

The woman looked at her curiously and then responded, "*Nimwega mono.*"

Chapter 7

As Kanini walked back to Kanwa, she realized that Gatiria had not given her many details about Njeri or her funeral. An arsenal of anecdotes might have made it clear to Mama that her sister had at least cared about her aunt's fate. Now Kanini would have to make things up to tell Mama on her sister's behalf, or it would appear as though Gatiria was only concerned about her own skin. Which, for all practical purposes, she was.

When she returned to Aniceta's place, she found the older woman out in the fields working as usual. Wordlessly, Kanini fell to work beside her. The heavy physical labor of turning over the soil and planting seeds felt like salve to a wound. Presently, Aniceta asked what had happened at the mission and when Kanini told her, she nodded gravely. "I hope you don't intend to return to Kajuki today."

Kanini shook her head. "If it's all right, I'd like to stay another night here, Aniceta. I'm feeling really tired, and there's no rush...now that we know where Gatiria is."

Despite the fact that her sister had accomplished her goal, Kanini did not feel light-hearted or buoyant as she set off the next morning. As she rode the *matatu* back to Kajuki, she kicked herself for not thinking to buy some fresh vegetables at the Kanwa market. She could have told Mama the food came from Gatiria, as a peace offering.

Upon entering the compound, she saw no one. Then she heard a humming sound and discovered Cucu in a shady corner outside her hut, sitting on the ground, her legs splayed out in front of her.

Kanini crouched down, clasped her grandmother's hand and swatted a fly away from her face. Cucu nodded; her slight smile did not alter and her glassy eyes registered very little. While unpacking, Kanini found an orange from the first day of her journey. She peeled it for Cucu and brought the juicy sections out to her in a dish.

Mama appeared, Mutwiri on her back, the small *mtungi* suspended below the baby on a trumpline. Gitonga was behind her, hauling the large *mtungi*. Kanini hurried to help Mama set down her load, wishing she could set her own load down as easily.

Mama looked at her in consternation as she untied the sleepy baby and swirled him around to her front so that she could nurse him. Kanini busied herself getting her mother a glass of water from the jar.

After some moments, Mama heaved a sigh and asked, "So, Kanini, you have returned. What news do you bring from that upper place?"

Kanini glanced at Cucu and Gitonga. "Maybe you and I should talk alone, Mama."

Mama closed her eyes, looking spent. Her mouth was now a thin line, her pretty smiling lips a thing of the past.

"Why? We'll all find out your news soon enough anyway."

As Kanini related what had befallen Njeri, Mama's stare never left the ground. After she finished, there was a long pause.

Finally, Mama found her voice. "Well, then, if Njeri has been dead for two weeks, what has become of my younger daughter?"

Kanini took care to keep her voice even; she was determined to stick only to facts and give nothing else away. "That was a mystery, Mama. No one knew where she was. Aniceta had given her transport money to return here the day after Carolina's funeral. But of course she never came."

Mama's face gave no hint as to her thoughts.

"Gatiria had talked to the *wazungu* at the mission up near Chuka, so I thought maybe they would know something about her," Kanini continued. "The next day—yesterday, I guess—I walked over there to see."

At this point, Gitonga interrupted her. "Did you see a *mzungu*, Kanini? What do they look like? Is their skin really pink?"

"I did see one, Gitonga, and her skin was pink and her eyes were blue." Gitonga's brown eyes seemed to pop out of his face.

"Had they seen Gatiria, Kanini?" rumbled Mama.

"Yes." Kanini took a sip from the glass of water her brother handed her. "She's been staying there with them."

Mama drew in her breath and looked faint. Her skin grayed visibly.

"Staying with them! Doing what?"

"She's working there, doing tasks to earn her keep."

"Earn her keep! How long does she intend to stay?"

"They're keeping her so she won't have to come home...to be circumcised," said Kanini. She'd tried to choose her words carefully, but they sounded blunt—even accusatory—all the same.

"What?" Mama's stare bored into Kanini. Kanini shrugged her shoulders and forced her arms to stay rigidly against her sides. Folding them in front of her would implicate her. She tried to ignore her feelings of guilt; nothing Gatiria had done was Kanini's fault. Even without her encouragement, her sister would have followed through with everything. Still, she was sure

Mama could see through her, could tell that she had somehow collaborated with Gatiria.

"How can they do this?" Mama's voice, low and ominous, penetrated the quiet afternoon. "She's our child!"

Kanini took a breath and plodded on. "Yes, but they say that circumcision for girls is illegal in Kenya, so Gatiria has the right to stay with them. As long as they are willing to protect her—"

"And how long will they be willing to *protect* her?" Mama spat out her words, which were more riddled with irony than Gatiria's had ever been.

"She says they've offered to let her attend secondary there at the mission. She'll pay her way by working for them."

Mama looked as though her worst fears had been realized. Her mouth went slack; she looked like she might become ill. Kanini suddenly wished, for her parents' sake, that Gatiria had been killed in a *matatu* wreck. Then they would have mourned her in sorrow, not been disappointed and angry as Mama was now. Would they ever forgive her?

Kanini reached out and Mama let her take her hand. "I asked what we could do to get her back. The nun said you and Baba would need to go up there and swear that you wouldn't force her to go through with *nyambura*. They said that—"

"I would not do that, Angela Kanini," Mama snapped, roughly withdrawing her hand. "You know Baba and I would never grovel before those people like that. Not even to get our daughter back." Mama gazed off into the distance, over the head of Mutwiri, who was still fiercely nursing. She lifted her chin with pride. "She has become one of them. She wants nothing to do with what we believe in so strongly, what binds us together within our culture. Without *nyambura* everything we believe in falls into chaos. She is lost to us, Kanini. There's nothing we can do. I'm sure Baba will agree with me."

With that, Mama got to her feet, the baby in her arms, and disappeared inside the main hut. Kanini felt terrible. She stared at Gitonga, so innocent and good-natured, as he squatted on his haunches beside the empty firepit.

"Do you know where Njagi is?" she asked him, finally.

"I think he's at the market," he answered in a solemn voice. Kanini swallowed the lump in her throat and proceeded into the *riko* to stoke the fire.

The afternoon and evening passed in a vacuum of unspoken words and unshared feelings. When Baba returned, he and Mama went on a long walk together, something they never did. Kanini remained at home with her grandmother and brothers, answering their inquiries in one or two-word mumbled responses.

The next morning, Mama went to inform the circumciser that there would be no ceremony at their home the next day. She was gone for many hours and when she returned, appeared distraught.

"What happened, Mama?" Kanini asked.

"I don't want to talk about it, Angela Kanini. Just be careful the next time you go to market."

Kanini found an excuse to walk to town that afternoon. As she passed the *wazee* and mamas she normally greeted, none of them would turn to look at her, let alone greet her. Their eyes were cast down; it was as though she did not exist. The circumciser must have divulged the news about Gatiria and it had spread through the town like a plague. Now, the townspeople had turned against their entire family.

She went directly to Florence's shop. The young woman looked up as Kanini's shadow fell over her. She did not glance away as others had, but the familiar light did not shine in her face. "*Muga*, Kanini," she mumbled.

"*Muga mono*, Florence. You know about what happened."

"Yes, Kanini. The whole town does. They're making you outcasts. It's very bad, very narrow-minded. I won't stand by what they're doing."

Tears filled Kanini's eyes. "You're very kind, Florence. Mama and Baba aren't to blame for what Gatiria did. It's not their fault."

"I know, Kanini. These people do not understand that. It may take a long time for them to ever understand it."

Kanini squeezed the hand of her relative in gratitude. Then she made her purchase, and caught Florence's eye one more time before walking away. Her chin was high, her gaze aimed directly in front of her. She knew the townspeople were watching her and she felt swollen with contempt. What had her family ever done to offend them? Weren't they going through enough grief without losing the support of their community, the same community that Kanini had believed in so steadfastly, had been so painfully initiated into?

She arrived to find Baba home much earlier than usual. She was surprised when he motioned her into the main hut. Heart thumping, she entered the dark gloom and sat down. Baba shut the door. It took her a moment to realize Mama was already seated there.

"Kanini," said Baba gruffly, but not unkindly. "Mama and I have been talking a long time about setting up a wedding for you. We were having trouble agreeing on when it would be, but now we're thinking it might be best to do it as soon as possible."

Kanini looked from one face to the other with trepidation. "As soon as possible? But why?" Kanini knew Mama had always objected to her getting married so soon. Her latest explanation was that she needed her around to help with the baby, especially with Gatiria healing from *nyambura*. Once Kanini was married, she would never live with her parents again; she would literally become the property of another family. Up till now, Mama had claimed to want to put this inevitability off as long as possible.

Mama did not look at her. "Kanini, it's best not to question our decision. The events that have just taken place—they've changed my mind. We need to prepare to meet this future husband of yours."

A new lump formed in Kanini's throat as she gaped at Mama. To get married so soon? To leave her home and family before the next planting and move in with a man she'd never met before? The thought of it terrified her. A mere twenty-four hours ago, she'd been commiserating with her sister, relieved that Gatiria had escaped the worst fate either one could imagine. Now resentment pricked at her. She knew that Baba had a certain man in mind for her. Perhaps he was worried that if this man understood the lowered status of her family—lowered status conferred upon them because of Gatiria's actions—he would reject them too. To hurry and arrange the marriage would insure that this potential husband would not be able to back out of it.

A short silence passed. Finally Kanini swallowed. "I understand, Mama. I am prepared to meet him."

Ishiara and Chuka

1990-1993

Kajuki Market
8 May, 1990

Dear Gatiria,

How are you, sister, there where the atmosphere is so different from ours? We hear you are getting some rain, while in Tharaka, it is too dry and not even a single maize plant is growing. Can you tell Ngai on the mountain to please send us some of that rain?

I am wanting to practice English, so I don't forget it. Let's write in this language, so that our conversation across the airwaves will keep me up to date.

Everything has changed since the time I returned here after seeing you at school. The people around our place have turned their backs on us. That is to say, they are no longer our friends. Maybe it's because of their ignorance. They think Mama and Baba could not control you, so you ran away and made them to lose face. They don't understand that a girl can be able to make her own decision about her life as you did, and that many others are doing the same now in different places. They are quite old-fashioned, really. Myself, I still accept what you have done and love you as my only sister.

Now, Baba and Mama are worried that because we have been outcasted like this, my prospects for marriage are decreased. Baba has therefore speeded up marrying me off. I am to meet this husband of mine in two weeks' time, on a Tuesday, which is the market day in Ishiara. We will take a vehicle there and then walk to the man's home. Baba and this one's father will discuss the marriage agreement. The man's name is Kathenge wa Kaboro, and he is a primary school teacher near Ishiara. Baba and Njagi have met him and they say he seems to be a hardworking man, moreover handsome. Mama has not yet met him.

How is life there at the mission? What are you studying in school? Are you far behind since you missed the first term, or can you be able to catch up? I am very happy for you, really, sister.

I am waiting to hear your reply the soonest possible.

Yours truly,

Angela Kanini

Chuka Girls High School
22 May, 1990

Dearest Kanini,

I can't believe my escape from there caused such a scandal! What is wrong with those people that they can't accept what someone else has done, even it is different than what they do? They are very narrow-minded, and it is better that Mama and Baba do not continue relations with them. What about Bwana Mkubwa, Florence, and all of those? Are they our enemies now too?

What have Mama and Baba said about my being here? Were they angry when you told them? How was Mama when you told her about Njeri? I am sure they will not come here to try and beg my case. I knew from the start they will never agree to let me go uncircumcised. How is Njagi doing? Is he also mad at me for leaving or does he have some sympathy for me?

I am shocked that you are to be married off so soon. All because of what I did? That makes me to feel guilty, Kanini. But nothing I can do now except continue with my studies, which are starting out difficult, by the way. Who knows? Maybe if I get a Form Four education, I can be of some help to you in the future, since you are the one helping others now.

Life is okay here, but not so wonderful. Not only classes are hard, but I must stay up late every night because I don't arrive at preps until two hours after the others. This is because I am washing *sufurias* after dinner until 8:00, while all the others go to study at 6:30. Then I have to stay until at least 10 or 11, whereby the rest have gone to bed. Brother Severino is even now working on a scholarship application for me so that I can be getting money from abroad. Then I can quit doing so much work and focus more on studies. You can wish me good luck! (And I will pray to Ngai to send more rain to Tharaka!)

I need to go, Kanini, my dear. Give my regards to anyone who still cares about me. I look forward to hearing from you again the soonest possible!

With love,
Lucy Gatiria

Kajuki Market
30 June, 1990

Dearest Gatiria,

How are you doing, little sister? I think of you everyday, and thank God you are somehow healthy and okay. I am happy to hear about your studies, however they are difficult and you are tired a lot. Keep up your good work!

To answer your questions about Baba and Mama. They were very upset and hurt to hear what you did. Mama said she can't believe you used your time with Njeri to plan your escape. She said it is better they never see you again. I am very sorry for their feelings and can only hope that after some time they will forgive you. They do not know that I am writing to you. Njagi has stopped thinking of you as a sister. He says he will not go visit you or give me money to visit you, since you have offended our family with your actions, even he was not too surprised about what you did.

My wedding date has been set. It will be in August when Kathenge is on holiday from school. We will not be doing in a church, but just following the traditional way. I wish you can be here to attend it. I will miss you horribly, but nothing that I can do about it.

Kathenge seems to be a good man. I am relieved about that, because I was worried he is cruel and cold. No, he is not. He is young and laughs a lot. His face is kind and he has nice eyes. You would like him, I know. I have only seen him twice. His place is in a good area, down in a valley by a small river. They get more harvest than we do, and his mother is a good farmer. She plants tomatoes, groundnuts, onions and other things you never see around here. They are giving one bull, two cows, one calf and thirty goats for the dowry, moreover eight large gourds of *uki*! Can you believe it? Mama and Baba will be rich! I can't believe they will be milking cows when you and I are not there to help them. We will be gone, yet they will be drinking that sweet, rich milk in their *chai*.

I cannot believe there is only one more full month for me to live at home. I send you my last warm wishes from here!

Sincerely,
Angela Kanini

Chuka Girls High School
3 August, 1990

Dear Kanini,

Ngai, sister, you are marrying a man you have only seen twice? How do you feel about that? Are you frightened? You seem satisfied with him, but who knows how he will be once you are married?

Does he not have a problem with your sister being a disobedient child and causing your family such disgrace?

So, Baba, Mama and our brothers will be getting the benefits of all that livestock, now that we aren't living there. That doesn't seem fair, somehow. But who am I to complain, since I ran away? You, on the other hand, have every right to feel somehow cheated, especially since you are the goods being traded for this new wealth of theirs. I am glad you are willing to tell me how you feel, Kanini. It is good to talk honestly. In our letters, we can.

Now the school has closed and I am back with Aniceta and the children. I am so relieved that she is willing to let me stay with them. Maybe she would be siding with Mama and Baba. I think she understands me better or maybe she appreciates that I can at least do some work around here. Anyway, she and Zacharia and Sylvia send you their warm regards.

By the end of the term, school was tough as ever. There is no scholarship for me yet, so I still must work like a slave, while the others only must work at their books. Sometimes when I am so tired, I feel annoyed. But then I think about how lucky I am to be here, and not at home healing (or dying!) from a useless circumcision, and I am satisfied. I really wish you can attend school here with me, Kanini. We could both be in Form One. Why not? You could be helping with the sciences, which you were always better at than me.

I only have one friend so far. Her name is Maisha and she is from around Chuka. When I told her about escaping *nyambura*, she could not believe it, since up here, they never circumcise girls. You know this already. We have our bunks near each other in the dormitory. Sometimes she is awake when I come back from preps, and then we talk for long times. It is very nice.

I remain, hoping to hear soon about your wedding, and how it is being with a man.

Yours,
Lucy Gatiria

Ishiara Market, via Embu
21 August, 1990

Dear Gatiria,

Thanks for your letter, which I received a week ago, right before my wedding.

I am having so much to tell you now! I am a married woman! My wedding was very nice, simple and quiet compared to some. It was located at my new home near Ishiara. Only a few people that we know were there, because so many who are not our friends now. Bwana Mkubwa and Florence came, as well as another wife of his, his three sons and their wives and children. I am very happy to know they have not outcasted us as the others have. Cucu's nieces also came with their families.

Kathenge's entire clan was there, I think. There were at least fifty people, including his brother, sister, brother's wife, and aunts, uncles and cousins. I felt very shy, since I knew no one of these people.

Everyone stayed all day, eating, drinking, dancing and talking. No one talked anything bad, only about what good luck we will have as a healthy young couple and how Ngai will smile on us, since we have followed Tharaka's customs. There was a ceremony to grant us fertile and many children. This embarrassed me more than anything, but my husband laughed and showed his white teeth, which made me to feel happy and hopeful.

When night came, most people began to leave. Only our family, which stayed to help clean up. They all slept in Kathenge's parents' house, which is much bigger than our parents' house. I went to stay with my new husband in his house. It is also large and very nice. Strange to be sleeping there with him instead of with my own family! But our family isn't us anymore. It is them. You and I are not a part of it now. I think about this and it makes my heart to feel heavy.

The next day, we escorted Mama, Baba, Cucu and the others to the path that goes to Kajuki. When I hugged Mama good-bye, I felt like a dry riverbed. I even felt sad to say good-bye to Njagi and Baba, even he was the one to force me into marrying so soon. He was very excited about getting the cows and goats they promised. Kathenge, his brother and father will bring half the amount to our family's home tomorrow.

About your concern whether Kathenge's family didn't want me because of our neighbors. They are happy to have me! They do not care what the people from Kajuki think! They consider those people backward just like we do! Kathenge even told me he doesn't care whether I am circumcised. If I was not, he wanted to marry me anyway. I am grateful to Baba really. He picked me a good one, I can tell you that. There are so many girls who are not as lucky as me.

I have too much to do, so I must go. Please be writing the soonest! I cannot wait to hear from you again!

Truly yours,
Angela Kanini

N.B. I am happy that you are at Aniceta's place for the holiday. Pass my regards to her and the children.

Chuka Girls High School
31 August, 1990

Dear Kanini,

I want to write before classes begin—tomorrow! Zacharia escorted me back to school this morning, whereupon I received your letter. I am thinking about it even now, everything about the wedding and Kathenge. Please do tell me, how is it sleeping with this man? Is he very demanding, you know about what? Remember when we used to wonder about playing sex? I am hoping you will tell me all about it, if you feel comfortable.

So, now I am happy to be returning to studies even I must work in the kitchen during the evenings. I am also waiting the arrival of Maisha to hear about her holiday. She has one brother who is at University in Nairobi and he was home the time she was. She will be telling us many stories about that big city, and if there are interesting ones, I will tell you too.

I have some more questions about that new place of yours. Who are you living with, meaning how many people and what are their names? Are there children, like brothers and sisters or nieces and nephews of Kathenge? I am very interested to know, since I want to hear all about your life exactly like it is now. What do you do everyday? How is your work different than at ours?

Sincerely,
Lucy Gatiria

Ishiara Market, via Embu
2 October, 1990

Dearest Gatiria,

Please forgive me for so long time I'm not writing to you. Even my English, it is somehow worse than before, with no one to practice. I appreciate your letters, as always.

Life is so different now, Gatiria. Sometimes is okay, but other things are hard and I miss our home and parents. I feel too young to be a wife. I am really fearing to get a baby. But what can I do? Kathenge and I play sex almost every night, for hours sometimes, and I can only wait to see if I will be *mimba*—how do you say in English? It is sure to happen soon.

I do not like playing sex, Gatiria. When I see the sun going down, I start to feel bad thinking about the night coming. Kathenge is really liking it. He says he lives for this thing, which to me is such a torture. I do not understand why men are wanting sex all time, even so many women do not care about it. And then it is the women who must suffer having the babies. At least the men could be having them if they like the sex so much! Truly, Ngai is not fair, and I do not understand Him.

We live together with Kathenge's parents, brother, Njoka, and his wife, Stefanie. There is also a younger sister, Gachwe. I think she is your age or maybe a bit older. She is in Standard 8 and is sitting for KCPE next month. She wants to be taken by Kabati Secondary in Embu. She is independent like you, but much more proud, I don't know why.

I get up everyday before it is light and make *chai* to take to Kathenge's mother, Bilibina, who never does anything for herself anymore. Now she has two new daughters around, Stefanie and me, she is ordering us to do everything for her. She is only forty-something! Younger than Mama and much younger than Aniceta. Yet they are working so hard. Not like this one, though she was somehow used to it before. She is like the chameleon in that folktale that changes its personality—you know the one.

After *chai*, Kathenge and his brother leave for their school. His brother is the headmaster there, so they walk together. I envy them because they do not have to follow Bilibina's orders all day. Only when Stefanie and I work in the fields, then we are free from her. Kathenge's father is not usually around, but sometimes comes for dinner. When Kathenge and I are finally alone, we don't talk much. Mostly, we play sex, and after that I am so tired I want only to stay sleeping forever.

Stefanie is *mimba sana* and will *kuzaa* soon. It is hard for her to do a lot of work. This will be her first child and I am happy for her. She is older than I am, maybe around 21.

Well, dearest, the kerosene has finished, so I need to say good night. Please write again soon! Your words bring the love and hope I need.

Truly,
Angela Kanini

Kanwa Market
30 November, 1990

Dear Kanini,

I hope you are doing okay and not pregnant! ("*Mimba*" is "pregnant" in English) Why must you fear this? If you are not ready to be a mother yet, just tell your husband to stop demanding sex all the time. Then you can stay without a baby.

There is also this thing called birth control, or family planning, that I was telling you when we were here together. I would like to get you some, but it is impossible here at the mission, since the Catholics don't believe in it. They want as many of themselves as possible, so why should they be helping others not to have children? I know there are other *wazungu* who support the use of it—*wazungu* are the ones who invented it, after all. They are the Protestants, who are over at Chogoria and Meru.

The Catholics talk about only one way to stop babies. It is a method whereby you count days on a calendar. I don't understand it, but it is something they can explain. I think a trouble with that one is you cannot play sex for some time during every month, the time when your body can be making a baby. Kathenge, he maybe won't like that, especially since he seems to want one. I will find some more informations so I can send you.

I started writing to you many times during the last term, but I never finished those letters. I will summarize some of what I said. They were mostly about what I learned was happening in our capital Nairobi, about the riots. I have learned so much about our ruling party, KANU, since coming here, not from the teachers, but in secret, from my classmates.

Do you know what Moi's government has done, Kanini? They are making the different tribes to fight against each other. They keep all the money from the small people, those with no power, reserving huge salaries for government officials. They traffic in illegal drugs, they arrest innocent people and hold them in jail without a trial—the corruption goes on and on.

So now, many who want multiple parties are demonstrating in the streets, but KANU stops them and arrests them. Our president is like a king here in Kenya, Kanini, I'm sure you are aware. He will not let any other party compete with him for power. Why is Kenya considered a democracy? We cannot say what we want about the government—many have tried and are taken to jail. When the elections come, we are forced to vote for KANU party again, always *Rais* Moi, as if he is the only one who can be able to rule. I think the disturbances will force some change. We cannot remain a single party nation forever. Soon there will be other parties and other candidates. I am looking forward to that day.

At school, at least every teacher is afraid to discuss these things with students. They are worried that students will tell their parents about what they say, and they could get in big trouble. So, here is all this history making in Kenya right now, but we are not able to learn about it. Only we girls lie awake at night in the dorm telling what we know from newspapers we see and stories we hear.

I will write more later when I have more energy. I am still very tired from the exams we finished yesterday.

Sincerely,

Lucy Gatiria

NB I have put Aniceta's address at the top, in case you write in the next month. I will be here until January!

Kanwa Market
12 December, 1990

Dear Kanini,

Here is the letter I promised to write, even I have not heard back from you.

Greetings of Christmas! What will you do during the holiday? I think you will be eating a goat there at your place with friends and neighbors, is it? Here, the holiday will be very quiet, with no money from Ezekial to buy anything new for the children. The man is very thoughtless and I don't understand how he can forget his mother and niece and nephew like this. But, I will not go on about that one, I become too angry.

So, I'm thinking back to the interesting things that happened last term, but I can't think of many. The stories Maisha told of her brother's life in Nairobi were very sad. Many people are getting bad cases of diseases such as TB and dysentery, bad enough to kill them. This is not normal, Kanini! What is happening? Maybe the conditions in that city are very dirty, worse than before. But how can a grown up person die from dysentery? It is very strange.

I asked Brother Severino about my scholarship, and he said he received a letter saying no more sponsors for the whole next year. So I will need to be working all next year. It is a hard life, Kanini. But at least I don't have to worry about pregnant or someone always asking sex from me. I admire and sympathize with you. You will be a good mother whenever you get a child, at least I know that.

I look forward to hearing from you again, hopefully while I am still here at Aniceta's.

Sincerely,
Gatiria

Ishiara Market, via Embu
15 January, 1991

Dearest Gatiria,

How are you doing up there at your school? Well, I hope. You are now in Form Two!! I am having hard time to believe it.

Thanks for the letters I received in December. I am very sorry I never responded them. I appreciated hearing all about the politic in Nairobi. We never hear most of that out here. Only if you get a newspaper and they are usually finished at Ishiara when I go to market.

You were kind to send Christmas greetings. Our Christmas was very small, no harvest yet, so we didn't have much money or food. I was very sad because my first Christmas being with this new family, I was missing ours so much, that I could not enjoy it. Better to be working like a donkey in the *munda* since there you cannot be able to think about these sad things.

I know you want good news, but I do not have much. On my side, I am suffering a lot. I was having pregnant last November, but I didn't know until just some weeks ago. Then I started to bleed and Bilibina told me the baby was coming out blood. Not a real baby. She told me it is common, especially for first babies. I stayed in bed all day as I passed the blood, and she fed me *ucuru* and gave me cotton wool to put down there. I never saw her so kind before! My husband was also kind. He didn't ask for sex at least four or five nights, since he was worried about the blood. He killed a chicken and Stefanie cooked for me. It tasted so good I ate almost half the thing myself!

Now I still am feeling weak and sick. Sometimes I sit down for an hour in the shade to rest. I play with Stefanie's baby boy while she works and I think about how I am too young to get a baby, and even Ngai knows it and that is why he made this one to die. I don't want to pregnant again for a long time, Gatiria! Please send me the informations about the birth control the soonest possible!

At least, we got some rain last season. The cotton we planted is doing well and we are having so many tomato plants! Enough to sell tomatoes at Ishiara market for extra money.

Please, I am waiting to hear your reply the soonest possible. I am feeling lonely and empty. I miss Mama, but she did not come when I sent for her. Maybe they did not receive my letter.

Faithfully,
Angela Kanini

Chuka Girls High School
29 January, 1991

Dearest Kanini,

I am so sorry to hear about what happened! How are you feeling now? Not so weak, I hope. Please eat as much healthy food as possible, plenty of beans and even meat. Are your cows giving milk at this time? You should be taking it like you were when you were healing from *nyambura*.

Four or five days doesn't seem like much time for Kathenge not to ask for sex. After a miscarriage (that is what happened to you), I think he would stay without it for at least two weeks. I hope you are not in pain, Kanini. I am including the information sheet on the Rhythm Method in this letter. I hope you can be able to understand it. If you have trouble, write and ask me.

Not much is different since last time I wrote. School is harder than last year. At least I didn't start the year late, so I am keeping up well enough. Maisha and I stick together. We have another friend named Mary, who comes from Western Province. Her tribal name is Tapkili, which means "the one with the good heart". I like the sound of her language. She speaks Kalenjin, same as President Moi. Though they are the same tribe, she also criticizes him, like I do! We talk Swahili and English together. It is good for us to practice, since Maisha and I were often speaking just only our mother tongue when we were alone.

I wish you can also get a good friend, Kanini! Maybe Stefanie has become a good friend. I hope so. I will be thinking of you as you become healthy again.

Love always,
Gatiria

Ishiara Market, via Embu
13 March, 1991

Dear Gatiria,

Please forgive me for not writing to you this long time. The work has been too much, even more than before. For two months I have been going to Ishiara market every Tuesday to sell the tomatoes. It gets us a lot of money (which mostly goes for school fees for Gachwe, Kathenge's sister), but tires me a lot. On Mondays I need to pick tomatoes all morning, on Tuesday, I go to market and on Wednesday, I just want to stay in bed. But then I hear Bilibina's voice screaming at me to make *chai*, so I must get up.

Kathenge does not come home every night after work now. He is staying with a friend, or maybe out *"kupiga maji"*, I know you remember what that means. Why do most men want just to drink beer and play sex during their free time? Sometimes I feel relieved because he is not home to bother me, but other times, I feel sad because I am not very big part of his life. Maybe if I have a son, but even then I will go from an elephant to a hyena in just a few short months. I guess this is the life of African women. I knew it before, but I thought it will be different for me. You were right, Gatiria. You knew what was coming. But what can I do now? Only follow the path that was shown to me by our traditions.

I am feeling better now than I was before. I do housework for Stefanie since she is full hands from caring for baby Riunga all day. One Tuesday she went with me to Ishiara and Bilibina watched the baby. She was feeling like on holiday because without the baby she could relax. Then later her *maziwa* became heavy gourds and she wanted only to go back home to feed the baby. It was a better day than others, for me, at least.

Forgive me if I write more in *Kitharaka* and even *Kiswahili* than I did before. It is because my English is so bad these days. No one here who is willing to speak it with me. I wish you can come down, just for a short visit. Can you get transport money from Aniceta during April holiday? Just a few days. It will be so great.

I am not having much to say. I miss you, Gatiria! Please see what you can do about a visit. I hope to hear from you the soonest!

Sincerely,

Angela Kanini

Chuka Girls High School
26 March, 1991

Dear Kanini,

I cannot be writing a long time because I have exams to study for. Regarding April holiday, I'm sure there's no money at Aniceta's place for me to travel with. I'm very sorry. I would also love to go there for a visit. But not this holiday.

I'm sorry that you have started to experience what is fated for so many African women, Kanini. I never condemned you for wanting that life, but I wondered how you would cope with everything. It seems like even the best men cannot remain home for long. Even if they have a job and can support their families, they still must go out to chew *miraa* or *piga maji* with their friends. Meanwhile, the woman stays home alone or with the children. Maybe polygamy isn't so bad, especially if the wives live nearby and are friends. But at least you are having Stefanie.

For now, I wish you all the best. I'll write more later!

Yours,

Lucy Gatiria

Chuka Girls High School
4 August, 1991

Dearest Kanini,

Oh, my sister, I have heard such terrible news, you will not believe it could happen in our country, even in our own Meru district. It happened up at St. Kizito's school, that place somewhere north of Meru town. It is attended by almost all Tigania clan members, but of course they are also *wameru* like ourselves. The case has been in all the national news, both papers and radio, and our people are made to look so shameful.

I guess some boys at this school were angry that the girls would not support them in striking to get funds for a sports event. The boys decided to attack the girls, so all 300 of them went to the dormitory where the 200-something girls were hiding. They had sticks and rocks and beat the door down. Then they dragged them out, beating and raping them. In the end 19 girls were dead, Kanini! They had been crushed beneath beds and other bodies. These boys murdered them!

Then to insult the injury, only 39 boys have been detained and even they are not charged against. The deputy headmaster told the reporter in the paper that "they meant no harm. They only meant to rape."

This country is so backward! In places like Canada and Denmark, men go to jail for raping women. Not here in Kenya. Women are around for men's pleasure only, or to do chores. You know how many girls are raped regularly at schools around Kenya, especially the larger ones? I did not know how many until I read these articles. I feel so lucky that I am at a girls' school and so nothing like that will ever happen. We are praying for those who attend mixed schools. May no more boys get these terrible ideas to rape their classmates! It astounds me how little punishment goes to them for their terrible acts!

Sometimes I am scared to grow up in our society as a girl who is educated and independent. I almost feel like I know too much. In some ways this education has given me a lot of frustration. I want to make so many changes! But how can I? Really, there is nothing I can do except live my life in a good way. And try to avoid trouble as much as possible! It does seem like trouble follows me, what do you think, Kanini?

I hope you too are able to avoid trouble, Kanini. Please write me soon. I need to hear your words to know that some things are right with our world.

Yours truly,

Gatiria

Ishiara Market, via Embu
4 September, 1991

Dear Gatiria,

I appreciate your letters, dear sister. I'm so sorry I have not been faithful to writing. Only that it takes time and precious kerosene, and I am so tired always, especially by nighttime.

I never heard nothing about that incident at the school near Meru town until I received your letter. When I asked Kathenge about it, he didn't answer me. I thought maybe he was feeling shame. I did hear Njoka say that it was too bad so many girls died. If not for that, no one would know what happened, and that school wouldn't need to feel so bad.

I never understood what rape is until you told me. It seems men can always take sex from girls, even if the girls are not wanting. Even myself and Kathenge, I usually am not wanting sex, but he takes it anyway. I guess this is not rape, since he is not violence with me and he is my husband.

Now I am writing to tell you I am having pregnant, nearly four months at this time. I am only telling you and Stefanie, since you know it is bad luck to tell people too soon. Kathenge is excited about it, so he is happy with me again. He comes home almost every night and we play sex as much as before. I tell him we shouldn't, since it can make me to lose this baby, but he tells me I'm being foolish, so we do anyway.

Bilibina is having malaria too much, almost every month. She is going to the health center at Ishiara, or sending me, and using a lot of money on *dawa*. This has been a bad year for it, I don't know why. How is the malaria up where you are? Since there is more rain in that place, I'm thinking there is more malaria, but maybe not.

Gachwe just left for school and I am relieved she is gone. She is so big-headed and treats Stefanie and me very bad. Even Bilibina is ordering us, it still feels very peaceful without Gachwe.

I received a letter, some two months ago, from Njagi. It had words from Mama in it. She said she was sorry for the miscarriage and wished she was here to be with me. She is also working very hard since the rain gave them a good harvest and no one but Gitonga to help her. Some of her old friends are talking to her again, also relatives. I am so happy about that, since her life is already so hard! She wants Njagi to get married, but Baba is worried about paying too much bride price. Mama said she is missing our help, so she needs another daughter. Now the cows and goats for my dowry had babies and so she and Baba can be using those animals for a dowry. If Njagi is to marry, I will go to the wedding. I miss our family too much, but especially you, Gatiria.

I am praying to get a girl baby. I know babies are a lot of work, but if I can have a girl to help me in a few years, it will make the life easier. I will name the baby Gatiria, and maybe she will even look like you!

Love always,
Angela Kanini

Chuka Girls High School
2 October, 1991

Dearest Kanini,

So, you are pregnant again, is it? I hope this pregnancy goes better than the last one. I guess that rhythm method didn't work, did it? Or maybe Kathenge, he ignored and you played sex for too many days. How are you feeling now? I hope you do not miscarriage again. I am praying everyday you get a girl baby, a strong one who can be helping you as soon as she can walk. How is Stefanie and her baby?

Here, my work is more than ever and I am always tired. I have been working at the clinic for many weeks now. There are more sick people coming than before and not enough nurses or aides. So I help with the patients, carry away their *mavi*, clean them and even feed them. Many of them are having dysentery and malaria and something called pneumonia where they are coughing and have a fever. I never heard about that one before, but it is a little like TB. It makes me afraid to help them, since I don't want to catch the disease from them. I wash my hands well and try to hold my breath when I am near them. To clean them, I wear gloves made from very thin rubber.

One thing very strange, is that these people get so sick that in no time, they die. Especially the old ones, they are dying night and day. When the family members come for them, we can only say we tried our best. Then we give them the bodies to take home. I never heard of a kind of malaria or dysentery that can kill healthy people like this. It is also very hard, because we do not have a real hospital here, just only a health center. When the people arrive very sick already, we try to send them to the hospital at Chogoria, but they never leave. Only sit waiting for us to cure them, which, of course, is impossible, without enough supplies and workers.

I only have time for maybe one hour preps at night, and then I go to sleep. I am getting behind in most of my classes, only Composition where I get high marks, because I always have interesting things to write about.

If I ever finish Form Four, I would like to be a newspaper reporter, Kanini, and live in Nairobi. They have such an interesting life and if you're a woman, no one who can tell you what to do (eg, husband.) That is the life for me. You can come and visit me and we can take tea together at those nice tea shops. I have heard so many great things about Nairobi, I cannot wait to see it, although I am fearing to be there right now due to all the disturbances which are happening, moreover diseases.

Well, Kanini, I love to write to you, but I need to go, it is late and there are too many things to do in the morning. I will hear from you again soon, I hope! Good luck with this pregnancy!

Sincerely,
Lucy Gatiria

Ishiara Market, via Embu
19 December, 1991

Dear Gatiria,

As usual, it was good to hear your words, despite I have not written in more than three months.

I am having very little to do now since this baby started *kuzaliwa* some days ago. I started feeling a lot of pushing in my stomach area and Bilibina called her sister. She is good at helping women birth babies. She told me I needed to be staying in bed maybe until the baby comes, or I can miscarriage again. This time, it would be really a baby, not just only blood, but somehow a dead baby.

So, mostly now I stay here *mucii* resting, cooking and playing with Stefanie's boy. Bilibina must take my place in the *munda*, however, she is still getting malaria now and then. I am very big in the middle—you will laugh if you can see me. I don't do any hard work and yet I am eating more than before. Even my arms, they are rounder now.

I am sorry to hear about all the sick people in Nairobi and up near Chuka. I agree it seems like something terrible is happening; maybe overpopulation is causing the problems. Here we are only having malaria, and that isn't even all the time.

I wrote to Mama to come in one month so she can be here when the baby comes. I rather be having Mama than Bilibina's sister, Aunt Celina. Maybe I will have them both. It scares me to go away by myself to birth a baby like Njeri did. I fear having the baby even with many women around who know how to do!

I will try to write again, probably after this baby comes. I will tell you all about the thing whenever it happens.

Love,
Kanini

Chuka Girls High School
22 December, 1991

Dear Kanini,

I hope you are taking good care of yourself! I am worried that even though you are pregnant, you are still asked to do too much work and have too much sex! You must say no, Kanini! It isn't worth your health!

I feel like writing to you even though I didn't receive anything from you for so long. Maybe you wrote a letter, which even now is in the mail coming. I will write again after I get that one.

I can't believe I finished Form Two. I was very sad to see my friends go this time. The December holiday is so long, you know, and with only our cousins and Aniceta around, I get lonely.

I have learned more about why so many people around here are getting sick. I asked a *mzungu* doctor from U.S.A. He didn't want to tell me anything, but I kept asking. He told me that these bad cases of TB, dysentery and pneumonia are brought by a larger sickness called AIDS, or *ukimwi*, as it's called in Swahili. This disease makes you very weak, and your body has no way to fight the other diseases like TB, so after a while you die. Doctor David said it happens because so many are playing sex with who they want, and the prostitution makes it worse. It seems that this was the disease Njeri had, but I do not understand how she had it. She was not in Nairobi playing sex with strangers, like a prostitute. I think it will go away soon, maybe like a cholera epidemic. Remember when *kipindu pindu* came to our place that time?

I need to go now, but trust my words, Kanini, and pay attention to this *ukimwi*! It is something serious! I hope you are feeling well and the baby is growing big and healthy. I will write again soon, before the start of next term, I promise.

Always,

Lucy Gatiria

NB I'm sure you have heard something about the political situation in Nairobi, even if you don't see the newspapers. All the protesting is finally forcing Moi to give in to a multi-party system! This FORD (Forum for the Restoration of Democracy) party has really done its work. Now I've heard that in Nairobi everyone is flashing two-finger salutes, showing solidarity with two parties. Could be next year during elections, no one will be voting KANU. I cannot wait to see that day.

Ishiara Market, via Embu
2 March, 1992

Dearest Gatiria,

How is going, dear sister? I miss you so much, wanting to tell you about everything, but no time to write. How I wish for a telephone—Kathenge wants one too, but of course, we are not having electricity.

So, I am now a mother. My daughter is having two months already! Her name is Josefina Gatiria, but we call her Gati. She born on 5 January, during the night. It was so wonderful, Gatiria. I can't believe I'm saying that, but it really was! Mama came and helped! It was so great to see her! I thought she won't come in time because the baby was so early. But, she somehow knew this baby was coming, so she came early too! She arrived the afternoon before.

Many women were attending me: Stefanie, Bilibina and her sister Celina. I was feeling the pains in my stomach, then Mama arrived, and I felt so happy, that baby really started to come out! Only two hours later she was here. It was a lot of work, but the pain was nothing compared to *nyambura*! And now I have a healthy baby girl. Even she was early, she was big, in fact. Everyone was very proud of her. I worried because I thought Kathenge will disappoint since she is not a boy. But he is happy with her. Of course, he went out *kupiga maji* the whole night, but I didn't care—all the women laughed and said that is what men do. It was so great to have Mama there with me. (Mama was surprised I named her for you, but she said nothing. She still isn't knowing we are writing now and then.)

Mama stayed one whole day and then left the next day. She told me so many stories, one about Mutwiri, who was bitten by a snake, but not a poisonous one! Also, about Gitonga, who helps her with everything, even grinding! Can you believe he is in Standard Five now? I wish he can be able to attend secondary. Maybe Bwana Mkubwa can sponsor him. (By the way, have they found a sponsor for you yet? I do not like thinking about you working in that awful health center.)

In regards your last letter, we are all horrified of this terrible disease you speak of. No one around here who is having it or even hearing of it. When I told Kathenge your words, he only laughed at me. Then he asked if I am not trusting him to just only play sex with me and not other women. I started fearing his anger and I said nothing more.

The other thing concerns the politic in Nairobi. We have only heard a little bit about all of that, even I know it is in the papers. It seems like some big changes are happening here in our country. I wish I can understand more, but at least you are explaining me. Thanks for that.

I need to go and feed this hungry baby. I wish you can see her, Gatiria, she is looking so much like you! And she is very loud, also like you!

Please write again soon, and I will answer, I promise.

Sincerely,

Angela Kanini

Chuka Girls High School
2 April, 1992

Dear Kanini,

Congratulations on the birth of Josefina Gatiria! I am very honored that you named her after me, your wayward sister. I wish I could see her! I am glad that you had no complications during the birth. The girls here are telling me that sometimes women who are circumcised have troubles. Ngai has kept you healthy, my sister! We can be thankful for that much, at least.

I am staying at the mission this holiday to help out at the health center. We are short workers here, so they asked me to please stay, whereby they will give me some small wage for my work. It will be strange to sleep in the dormitory all alone!

I now know more about this disease, AIDS. It is something passed only through blood or other liquids in your body. So, if you play sex with someone who has it, you can get it, or if you transfer blood with someone, the same. Those are the main ways. If people only play sex with their husbands or wives, they will not get it, but the problem is that so many are going with others around. Now they are suffering severely for their sin—this is what the Catholics say—and there is no way for them to be cured.

I wish people can believe about AIDS. No one talks about it; only they say they have dysentery or malaria and they will get better soon. Then, they diarrhea or cough so much they get too weak and die. We need to make people understand how dangerous this *ukimwi* is! There is a saying in both English and Swahili that prevention is better than cure. Why does no one want to practice a prevention of this disease?

Ukimwi makes me want to never play sex with anyone ever, Kanini. You know how these men are. Maybe I will only play sex with my husband, but what if he is playing with another woman, one who has *ukimwi?* Then he can give it to me. It is passed that easy. I am sure that's how Njeri got it. Her husband probably went with a prostitute in Mombasa. So, I'm telling you, Kanini, be careful. Tell Kathenge about it again and make him believe it. He must stay faithful to only you, not go with other women.

Ngai must be angry with us here in Kenya. Usually we are not getting enough rain, now the rain doesn't want to stop. Our crop at the mission was washed away and there will be no vegetables for the students next term. There have been three *matatu* wrecks in one month's time due to the mud. (Some are saying they fear *matatus* worse than *ukimwi!*) And, like you wondered, we have more mosquitoes than usual, so there is more malaria. I feel lucky that I have not gotten it, not even one time. Maisha is having it now and then. For a whole week, she was so sick she was not able to attend classes. Finally she got better.

One thing is that the people with HIV infection, this thing that gives you *ukimwi*, they cannot come as often to the clinic due to the rains. Therefore, we are not as full here, but this means they must be very sick at home, with nothing to make them feel better. It is very sad. For a while, people with the HIV can live regular lives, without pain or other diseases. Then, their bodies start to get weaker, usually the older ones first. After they get the AIDS is when the other diseases enter their bodies and start to kill them. It does not take long, especially if they cannot eat, or if the water is bad.

What we are worried about now is all the children who will have no parents. What can they do with both parents dead from *ukimwi*? (At least Zacharia and Silvia have Aniceta.)

Brother Severino has told me that there will be no more sponsorships due to these people in the overseas countries fearing to send money to Kenya. They are afraid, because they think we are just only using their money to treat the people with HIV, which they think is a hopeless cause. Even though he tells them that their money goes to keep children in school, they don't believe him. So, here is my fate—no scholarship. But, at least now I am more than halfway finished with secondary.

I am not looking forward to this holiday. Maybe you can come my way for a visit, Kanini. I know you have the new baby, but a trip will be good for you. Think how wonderful to see each other again! I will pass encouraging thoughts to you through the air currents.

Love always,
Gatiria

Ishiara Market, via Embu
15 September, 1992

Dear Gatiria,

So many months have passed I cannot even count them! Yes, I received your letters of April and August, and I have no excuse about why I didn't reply them. This baby and all the *munda* are just taking too much time. One thing, dear sister—your words are becoming somehow too difficult to understand. I am using a dictionary every time I get a letter. Please be using some easier vocabularies. Thanks a lot!

Kathenge went to Nairobi during August holiday, for a teachers' meeting. He was gone more than a week, and it was a holiday for me too! Stefanie and I worked together and played with the children. Bilibina ordered us, as usual, but she didn't annoy us. This was because I was always happy and sleeping like a cow at night, so the daytime, I wasn't feeling bad about nothing. Without Kathenge, is really an easier time, just like when Baba was gone, remember?

I will try to add more to this later, but maybe I won't be able.
Always,
Kanini

Chuka Girls High School
9 December, 1992

Kanini,

This time it is I who have stayed so long without writing! Form Three is somehow harder than Form Two, so I have been studying a lot. I finally got a good mark in biology this term, but still not so good in maths or physics. Those will never be good subjects for me.

I am sorry that you don't like to play sex with Kathenge. In the dormitory one night we were talking with some other girls about playing sex, and many of them have done it! Some of them like it a lot and do it whenever they go home for holiday. I asked how they prevent pregnancy and a few said they cannot get pregnant because they aren't married! I wondered at their ignorance. The doctors say it is easy for young girls to get pregnant any time, married or not.

Later, I talked to one of the girls who said that she knows how to prevent pregnancy, even with no birth control. When the boy's juice is about to spill inside her, she tells him to take his *nini* out very quickly, so his juice will spill on the ground. I told her how you don't like sex and she said it is because you are circumcised. Could that be the reason? I think that is very sad, Kanini. Perhaps you would like it if only you had been left whole, like these girls. Instead, you hate it and feel like Kathenge is raping you. So you prefer him to leave you alone, but then he may be out with other women or prostitutes getting diseased. The whole situation is very depressing.

On the other hand, these friends of mine could be getting diseased themselves when they go playing sex during holidays. Myself, I think I will stay virgin the rest of my life. It is not worth getting a disease just to experience this sex. What do you think?

One other thing, Maisha's brother may be having AIDS himself. He has dropped out of University and is right now home with his family, very weak with a high temperature. He tells everyone it is malaria, but I wonder how malaria could make someone so young and healthy drop out of University. Maisha also thinks it may be AIDS, but she has said nothing to her family.

I need to go, but I will see you soon! The minute I am finished with KCE next November, I am coming your way, Kanini! Then we can talk all night, about all these things and more. We will be reunited soon, I promise; I cannot wait for the day. In the meantime, greet Stefanie and all the family members and give Gati a big hug!

147

Your loving
Gatiria

Ishiara Market, via Embu
16 February, 1993

Dearest Gatiria,

Thanks for your letter of December. I have read it again and again and I appreciate your understanding words. Thanks too for telling those friends of yours about my situation and getting stories from them. I like to hear how other girls my age are living, the ones in a different world from my own.

About whether you should stay virgin all your life, I think it is a good idea, that is, if you never want to be married. For myself, I cannot imagine sex bringing any joy, it is usually boring and uncomfortable and prevents me sleeping! On the other hand, you are not circumcised, so maybe you could be enjoying sex like your classmates, that is if you get a nice man to share with. Finding a good one is hard—like you said, how to know if he is faithful or not? Since maybe you can be the one to make your own decision about a husband, it might go better for you.

So much news to tell, some of it sad. Kathenge's father, Kaboro, is very sick and may be dying. It seems like the disease you talk about, but everyone here is saying is only malaria, so I don't disagree them. He is coughing a dry ugly cough, like I think Njeri and Carolina did. He is also very thin and weak now. I didn't know him very well before because he was never around. Now he is in his house all times, and Bilibina is very busy caring for him. We don't see her much, but when we do, she is more difficult even than before, with too many orders.

A better news is that Njagi is to be married on 12 April. His wife will be Mukami! Can you believe it? I was not sure I understood right. Mukami and I have never written letters. In fact, I wasn't sure if she is still living in Kajuki. But she is, and will soon be Njagi's wife! Baba is giving four cows and twenty goats for her, half of his herd. He will give 28 more goats within the next two years.

Mama is also happy, since now she and Mukami's mother will be relatives! I am so relieved to know that Mukami's family never stayed angry with us for a long time, like some others. Some of them even now are not talking to us. Our real friends from then are really our only friends now.

I am feeling excited about this wedding, not like my own when I was so nervous and shy. There is one tailor in Ishiara, who is making me a new dress and one for Gati too. We will be going together with Kathenge. I will tell you everything after it is done. If only you can take a *matatu* down for that one day; maybe you can be wearing a *leso* over your head like a Muslim, so no one will know is you.

I am counting down the months until I see you again. Only nine more! It is such a short time really, compared to the time already gone. I will be thinking of you during this first term of Form Four. Good luck!

Love always,
Kanini

N.B. My first time I got to participate in our national election, on 27 December! While I was waiting to vote, I was thinking of how it should be you voting instead, but you are not yet eighteen. What do you think about the results?

Chuka Girls High School
3 April, 1993

Dear Kanini,
The April holiday already! I am so ready for it. And this time I am to go to Aniceta's, not like the other two holidays when I stayed at school. I really need a break!

So! You voted for the president in this historic election! I am envious. How was the voting? I won't ask who you voted for, but you know I was for the opposition, I didn't care which one. How frustrating that we will have Moi another five years, with all his corruption and playing favorites. It seemed so hopeful that he would lose and another candidate take his place. The problem is that the opposition was divided. Moi only won with 38% of the vote, while Matiba had 26%. If all the opposition candidates put their energies together, I'm sure they could have defeated that king of ours. I am almost sure there was fraudulence. Maybe Moi paid people to vote for him, or even had extra ballots with his name on them put into the boxes. So corrupt! We can talk more about this when we are together again.

I have news, Kanini. I have been offered a position as a primary schoolteacher over near Chiakariga, that place east of the Mati road. Every one of the previous teachers has left, due to poor pupil attendance, lack of transportation and other things that I'm sure I will find out more about when I get there. Now there is only a headmaster who is trying to teach all the classes himself. The situation seems worrisome, but Brother Severino says to have faith; God will watch over me and make sure all goes well.

I'm not sure I believe in a God anymore, Kanini. Why would He make so many troubles for people who are already suffering so much on this continent? The Christian god is for the *wazungu* only, since Africans do not seem to get any of the benefits of believing in Him. It seems our Ngai up on Kirinyaga has also forsaken us and maybe won't answer our prayers until we live our lives in a better way. With all these droughts, floods, diseases, etc., it seems as though we are doomed here in Africa. What do you think about this?

I'm sorry to be so depressed. It is hard not to be when I look around and see all the misery. Now I have studied and worked hard for four years, all so that I can go to a poor community and work to teach children who may drop out after a few months. It is so sad! I'm not sure how long I will last there.

Anyway, I plan to leave here on 1 December, that is the week after we finish KCE, and take a vehicle straight to your place. I would like to stop by Kajuki, but I won't at this time. I would love to stay with you a long time, but maybe four or five days will be enough. How long are you thinking I will stay? Then, I want to travel to this new area where I will be teaching and get myself settled. I will need a house, furnitures, etc.

Brother Severino has talked to Brother John over at Materi, and he says there is nothing set up for a teacher who is not local. So, I will need to be accommodating myself. Maybe I will have to rent a room in the town, or stay with a family nearby. I wish you could come with me to see the place. Do you think you would be able? Please write soon and tell me.

How was Njagi's wedding? I am so happy to hear he married Mukami. It must have been wonderful for you to see her again after so long. Now she is living at ours, isn't she, and you can be going to visit there sometimes. I wish I could go too. Do you think Mama and Baba have forgiven me by now? Did you ask them how they are feeling about me? If so, please tell me what they said.

It sounds like your father-in-law has AIDS. Is he still alive, or has he died already? I can't believe the people down there are still denying so much about this disease. It is very real and is being passed very quickly, not only in cities, but out in the bush as well. Everyone needs to understand and try to prevent it. Otherwise, it could kill off our entire population! When I come to visit, I will be bringing some pamphlets and other informations, to show your husband and family. I wish I could bring some condoms, but there is nothing like that here.

These Catholics are also denying too much! They would watch all their people die of AIDS, just so that people don't wear condoms! I want to get the word out: this disease is deadly and it is serious! It is not something to take lightly.

You say Kathenge goes out at night and doesn't come home? Where is he going, Kanini? What is he doing and who is he staying with? You must be finding these things out. Could be he has another woman he is sleeping with, or maybe he is going with prostitutes. What did he do when he was in Nairobi? I know our culture makes it impossible for a woman to ask her husband these things. But at this time, Kanini, it could be a matter of life and death for Kathenge and *you*! I am worried, Kanini, but I will talk more about it when I see you.

And we will see each other soon!

All my love,

Gatiria

Ishiara Market, via Embu
17 June, 1993

Dear Gatiria,

How are you, dear one? I am happy to hear that you will be working in Chiakariga. That place is not far from here, maybe only a day's walk, or an hour *matatu* ride. Which side of Chiakariga is it? This side, I hope. We can be visiting each other maybe two or three times a year!

Everything is going as usual here. Only Kathenge's father who has died, which you predicted. I am sure it was *ukimwi* that he was having. But no one wanted to say so, and he was buried without anyone knowing. I wonder how he got it—maybe he had other women he was playing sex with, like you said. He was so old, fifty at least. I guess men always need sex, whether old or young or what.

Kathenge says for sure he is true to me and only goes to friends' houses after work to eat supper and sometimes sleep over if the time becomes too late. On my side, I must trust him as I don't have a choice. What can I do, follow him everywhere?

Actually, he is also here a lot of the time, and he plays with our daughter and helps with projects around the compound, now that his dad is dead and his mother is so depress. Bilibina doesn't do any work now; she is just only staying in her house everyday, calling for *chai* and *dawa* and sleeping in her mosquito net. I know her malaria is bothering her too much, so we must be patient and serve her.

My daughter is growing bigger everyday, and looking so beautiful, so much like you, Gatiria! I cannot wait for you to see her! She is walking everywhere, even to the river with me for water, and never complaining She plays all day with her cousin, Riunga. I am very happy to have him around so that Stefanie and I can work. I will wait to tell you more when I see you personally.

I want to tell you about Njagi's wedding now. It was very wonderful, the best one I ever saw. So many people were there! I was thinking maybe no one who will be coming, but it is like everyone is our friend again now. Maybe not everyone, but everyone we want to know. Mukami and I cried to see each other and she was holding Gati for long times. She says she can't wait to be getting a baby herself. Her baby will be our niece or nephew, Gatiria! She is like another sister now.

We roasted at least two goats and there was rice and *ugali* and a lot of soda and *pombe*, even the store-bought kind. Everyone stayed very late, some sleeping on the floors or out by the fire, like at Njagi's circumcision. Mama and Baba were very happy, more happy than I saw in a long time, however they are looking somehow old.

One thing I don't know if I told you. Cucu died some months ago. She passed without pain in her sleep, Mama told me. So only her spirit attended Njagi's wedding. I thought you will like to know that, Gatiria.

Gitonga is now in Standard Six and already talking about going to secondary. If the goats and cows keep birthing, they will be selling them, so the money will be there for him to go. I am very happy for him; he is smart and aware like you are. If he can go to secondary, I'm sure he will get a good job and be the one supporting Mama and Baba when they are too old. On Njagi's side, he is still writing letters and selling charcoal in the market. He is saving to buy a truck so that he can start a business transporting goods from Chuka.

I talked with Baba and Mama about you. I told them I am writing to you sometimes and they were surprised, but interesting to know how you are doing. When I told them you are coming this way to work in Chiakariga, Baba looked away but Mama looked like crying. I think they will like to see you sometime soon. So many of our friends and relatives forgave us, I think they have to forgive you someday. What is that *Kiswahili* proverb? *"Mavi ya kale hayanuki."*

Well, I need to go soon because the animals need to go out, and I see Gati playing near the fire. Send me one more letter, at least, before you leave that place. I need to know the exact time when you will be coming, how you are arriving and all of that.

Sincerely,

Angela Kanini

Chuka Girls High School
15 October, 1993

Dear Kanini,

"Old droppings don't stink." I can't believe you remembered that saying, Kanini. I guess you're right. Someday, Mama and Baba may see that what upset them so much all those years ago is really only a pile of manure, drying in the sun. I have to hope that what you predict will really happen.

So, I am about to leave this place and visit you after so long a time. Did you get my letter of August, while I was on holiday? I have not heard from you since June, but that's okay. I'm assuming all is well with your family, and I will be there soon to see for myself!

My plan is to get a vehicle early on 1 December, since it is a market day in Kanwa. I will be arriving at Ishiara around lunchtime. Can you meet me there? If you get this letter, please send me one to tell me so. Also, I will have a lot of possessions with me, at least everything I own, packed into one trunk and a few bags. Maybe you can bring someone along to help us carry the things. How far is your place from Ishiara, by the way?

I have not much more to say at this time. We are very busy studying for KCE; in fact, I don't have to work very much in the clinic these days since the brothers and sisters have all taken pity on me and are letting me study. I want to get a good pass on this exam. If I can get a pass of Division 1 or 2, maybe I can do a diploma course or even go to University. (I am still hoping to be a reporter someday!)

I hope to hear from you as soon as possible. Good tidings, until I see you in person, dear sister. Only six short weeks from now!

Sincerely,

Gatiria

NB I hope you are still practicing that rhythm method. I'm sure you don't want to get another baby too soon!

Ishiara Market, via Embu
28 October, 1993

Dear Gatiria,

Please forgive me, sister, for not writing to you sooner. I never received your letter of August, but should be I wrote you anyway. Everyone was very sick around here, though not with *ukimwi* or even *kipindu pindu*. It is malaria again, and it has affected everyone except Kathenge and me, I think. Gati was very sick for around two weeks, and I worried so much, I thought to die! She lost a lot of weight and even now is looking very weak and thin, with her skin somehow pale. Stefanie and Riunga both were sick, and of course Bilibina. Even Stefanie's husband, Njoka, stayed with it for some days and did not go to school during that time.

We are getting more mosquito nets as soon as the shop at Ishiara receives some. Right now, just only Bilibina who is having one. You should bring one with you when you come, and if possible, bring some extras!

I have gone to Ishiara many times to get chloroquine, but it doesn't help anything, I think. Please, if the *wazungu* have anything better up where you are, bring some of that *dawa* to us. I know there are better things, but I don't know what they are. What are these condoms you wrote me? Can they be helping with malaria?

I have not been tending the crops, and they are all weeds now, and maybe no tomatoes like we were having the other seasons. There were some insects eating the leaves, and I could not be out picking them off like before. So those plants are no good now, and nothing we can do.

I will tell you, Gatiria, if you can stay here with us a long time, *karibu sana*. We need anyone who can work, especially one who knows so much as yourself. You can be helping us a lot, and at least everyone will appreciate.

So, please you come and stay long as you can, and we will be very happy about it.

Kathenge and I, we are trying to follow that rhythm method, but it gets hard sometimes. If he wants to play sex while we are not supposed to, what can I tell him? Go find someone else? Sometimes I wish he can take a second wife, one who is virgin, of course. Then I can just stay alone for long times, a relief for me!

Stefanie and I are planning to be at Ishiara that day, 1 December, to meet you and help you with your luggages and to show you the way home. The children will stay with Bilibina, if she isn't too sick by then. We want to stop at one *hoteli* for a lunch of roast meat and *chapatis* before leaving. I'm sure you will like that place, and it will be pleasure to give you a nice meal after so long, sister.

I look forward to seeing you on that day, around noon, at the *matatu* stand. I will be wearing a new head square Mama gave me—a green one. I will surely know you with your large trunk. I am so excited to see you after all the time that has passed.

Love always,
Kanini

Ishiara and Chiakariga
1993-1995

Chapter 1

Kanini had been waiting at least a half an hour at the windy *matatu* stand in Ishiara for Gatiria to arrive. As she jiggled her daughter on her back, she squinted down the dusty road, wondering what her sister would look like. It had been nearly four years, after all.

Finally an open-backed pick-up stuffed with passengers rattled off the main road and came to a stop before her. After blinking away the dust, her eyes fell upon a striking young woman climbing out the back of the dented vehicle. Her first impressions of Gatiria were: clean, neat uniform, slim figure and evenly plaited corn-rows. Struggling to swallow her usual self-consciousness and the bite of envy, she crooned, "Look, Gati, it's Auntie Gatiria! Just there!"

A slow smile started across her sister's face as Kanini caught her eye. Gatiria moved toward her and they embraced each other. Kanini could smell the sweet scent of lotion or hair gel, she didn't know which. Gati squirmed impatiently then giggled as she succeeded in grabbing a handful of Gatiria's braids.

"You brought her with you," Gatiria breathed, her eyes drinking in the cherubic face of her niece. "She's so beautiful, Kanini. But I don't think she looks like me as much as she looks like you."

"It's odd to hear you speak *Kitharaka*." Kanini still hadn't taken her eyes off Gatiria. "It almost seems like *Kizungu* had become our language."

Gatiria gave a short laugh. "It's amazing that our entire relationship for four years took place through letters written in the white man's mother tongue!" Her voice, always loud, resounded in the hot, dry air. A pair of scruffy men looked their way as their tire sandals slapped through the dust. Kanini lowered her eyes.

The bright yellow form of Stefanie stepped into view. She had just finished shopping and was loaded down with bulging plastic bags, a *kiondo* and a *mtungi* of kerosene. Riunga, her plump, fist-flailing son, was tied to her back, sucking on a slimy piece of steamed arrowroot. In contrast with Gatiria, whose oiled skin and graceful figure were so refined, Stefanie looked dusty and coarse. As she approached, a frown was plastered across her blunt features and her eyes were skewered into slits against the sun.

"Stefanie, this is Gatiria, my sister. And Gatiria, my sister-in-law, Stefanie. She's been...so nice to have around for the past few years." As the women shook hands, Kanini's heart felt full to overflowing. Blinking tears away, she suggested that they head to the restaurant to get out of the sun.

"Wait," said Gatiria, as the *matatu* gunned its engine. "I need to make sure all my things are here." Her trunk had already been removed from the bed of the vehicle and placed nearby. She glanced back in and grabbed a plastic *kiondo* off the seat. Then she waved the driver on.

"Kathenge and Njoka will come through town later, after they finish work," Kanini said. "We can keep your trunk at the *hoteli* until they get here."

A few interested onlookers watched the three women haul the trunk over the rutted ground, but no one offered to help. People were too busy selling their wares or fixing broken shoes, watches or *jikos*. The few men who were lounging in the shady doorways of shops only leered and took long draws from their cigarettes.

The smell of roasting beef blew in from the back patio of Kanini's favorite *hoteli* and enveloped them as they sat down inside. Kanini and Stefanie took the children off their backs, and they scooted down onto the dirt floor to play with a scraggly cat.

"I thought you'd leave the children *mucii*," Gatiria said, her eyes following their every move. "I'm so glad you brought them."

"Bilibina wasn't up to watching them," said Kanini. "She's been so sick lately." She glanced over at Stefanie, and then back at Gatiria. "We're hoping it isn't the same thing her husband had."

Gatiria's face instantly became grave. "What are her symptoms?" she asked.

"She has a high fever most of the time," said Stefanie. "For awhile we thought it was malaria, but nothing we did helped. Now she seems to have a chest infection and coughs, like her husband did." Her eyes met Kanini's. "She's often confused and doesn't know what's happening around her. We're afraid to leave the babies with her anymore, since she might neglect them."

"Did these symptoms come on very quickly?" asked Gatiria.

"Oh yes!" Kanini exclaimed. "A month ago, she wasn't this bad. It's all happened during the last few weeks. Everyday she seems to get worse."

"It sounds like she has AIDS," Gatiria said in a lowered voice. "There's no other explanation for it. She must have gotten it from her husband."

"Do you think she'll die, Gatiria?" asked Kanini after a moment.

"She's so sick. She probably has pneumonia now; that's what often kills people with AIDS."

The women sat solemnly as a young waiter brought plates of *ugali* and *chapatis* to their table. Kanini had been looking forward to this meal for so long; indeed, she'd ordered it even before Gatiria's *matatu* arrived. Now she felt like they should hold off before indulging, out of deference to her mother-in-law. When her steaming mug of beef broth was set before her, she watched the steam as it curled upward, but waited to lift it to her lips.

Gatiria took a deep breath and asked, "How is your husband, Kanini?"

Kanini shrugged. "Oh, mostly the same. He and Njoka are going to Embu this week, for another teachers' meeting."

"They must be close friends, your two husbands," Gatiria observed.

"Oh yes," said Stefanie. "They go everywhere together. And—don't always tell us where they're going."

Kanini glanced at her sister-in-law and then over at Gatiria who was looking from one to the other. "What'll they do during the December holiday?" she asked.

"They'll stay out a lot," Stefanie said, a trifle wistfully. "Maybe we'll see them in the evenings."

The women ate silently for a while, savoring the chunks of goat meat that had arrived on a single plate. Gatiria refused to take more than a tiny amount, encouraging the others to eat more. "You're breastfeeding," she protested. "You need the protein."

"Yes, but you're so slim, Gatiria," said Kanini. "You have to put more flesh under your skin. Otherwise, how will you survive in that poor place you're going to?"

"We'll fatten her up *mucii*," said Stefanie. "You are staying the whole holiday, aren't you, Gatiria?"

Gatiria looked at Kanini. "The whole holiday? I thought I might stay a week or so..."

Kanini laughed. "You have to stay longer than that! I haven't seen you in ages! And, we'll appreciate your help. Did you bring any *dawa* with you, by the way?"

"Only some simple things, like cough suppressants and pain killers. Things that can't really help very much. For Bilibina, there's nothing that can save her. You can only give her some pain medicine to make her comfortable."

"What about those things you told me about...'condoms'?"

"Those are a form of birth control, Kanini... 'Family Planning'. For men to use. Of course, most men don't want to use them, because they make sex less enjoyable. Have you ever heard the saying 'the candy tastes sweeter with the wrapper off'?'"

Methodically, Gatiria tore pieces of *chapati* into strips and lay them in rows on her dish. Under the table, Gati pulled the cat's tail and it yowled. Stefanie tried to push the cat away with her foot, but Riunga lurched after it and grabbed it again.

Gatiria barely noticed the commotion. "Condoms can also protect the man from getting AIDS if the woman is infected, or protect the woman if the man's infected," she went on. "If people used them every time they had sex, they wouldn't pass the virus."

It was hard to understand Gatiria, with her constant use of English terms. Kanini was beginning to lose her appetite, though there was still plenty of food left. Stefanie's attention was on the children. She picked up the bones and cups they'd dropped and tried to wipe her son's greasy face. Over the jangling radio and the clatter of teapots and dishes coming from the kitchen, Kanini struggled to focus on what Gatiria was saying, but finally gave up.

"We should go soon. The children won't last much longer," she said.

It took them a while to finish up and leave, but it was a relief to be back out in the open air. Stefanie led the way to the path that would take them to the *munda*, an hour's walk away. They looked like peddlers, so loaded down were they with bags and jugs, umbrellas and babies.

Gatiria looked out over the brown and green landscape and sighed. "I've missed this land more than I ever thought I would. I love those tall termite hills and the gullies that never have water in them. There's so much open land here; you can go for hours without seeing anyone. Then, when you least expect it, there'll be an old mud building with a *mzee* inside selling *chai*."

Kanini and Stefanie looked at each other, eyebrows raised. Gatiria had a knack for glorifying the dullest things, when she felt like it. "I suppose it's quite different from where you've been living," remarked Stefanie.

Gatiria nodded, but her eyes were following a distant bird as it swooped and glided on an air current, and she didn't respond.

Kanini breathed in the fresh, sweet air and scanned the vast horizon with a sweep of her eyes. After the rainy season, new growth was springing up everywhere, in the delicate film on the branches of the acacias, as well as the bright yellow flowers winking from the cactus. Kanini had always appreciated this land, had counted on it to come through for them. Which it had, many times over.

Kanini realized that she hadn't even mentioned the family. "Mama and Baba are doing very well now. They've had good harvests, and when they missed one, there were goats and cows to sell—"

"Goats and cows from your dowry, I suppose," quipped Gatiria.

"Yes, but I'm not the only one who's helped them," Kanini quickly added. "Gitonga has been a real help, more than Njagi ever was. He's the one that cares for the animals and does most of the planting and tending. He doesn't seem scared of hard work like most boys his age. I can't wait for you to see him."

There was a pause as the women walked and breathed together. "I'd like to see him too," Gatiria said, her voice hollow.

Their feet crunched the underbrush. Both little Gati and Riunga fell asleep and their heads flopped about on their mothers' shoulders. Kanini noticed Gatiria's eyes on their soft faces and wondered what was on her mind.

Her sister seemed happy to be with them, but her thoughts often seemed to flit to a distant place. Kanini regarded the smooth skin of her profile, glowing with lotion. Had Gatiria's Form Four education changed her, or simply accentuated her natural tendencies? She'd had a hard time fitting in even before going to live among foreigners and members of different tribes. Now she would be teaching school in the tiny village of Chiakraiga, fifteen kilometers further down the mountain, in the heart of Tharaka Location, a place more impoverished and traditional than theirs. How would she handle such a place? How would the people handle her?

Back at the *munda*, Kanini took pride in showing Gatiria around, trying to remember what it felt like to see the place for the first time. Gatiria was impressed with the fine buildings, the herd of animals and the extensive garden. Gachwe was there, crocheting in the shade of one of the huts. She got up to shake Gatiria's hand and looked her up and down in admiration. Compared to Gatiria, Gachwe looked like a country bumpkin, Kanini thought a little smugly.

"Kanini tells me you go to school in Embu," Gatiria said with interest.

"Yes, I'll be in Form Four."

"I just finished Form Four. What a relief! The KCE was difficult."

"Do you think you'll get a good pass?" asked Gachwe.

"I'm not sure. I'm really hoping for a Division Two. If I get a Three, I can only take a teacher's course or secretarial course. I'd rather do something else."

"Like what?" asked Gachwe, with geniuine curiosity.

"I want to be a newspaper reporter in Mombasa or Nairobi. I need to go to college for four years to do that. I don't know where I would get the money. But that's my dream."

"There's a lot of competition for those jobs," said Gachwe. "I'd rather open a shop of my own. I want to sell clothes and nice things for women. I'm good at maths, so I could do all the accounting myself."

Kanini hadn't known that was what Gachwe wanted to do. Leave it to Gatiria to bring out in her snobby sister-in-law what the other women couldn't.

Gatiria settled in—she would be sharing Bilibina's and Gachwe's hut—as the afternoon's heat peaked and waned. The sun was starting to sink when Kanini headed down the hill to the river, a plastic *mtungi* in her hand. She heard footsteps behind her and turned to see Gatiria hurrying to catch up.

"Stefanie gave me another *mtungi*. I haven't collected water very much lately, Kanini, but I'm sure I haven't forgotten how." Gatiria was now wearing an old dress, rubber slippers and a faded head square.

"Did you have pumped water at the mission?" asked Kanini.

"Yes, and electricity. You start to take those things for granted. A few times when they weren't functioning, we had to light the lamps and someone had to go for water, but it wasn't me."

"You must've gone for water at Aniceta's place."

"Yes, but that was nearly two years ago now. The few times I've been back to visit, she wouldn't let me fetch water; it was Silvia who went."

Kanini said, "I'm glad you changed your clothes. You should keep your uniform for good. And the shoes."

There was a pause. "Kanini, I was just with Bilibina. She looks bad. Very sick and weak."

"Like the people at your health center?" asked Kanini.

"Yes, like some of the worst ones. Stefanie says she's having diarrhea now and then, and can hardly eat. We tried to get her to take water, but she could only drink a few sips. Her lips and skin look so dry. And the sores on her face—"

"Could she take some of the *dawa* you brought?"

"Kanini, that medicine won't cure anything. It'll probably do nothing for her; she's in such a poor state. I gave her some and it might make her feel like it's helping. But you and I will know..." Kanini caught her eye. "When did you say her husband died?"

"I think I wrote you...It was before Njagi's wedding, maybe last March or April."

"She's probably had the HIV for a few years. The malaria weakened her, and finally the pneumonia took over. If her body were stronger, it would be able to fight off such infections." Gatiria gazed off across the river. "But she's obviously suffering from lack of resistance to—"

Gatiria had stooped to fill the *mtungi* and nearly lost her balance. After plunging one foot into the water, she tried again and this time was able to fill the container about halfway. Kanini said nothing as she watched her sister. "Ngai! I've forgotten how to fill a *mtungi*! I can't believe it," Gatiria exclaimed.

Kanini stepped forward and easily filled her own jug without dampening her feet. She covered the spout and swung the load onto her back, as Gatiria continued struggling with hers. Finally, after Gatiria had filled the jug as much as she could, Kanini screwed on the ragged cap for her and helped center it on her back. Then they started up the hill.

Despite the exertion, Gatiria would not stop talking. "Kanini, you must think back to your time with Bilibina and your father-in-law. Was there any time that either of them had a sore and was bleeding? Could there have been any contact with any open sore on your own body, or on Gati's or Stefanie's? This is another way AIDS is passed, between open cuts. If your blood came into contact with theirs, you could be infected."

Kanini wondered why her heart was beating so hard; unlike Gatiria, she was used to this climb. In her mind's eye she could see Bilibina's dry lips splitting open and blood trickling out. The vivid memory sent a shiver up her spine.

"I brought some of the gloves I used to wear when working with the patients at the hospital," Gatiria went on. "You can wear them when you tend Bilibina, and so can Stefanie. They'll protect you from any saliva, blood or other fluids coming from her body."

Usually Kanini felt at peace at this time of day, when the hot sun cast its late afternoon shadows over the purple hills and the stillness of the surroundings encased her in a timeless reverie. Now, she wasn't sure how she felt. Would her new family be able to get along with Gatiria for a whole month, or even two weeks? She had so looked forward to her visit. She'd had visions of the two of them working side-by-side, playing together with Gati and chatting with Stefanie. Would they be able to indulge in these pleasant pastimes, or would the reality of the AIDS disease intrude on every moment they spent together?

"Thank-you, sister," said Kanini and fell silent.

At the top of the hill, they heard the sound of male voices behind the thorn fence. Kanini pushed open the gate and spied Kathenge and Njoka, standing by the fire pit with Gatiria's trunk between them. They were guffawing and slapping each other on the shoulders, as though one of them had just told a joke. Their shirts were damp with sweat and the tendons in their forearms were bulging.

"*Mugeni*," Kanini greeted them, forcing her voice to be cheerful, though her heart was beating erratically. "Here's my sister to meet you. Gatiria, my husband, Kathenge, and Njoka, his brother."

The young men turned to face them. Sweat dribbled down one side of Kathenge's face and his hair looked woolly and disheveled. Encircling his mouth was a dark shadow of beard that accentuated his square jaw. He extended his hand and Gatiria shook it in gratitude. Then she shook Njoka's.

"Kathenge. Njoka. Thank-you for carrying my trunk all that way."

Kathenge turned to Gati, who was playing with Riunga. He swooped her up over his head and flew her around, to her obvious glee. Then he sank into a bowed-wood chair and bounced her on his knee. Kanini smiled ruefully at Stefanie who had just emerged from her hut. She guessed that their husbands had stopped for some local brew on the way home. It was a wonder they hadn't gone off and forgotten the trunk.

Njoka sat down as well and lit a cigarette. "Does anyone know how Mother is?"

Stefanie shook her head and clicked her tongue. "She's not well. She wouldn't eat anything today and only drank a little."

"I think the malaria has really taken hold of her this time," Kathenge said, shaking his head. "It'll likely kill her, like it killed Baba."

Gatiria raised her eyebrows and looked over at Kanini; her pursed lips spoke volumes. Kanini shrugged and looked away. Stefanie continued in an upbeat tone.

"I think Mama Njoka will improve. Gatiria brought some medicine from the clinic to give her. I'm cooking a chicken and we'll make her take some of the broth." With that, Stefanie disappeared into the *riko*. Kanini followed, not knowing what else to do.

She lit the lamp and started chopping onions, while Stefanie plucked the chicken, its limp body submerged in a basin of hot water. It wasn't long before they heard loud, disturbed voices outside in the murky shadows. They looked at each other, but continued at their tasks.

Within a few minutes, Gatiria exploded into the kitchen.

"I can't believe these husbands of yours! They refuse to admit that the AIDS disease exists!" Her voice trembled; sparks seemed to shoot from her eyes. "At first, they pretended to not even know what I was talking about. Then they admitted to hearing about it in Nairobi and Embu, but they don't believe it's anything serious. Or anything that can affect *them*!" Her gaze flitted back and forth from Stefanie to Kanini. Stefanie had stood up when she entered, but now settled back onto her haunches and continued stiffly plucking the bird. Kanini stayed leaning on the counter and stared down at her hands.

"They think the *wazungu* developed the disease to kill off the Africans, but that you're only at risk if you go to *wazungu* establishments or spend time with them. Since they say they never do that, they think they're free from getting sick."

Kanini didn't even know her husband thought this. She'd brought up the topic a few times with him, and each time, Kathenge ignored her. "What else did they say?" she asked in a low voice.

"When I told them that Africans are passing it to Africans at a very fast rate, they said I was lying. They said they would never wear condoms because they're made by the *wazungu*, and they probably plant the virus inside to infect us." Gatiria's hands gestured wildly as she spoke. "I told them the virus can't live in a condom, but they laughed and asked what did I know, a schoolgirl? I told them I couldn't believe what they do *not* know, being schoolteachers!" Gatiria stopped abruptly and stood quivering. "I'm shocked, Kanini. They're remaining ignorant on purpose! How can this be? They are educated people!"

Her words, ringing in the dim light of the *riko*, jarred Kanini's senses. She murmured, "I'm sorry our husbands are so stubborn...but there's really nothing we can do about it, Gatiria."

"Nothing you can do! You can give them the material I brought to read. If they claim it's *mzungu* propaganda, you can tell them to visit the AIDS Resource Center in Nairobi. If they refuse, you can tell them...you can tell them that you will not have...relations with them anymore until you can trust them!"

Kanini's heart skipped a beat. She looked at Stefanie. In the leaping lamplight, her sister-in-law's face registered alarm and dismay. Stefanie took a deep breath and said, "We women cannot refuse our husbands, Gatiria. We can only pray that they remain faithful to us."

Expecting another outburst, Kanini glanced over and was surprised to see a change transforming Gatiria's face. The look of outrage had softened to one of frustration mixed with genuine sadness. When she spoke, her voice was calmer. "I think I know how it must be for you. There's nothing you feel you can do, only hope that the men act responsibly. The problem is, so many men *don't* act responsibly. They never have. Now there's this disease, which they refuse to believe even exists. It's too threatening to their habits, their lifestyle...and the power they have over us women." Gatiria's hands had balled into fists, which she hit against her sides.

Kanini flailed about for something to say, but nothing came to her. Suddenly, Gati pushed open the kitchen door and ran to her, crowing, "*Iria, iria!*" Kanini caught up her daughter and retired to a corner to nurse her. When she looked up again, Gatiria was gone.

Stefanie stood with her arms folded. Her face looked haggard. "What are we going to do about your sister, Kanini? She's been here less than a day and already she's making things difficult. Maybe she shouldn't stay so long."

Tears welled up in Kanini's eyes. "I know she can be annoying...but I want to have her here. Maybe she'll calm down in a few days. She has so much knowledge, so much experience. She wants to share it with us...I know her intentions are good."

"But she says everything that comes into her head. It's shameful—" Stefanie sniffed and looked away. "If she makes Kathenge and Njoka angry with us, they might do something regrettable."

Indignation rose in Kanini. "I'm sure they've already done regrettable things," she said, not daring to catch Stefanie's eye. "I think it's time they admitted some of them. Kathenge has assured me he's never gone with another woman. I want to believe him, but how can I? Men do it all the time. If they were afraid of this disease, maybe they wouldn't. But if they keep denying...I don't know, Stefanie. It makes me tired...and sad." Kanini stroked Gati's short clumpy hair as her daughter's eyes closed.

"It makes me sad too." Her sister-in-law moved back toward the mud stove. "But how will your sister get them to believe what she says? They're not going to read her materials or visit a center in Nairobi." She looked down at the basin where the bald chicken floated. How pathetic it looked. And so vulnerable.

"I know they're not," agreed Kanini after a moment. "We need to keep Gatiria out of their way. We'll be the ones to get the information from her and tell our husbands...when...when they're ready to hear it."

"It sounds like you have everything figured out, Kanini." Stefanie's head swayed back and forth. "I'm still worried. I love Njoka. I want our lives to continue as they are."

"I want that too, Stefanie," Kanini whispered. There was a heartbeat's pause. "I only wish I loved Kathenge like you love Njoka."

Stefanie's eyes, luminous marbles in the dusky light, darted back to Kanini's face. "I'm sorry, Kanini..."

As Kanini sat straighter, her nipple slid out of little Gati's mouth. "It's all right, Stefanie. Gati's asleep. Maybe I should start making the *ugali*."

Chapter 2

The day after Gatiria's arrival, Kathenge and Njoka left early in the morning to attend the teachers' meeting in Embu. With the men gone, the women fell into a comfortable routine. The harvest was great, and as Gatiria worked alongside Kanini and Stefanie for hours at a time, she commented on how different things were from Aniceta's farm and the farm she and Kanini had grown up on. The time went faster with the fresh stories and perspectives.

Gatiria also enjoyed tending Gati and getting to know her. Kanini was astounded to hear their exchange one morning as she arrived home from the field.

"*Habari gani?*" Gatiria was asking her namesake, emphasizing the Swahili words so Gati could understand. "That means, '*Muga*'. *Unafahamu?* Do you understand?"

"Gatiria, what do you think you're doing? Gati can hardly say anything in our mother tongue, let alone Swahili." Kanini set down her basket and wiped the sweat from her face with her handkerchief. She could barely perceive a light breeze touching her hot skin.

"At secondary, we talked about how this age is the best for learning language. Gati can speak two or three languages like a native if she learns them now. If she waits till she attends primary, it'll be too late."

"But who'll continue teaching her after you leave us?" Stefanie joined the conversation, as she swung a load of green grams off her forehead and leaned her *panga* against the hut she shared with Njoka. She plopped down into the shade next to Gatiria.

"Kanini will do it, won't you, sister?" asked Gatiria. "Think how great it'd be. To already know *Kizungu* when you start primary school!"

"English too? There's no way I have the time or energy."

"But what about at night? There's nothing better to do than sit around and teach vocabulary and grammar. Riunga can be learning too and they can talk together!"

"You live in a world of dreams, Gatiria," scoffed Stefanie. "People want to relax during their time off. Not learn foreign languages."

There was a pause as Gatiria's mind switched to a different track. "I bet if you teach these children English, you'll gain such respect from your husbands. They might want to join you; they are teachers, after all. They would never go out *kupiga maji* again."

"They might take an interest in it for a while," said Stefanie. "But soon they'd get bored with it, and return to their old ways. They always do."

Kanini caught her sister's eye and shrugged in agreement. Without another word, Gatiria got up to help her niece gather banana leaves.

Kanini turned back to face her sister-in-law. "Sometimes I feel like I'm speaking a foreign language with your sister," Stefanie said under her breath.

One day the conversation took a different turn. The women were taking a break from harvesting millet and had sat down under the shade of an acacia near the field to drink water and feed the children. Gatiria took a deep breath and plunged in.

"So, Kanini, I've been wondering. Will you and Kathenge make Gati get circumcised when she comes of age?"

The question took Kanini by surprise. She thought a moment before she said, "What do you think, sister? Since you're her namesake, I'd like you to have a say in the matter."

"Well, you know my opinion on the subject. I would hope that you leave my little niece completely whole, so that she...I guess I hope that you at least give her a choice." Gatiria had started fiddling with some sticks that lay nearby. She watched Riunga and Gati as they chased each other among the rocks.

"I've thought a lot about this, Gatiria. Ever since my daughter was born, in fact," Kanini told her. "Kathenge agrees with me that once she comes of age, we won't have her circumcised."

Gatiria looked at Kanini, her face registering immense relief. "Oh, Kanini, I'm so happy to hear that!" She leaned back against a large boulder. "So often women claim to want to stop the tradition. Then when the time comes, they perform it anyway on their own daughters. They feel the pressure of the community, or maybe their own mothers or husbands." Gatiria dusted her hands off. "I hope you don't give in, Kanini. It may be hard to go against what is commonly practiced, living out here where you do—"

"I don't think it'll be so hard. Things are changing, Gatiria. Even here. Not as many girls in these areas are being circumcised. Kathenge goes to towns of all sizes. Most people he meets there consider the custom out-dated, even barbaric."

Stefanie's voice was low as she joined the conversation. "Njoka is not against it. I once heard him and Kathenge arguing about it, Kanini, right after Gati was born."

"What did he say?" demanded Gatiria.

"He asked Kathenge what he would do if Gati got pregnant while in secondary school, or even before. At their primary school, a few Standard Sevens and Standard Eights have turned up pregnant, girls who were never circumcised."

"So, they think that if the girls had been circumcised, they wouldn't have gotten pregnant?" sputtered Gatiria.

Stefanie and Kanini looked at each other. Gati climbed onto Kanini's lap. Kanini opened her dress and absently began nursing.

"I know uncircumcised girls can sometimes be more interested in having sex than the circumcised ones," Gatiria contended. "But today, even circumcised girls have sex before marriage, or get raped at their schools. So they can turn up pregnant too. And uncircumcised girls can be just as chaste as the others, depending on their upbringing. Circumcision isn't the only thing that keeps women...keeps women from going with men."

"Well, Kathenge told Njoka something like what you just said. I didn't know he even believed it, so I was surprised," replied Stefanie.

"I guess my husband does have something in common with you, Gatiria," Kanini said, a wry smile curling her lip.

Gatiria barreled on. "What do you think Mama and Baba will say when you tell them? Won't they try to persuade you to circumcise her?"

"I haven't really thought of that," said Kanini. "Maybe we can just tell the people in Kajuki we had it done, but not really do it."

"Hmm," Gatiria mused. "I think people will know the truth, Kanini. They always seem to. '*Macho hayana pazai*'... 'People make it their business to know others' business'."

Kanini knew that what Gatiria said was true. This event was so far in the future that she couldn't bear the thought of it now. She would deal with it later, when the time came. She felt confident that her husband would continue to stand by her. And maybe peoples' mindsets would continue to change, even in her backward hometown.

After the husbands returned from their meeting, the routine remained basically the same. The men would go out late in the morning and return at suppertime, or later, if the mood took them. They did not usually stay out all night. Kanini noticed that Gatiria tried to avoid them as often as possible. She knew her sister would have trouble keeping her temper if she got into an argument with them again. Gatiria did not usually share supper with Kanini, Stefanie and their husbands, preferring to eat with the children, Gachwe or Bilibina. Indeed, Gatiria had become Bilibina's most dedicated nurse.

One morning around daybreak, Kanini awoke to Gatiria's voice calling softly from outside her hut. She heaved herself out of bed as Kathenge continued snoring.

Kanini opened the door, her eyesight still fuzzy. "*Ngai*, Gatiria...What got you up so early?"

"I needed to go to the toilet...I glanced over at Bilibina on my way past and...let's go over there, Kanini."

As they entered the hut, Kanini knew what to expect. Her gaze wandered to the thin, lifeless form lying on the bed, covered with a *leso*. A light breeze blew the mosquito netting so that it billowed like a ghost. Her heart thudded in her chest as she lifted it.

"Well...at least she's no longer suffering," Kanini mumbled. Gatiria nodded as she replaced the *leso* and patted Kanini's arm.

Within two days, Bilibina's shrunken form was buried beside her husband in a ceremony presided over by one of the local priests. A small group of friends and relatives attended, having brought pots of food and bottles of soda with them. The smell of a roasting goat permeated the gathering.

The priest spoke in an upbeat manner about Bilibina's life. He commented that now her suffering was over, she was much happier in the place where she had gone. He then led the attendees in calm prayers and songs. No one wailed or cried as in the past. The priest made it clear that it was preferable for Bilibina to be in heaven with her husband. Afterward, as everyone feasted, Kathenge and Njoka shared stories about her life. They were joined by relatives and neighbors, each of whom had an anecdote about Bibi Bilibina.

The next day, the old woman's bedding and clothing were washed and hung to dry, whereupon everything was folded and put away, to be used again in some future time when her life had become a distant memory. As it was now, her spirit was still very much with them, having leached so much of their own spirits for so long.

Kanini knew Bilibina would remain in their midst for quite a while to come. As she came and went from the compound, she often thought she heard the voice of the woman who had dictated so much of her day. After a moment, she would realize it was only the squawk of a bird or a cry from one of the children. She would glance around, wondering if Bilibina were talking to her through some other medium. Sometimes she wondered if the spirit could perceive the intense relief Kanini felt at her departure. She tried not to acknowledge or admit this feeling, even to herself

Once she asked Stefanie if she ever heard their mother-in-law's voice. "Sometimes I think I hear her. Once, I even thought I saw her lying under a *leso* in the hut. But it was just a blanket that had been left there."

"I'm sure we're just not used to her being gone. Our minds are playing tricks on us," Kanini said.

"No, I'm sure her spirit is still around. She lived here for so many years... It'll be a long while until it's gone to its final rest."

Gachwe and Gatiria now shared the hut alone. At times Kanini worried that Gatiria would disrupt the departing soul, since she was only staying temporarily. Kanini dared not say anything about this to Gatiria. She worried that her sister would look down on her for her old-fashioned superstitions.

The days preceding Christmas were quiet and uneventful. The last of the millet was harvested and the women took turns grinding it into flour so that *ucuru* and *ugali* could be prepared. There were collard greens growing by the river, *nthoroko* and green grams recently harvested and tomatoes and onions that were ripe and succulent, all from their *munda*. Kanini and Gatiria walked to the market on a Tuesday and bought potatoes, pineapples, mangoes and a papaya so that their holiday feast could be complete.

On Christmas Eve they skinned, peeled, ground and chopped. A pile of potatoes stood like gleaming cotton balls on the table, alongside a large bowl of freshly ground millet flour, one of threshed green grams and another of hulled cowpeas. A few chickens would be slaughtered in the morning, quick-fried and then boiled with onions and curry powder.

"Are we going to church in the morning?" asked Gatiria.

Having never attended the Christian institution as children, Kanini wasn't in the habit of going, even on Christmas. "We've only gone once since Kathenge and I were married," she said. "That was our second Christmas together."

"So, do you want to go tomorrow?" asked Gatiria.

"Do you?"

"I've spent so many Sundays and holidays at church that I'd be content not to. But...whatever you want to do."

Stefanie overheard their conversation and joined in. "Perhaps we should attend church this year, Kanini. After Bilibina's death and everything. Maybe we could even get the men to go."

"I think it'd be nice to join the singing," Gachwe piped up.

Kathenge and Njoka protested loudly when Stefanie brought it up, but ultimately they were persuaded. They arose obediently the next morning, combed their nappy heads and put on their best slacks.

As the family set off, the men walked ahead, swinging their empty hands as they conversed with one another. Gachwe followed with Gatiria, one carrying a gunnysack of cowpeas and the other one of green grams, as offerings to the hungry. Kanini and Stefanie donned their cardigans, slung the young ones onto their backs, and followed in silence.

Kanini had been feeling both relieved and melancholy, due to the recent death of Bilibina and the impending departure of Gatiria. At this moment, however, with her entire family out on this special holiday, she felt content. What else could happen to disrupt their lives, at least right now? Kanini ticked off in her mind all the things they had to be thankful for: the full stores of food, the healthy livestock, their own good health and Gatiria's nearby work location. Life could be so much harder.

The sun glared off the tin roof of their boxy white church, as the brightly-dressed women milled about. In the midst of it all, a pointsettia tree bloomed. Gatiria explained to Kanini that this was a good omen; stories from other cultures depicted these cheerful red flowers as a symbol of hope and peace.

A large group of women and a smaller one of men hovered about the building, awaiting the arrival of the priest, who would come by motorbike from another church. A lot of time went by, and Kanini worried that their husbands would wander off somewhere. When the priest finally arrived, he swung his leg over his *piki-piki* and, with a beckoning wave, led the entire crowd into the church.

After the long service, everyone flocked back out into the sunshine. Kanini greeted acquaintances and introduced her sister around. A number of people who had not come to the funeral expressed condolences at the death of Bilibina. Kanini was shaking the hand of one of Kathenge's distant cousins, when the woman drew everyone's attention by launching into a tale in her high-pitched voice.

"We've also had a death in the family. My brother just died from a very strange disease. It wasn't malaria as we thought at first. He coughed a lot like he had T.B. He was only twenty-eight years old, with two small children! It's one thing when an old woman like Bilibina dies, but another thing when such a healthy young man dies."

Kanini tried to ward her sister off with her eyes, but Gatiria was moving in on the discussion and would not be deterred. In her loud voice, she asked point blank, "Excuse me, but have you ever heard of *ukimwi?*"

The woman took a step back and glanced at someone standing next to her. "*Ukimwi?* What are you talking about?"

"It was brought over to Africa a few years ago by the *wazungu*, or maybe it originated here. No one really knows. But Kenyans are contracting it and dying from it, by the thousands!"

Kanini silently begged Gatiria to stop. If she wasn't careful, someone might drag her off, assuming she was a lunatic.

"I've never heard of that," the woman said in a small voice. The crowd glared at Gatiria with suspicion. Kanini dared not look around for her husband.

"Well, you need to start believing that it's real. Healthy twenty-eight year-old men don't just up and die. He was probably engaging with a prostitute somewhere and got it from her. That's how the disease is passed. Now his wife probably has it as well."

"How dare you say such a thing?" The woman looked close to tears. "Who are you, anyway? Kanini, if this is your sister, make her go back where she came from." She turned and shuffled away, a number of onlookers in her wake.

Kanini's heart sank. How typical of Gatiria to not only turn their husbands against them, but then repeat the action with the community. How would Kathenge react? She shot her sister another look and swung Gati onto her back, tying her on with a *leso*. Kathenge approached Gatiria and in a low, ominous voice, said something that Kanini did not hear; whereupon, he turned and stalked off. Njoka hurried to catch up with him, followed by Stefanie, a troubled look on her face. Gachwe was nowhere to be seen; Kanini could only hope she had already started for home.

Kanini waited until the family members were ahead of them and all the churchgoers had left, then turned to her sister, who was still standing, as though riveted to the spot. "Gatiria, how could you say all that? The people here aren't ready to hear it."

"When will they be ready, Kanini? In five years when half the adults have contracted the virus? I hate this notion that rural people are so traditional, they can't handle any new information. Why are we so stuck in our ways? Our traditions are going to kill us; they already are!"

"Yes, but there's a time and place to let people know about difficult things, Gatiria. After church on Christmas isn't it."

Gatiria sighed. "Well, I am sorry if I embarrassed you and your family. I just can't stand people living in stubborn ignorance! It makes me want to scream!"

"I just hope Kathenge doesn't make my life wretched after you leave us," muttered Kanini. "His stubborn ignorance could be the road to my misery."

Chapter 3

Two mornings later, Kanini and Gatiria lugged Gatiria's trunk to Ishiara market to catch the bus to Chiakariga. Kathenge had originally offered to help them, but after Gatiria's outburst at the church, he reneged on his offer. Thus, the women were obliged to haul it the entire way themselves.

They arrived just as the enormous OTC bus coughed up to a stop, black smoke engulfing the horde that scrambled to get on. Kanini boarded while Gatiria waited for the driver to thrust her trunk into the belly of the battered vehicle. Babies wailed on laps and chickens squawked under the seats. The stifling heat was overwhelming, as was the odor of bodies, dressed in multiple layers of unwashed clothes. Kanini could see dust swirling in the shafts of sunlight that streamed in the windows. As the bus heaved itself onto the road, the shops of Ishiara receded into the distance.

Kanini had planned from the beginning of Gatiria's visit to escort her to her new place and help her settle in. After the unfortunate incident on Christmas, she wasn't sure her husband was going to allow Gatiria to stay on, let alone allow Kanini to escort her. Indeed, he withdrew so completely that she couldn't even talk to him until the following evening. He tried to forbid her to go at that point, but she was already packed. It didn't take a lot of pleading to get him to change his mind; he probably needed a break from her as much as she needed one from him.

Her heart felt lighter once they were on the road. She clung to Gatiria's arm as the vehicle trundled along, tossing its occupants around with every turn or bump. They alighted from the vehicle after an hour or so, a good thirty kilometers from Ishiara. Their stop was just a bare spot next to the road, marked by a windblown canopy of thatch atop four rickety poles. Snaking away from the little shelter was a dusty track, which the bus driver assured them led to Chiakariga.

Struggling with the trunk between them, the women started off. A *mzee* passed them, carrying a *panga*, and when Gatiria asked how far the place was, he answered in two words: "*Huko tuu.*" Just there. It wasn't long before Kanini glimpsed the shiny roofs over the trees, indicating the outpost. The little square buildings that marched in a half circle around the center were painted in bright, cheerful colors. There was not much activity; the only person visible was a tailor treadling his sewing machine outside a *duka*. Most of the buildings had padlocks on their doors; only one open doorway led into the cool gloom of a *chai* shop.

"I'm sure someone here can tell us where the school is," Gatiria said. A slight tremble rippled through her voice.

They left the trunk under the paltry shade of an acacia and walked toward the open shop. Inside, they found two women, one young and one older, with babies on their laps, sipping tea. "*Mugeni*," said Kanini politely.

"*Mugeni mono*," answered the *cucu*, her smile polka-dotted with toothless gaps. "*Karibu chai*."

Kanini and Gatiria sat down and ordered cups for themselves. The other woman asked where they came from and what they were doing in Chiakariga. After Gatiria told them, the older woman indicated the doorway with pursed lips.

"That school is not far. It is just there."

"Do you know anything about it?" Gatiria asked.

"Well...it used to be a good school," the younger woman answered. "The main problem now is that so few children come anymore. First, the teachers left, so the headmaster was teaching by himself." She looked uncertainly at the *cucu*, as though wondering how much to tell. "Then, there wasn't enough food, so lots of the children had to drop out in order to look for *mburu*, those fruits that grow in higher areas. Now, we hear that some of the children's parents have become sick, due to malaria or lack of food, we don't know."

"The school has a curse," whispered the *cucu*. "Things aren't normal there." She shook her head. "If you can bring back the children, we'll be very grateful." Both women looked from Gatiria to Kanini and then back again. Their eyes shone like pale marbles.

"*Nikwega mono*," said Gatiria, finishing her *chai*. "Let's go, Kanini."

They followed the women's directions and walked behind the row of buildings to a grove of spindly mango trees that grew in a ravine. They could see the school on the side of a hill, pieces of its tin roof flapping and clanking in the wind. Its mud walls were in desperate need of repair.

"It looks a little like Kithinge—" began Kanini.

"Only worse," Gatiria intercepted. "I wonder if the headmaster is anywhere around. Maybe he's still on holiday."

"Could be he lives nearby and we could easily find him."

"Maybe someone in town knows where he lives. Otherwise, we can go to Materi Girls' and ask Brother John. I've never met that priest, but he's friends with Brother Severino, and I'm sure he would help."

The women checked the door of the four-room school, and found a padlock hanging from it. There were no other buildings except for a wooden *choo* off in the distance, far enough away that no smell emanated from it. "No room even for teacher preps or an office," muttered Gatiria, almost to herself.

Back in town, the women in the *chai* shop had left, but a few men were milling about and they seemed willing to talk.

"We know the headmaster," one man lisped through mostly vacant gums. "His name is Mugambi Kiburu. He's not here now; I think he went to Nairobi or Embu."

"Is he from around here?" asked Gatiria.

"No—I think he's from somewhere up—near Meru, maybe. He rents a room in the market." With his chin the man indicated the cluster of tin roofs.

"That's what I'll probably have to do too, since there don't seem to be any teacher houses," Gatiria said to Kanini. "I think we'd better go to Materi. I'm sure they can put us up for the night. We'll get some more information there."

They made arrangements to leave the trunk in the available room behind the *chai* shop then started the trek back out to the Mati road to flag down another vehicle. Gatiria did not say much as they walked along, and Kanini felt sorry for her sister. Though Gatiria had not had high hopes for this job, she'd been excited to at least have work. Now she seemed to be seriously wondering how practical the position would be.

Getting a vehicle took a very long time. The women walked north, turning to flag down every passing lorry or land rover that went by. In a two-hour period, six or seven private vehicles raced past in clouds of dust, but nothing stopped for them. Finally, a lorry groaned to a stop and they clamored aboard.

The lorry was headed to the mission with its cargo of supplies. When Kanini saw how far from the Mati road the place was, relief washed over her. They would never have made it by nightfall on foot.

"This looks a lot like the mission where you lived," said Kanini, upon arriving at the main office. Gatiria gave her a wan smile as they slipped off the seat. She glanced around as they approached the office door.

Brother John was in, they were told, and not too busy. A young girl showed them into his office after only a ten-minute wait. Kanini looked around in astonishment. So many photos and knick-knacks, papers, books and notebooks, all stacked in disarray on shelves and tables. How could one person possibly deal with so much? Her eyes finally found their way to the man's face.

Brother John was a white man with thinning gray hair and soft, flaccid cheeks. He had wire-rimmed spectacles that perched on his nose. Kanini couldn't tell what the man's age was; it was hard to tell with these *wazungu*. He swiveled in his large, plush chair and faced the women with a gentle smile. He did not stand, but reached out his hand to each of them in turn, as they introduced themselves.

"It's very nice to meet you, Gatiria, and you too, Kanini." His English had a strong accent, which Gatiria later told Kanini was American. "Severino has told me a lot about you, Gatiria. He says you were a very bright student, with a lot of talent for words and ideas. We're happy to have you in our area as a teacher."

"Thank-you, Brother John," said Gatiria, with deference, her English clear and easy to understand. "But I am wondering about this teaching assignment. They told me at the Chiakariga market that very few of the children are coming to school, due to hunger and sickness."

"Why don't you both have a seat?" Brother John indicated chairs on the other side of his desk, and they sat down. "The school is very needy, but there are still enough children to warrant two teachers. Last term the headmaster was teaching two classes, one with about fifteen Standard Ones, Twos and Threes, and another class with about twelve older ones." Brother John leaned back in his chair and pressed his fingers together in front of him. "He was hoping you'd be able to take the younger class so he could concentrate on the older one, Gatiria. He also wanted to work at encouraging the other pupils—the ones who've dropped out—to return to school."

Kanini looked at her sister to see what she would say. She had only understood about half of what the man said.

"Well, now I'm learning a little more about what this assignment is," said Gatiria. "It sounds like there were more students last year."

"Yes, there were more, maybe thirty-five or something. That was why the headmaster was having such difficulty trying to teach all of them. A few years ago, there were over fifty pupils and he had two other teachers helping him. But one by one, they left, and so he's been teaching alone."

"I heard about that," said Gatiria. She took a deep breath. "Well, maybe I should plan to go up to Meru tomorrow to buy some furnitures and other things for the room I will rent."

"You could, or...I think we probably have a few things we're not using here, if you want them. Chairs and maybe a table and a bed."

A smile lit Gatiria's face for the first time all day. "I would gladly accept them," she said.

"Now, it's getting late. You two must stay the night here and start back tomorrow." Brother John rose and walked to the door. "Why don't I find you a room to stay in and then you can wash up for supper?"

Kanini was touched by the man's sincere desire to help them. She and Gatiria followed him out of the office, past a few closed doors, and out into a little courtyard with a paved walk that led to a small stone building. He took out a large key ring and opened the door, then led them to a room on one side. "This is one of our teachers' houses," he said. "They're not back from holiday yet, and we're still waiting for the new teacher who's moving into this room. In the meantime, you may use it."

The room was clean and plain with cotton curtains covering the screened-in windows and a good-sized bed. There was no need for a mosquito net. Kanini jumped when John switched on the electric light.

"The lavatory is down the hall, and you'll find towels there. Our dining room is back near the office where you came in. Supper will be served in a little while; I'll send someone for you."

He left them and they both sat down on the bed, exhausted. "I can't believe we're really here, Gatiria," breathed Kanini. "Brother John is so kind! It's almost like he was expecting us."

"He's been here many years," said Gatiria. "At least as many as Brother Severino. They come to expect anything at any time, these men."

"He seems very...thoughtful. So different from most Kenyan men."

"It's because he's a priest. If he were a regular *mzungu*, he'd be more like our men. Most men are alike, Kanini."

Kanini nodded in silence. After finding the lavatory and washing up, they were met back at their room by a younger girl in school uniform. As they followed her to the dining area, Kanini wondered how it must feel to attend a school like this, where you could focus solely on studies, with nothing else to trouble you.

The aroma of a hearty chicken stew greeted them as they sat down at a large round table. Two women flanked them, a Kenyan and a European, and two young Kenyan men and Brother John sat across from them. Everyone introduced themselves and Kanini noticed how comfortable the Kenyans seemed, as if they were used to sharing meals with *wazungu* on a daily basis. Feeling less than comfortable, Kanini did not talk much, though she answered the questions put to her as politely as she could. The Kenyan woman sitting next to her was a nurse who worked at the clinic. Her name was Muthoni. Her large eyes and brilliant smile lit her entire face; she was so stunning Kanini could hardly pull her eyes away. The white woman was also a nurse, a visitor who had come down from Meru for the evening. She was plump and flush-faced with thin, wispy hair. Kanini wondered why she didn't wear a head square to keep it in place.

The talk was all in English, and at first Kanini paid rapt attention, straining her ears to catch whatever words she could. After awhile, her mind dulled with the constant thud of the foreign sounds. She focused on her stew instead, feeling the savory warmth of it fill up her empty stomach. It was strange eating the soft bread that was served in a basket. Bread was usually reserved for *chai*, while *ugali* or rice was eaten with meat.

She didn't notice that Gatiria had started talking to the entire table until a laugh jolted her out of her reverie.

"—believe that KANU is in power another five years. We will bury Moi in office with the way things are going..."

Gatiria was spouting her own opinions about the current political situation. How could she be so brazen? Kanini stared down at her plate as the company listened intently. It wasn't until Gatiria had finished that Kanini noticed Brother John and a number of the others chuckling and nodding their approval. Gatiria turned to talk to the woman on the other side of her, but Kanini said nothing for the rest of the meal.

She decided not to mention anything disapproving to her sister. What was the point? Gatiria was an adult and had made it this far with her outspoken character. There was nothing Kanini could do or say to guide her to more proper comportment, especially in a foreign environment like this one. Even with her own family and community, Kanini had found it impossible to prevent her sister's inappropriate behavior.

The next day, Kanini awoke confused and disoriented. She had dreamed that she was sleeping beside Kathenge, but he was telling her he couldn't stay married to her. When she asked why, he told her it was because of a secret he had, a terrible secret that he couldn't divulge. As she struggled to wake up, the feelings of terror and confusion subsided somewhat, and she felt calmer seeing Gatiria asleep beside her. She took a few deep breaths as she stared up at the bright white ceiling. When Gatiria awoke a few minutes later, she related the dream to her.

"That dream says a lot," said Gatiria. "What do you think his terrible secret is, Kanini?"

"That he has gone with other women…that he may be infected…with that sickness."

"With the HIV. Your dream tells you he is. I sincerely hope that he is not."

"Can a person find out if he's infected, Gatiria? Is there some sort of test?"

"Yes, there's a test, but it's not always reliable. It's hard to get and it takes months for the results to come back." Gatiria lay on her back, her hands clasped under her head. "If you were afraid you were HIV positive, you could go to one of the clinics, and they would test you. But they won't just test anyone. As a woman you'd have to be a prostitute or something. I think it'd be hard for you as a married woman to get the test, though maybe Kathenge could get it."

"I wish I could persuade him to go, but he would never—" Kanini thought a moment. "Are there some early symptoms that we could be looking for?"

"Well, the early symptoms are hard to distinguish from a mild case of malaria. The person feels achy and has a headache and a fever. Sometimes he or she has stomach upset as well, with diarrhea or vomiting." Gatiria listed the symptoms off as though she was discussing what vegetables they needed to buy at the market. It always amazed Kanini how easily her sister could discuss this frightful topic.

"This slight case only lasts a few weeks," Gatiria went on, turning to face Kanini. "After that, a person can live unaffected for many years, up to eight or ten, in fact. It's usually the older or weaker ones that get AIDS earlier, after only a year or two. Healthy people like Kathenge could be carrying the HIV virus around, infecting every person he has sex with, and never know he has it." Her eyes rose up to the ceiling. "Then when he's thirty or thirty-five, suddenly he'll get hit with a bad case of dysentery or pneumonia, and his body can't resist it. I've seen healthy men that age die in just a few weeks, Kanini. That's all it takes. There's nothing anyone can do."

"Well, I haven't seen Kathenge with any aches or fever. When all of us were sick with malaria, he was the only one who didn't get sick at all."

"Not all people who've just gotten infected with HIV get these symptoms, Kanini. Or his symptoms could have been so mild you never noticed them." Gatiria sat up in the bed and folded the blanket down neatly. "You do have a lot of reason to hope. Kathenge and Njoka are educated. Though they don't want to admit anything about their behavior, we have to hope they are using decent judgment."

Kanini said nothing as she looked at the curtains that fluttered before the window. She sighed deeply and breathed in the fresh morning air. Gatiria reached over and squeezed her hand.

Within half an hour, the women were washed and on their way to the dining room where they could smell toast and *chai*. Brother John and Muthoni welcomed them to breakfast. Muthoni introduced her brother, a bright-eyed young man with a smile that seemed to swallow his whole face. They assured Gatiria that they would find some furnishings for her new home, as well as see to it that they were loaded into a land rover and taken to the site. Gatiria was so delighted, she actually sat in silence and gazed at the woman and her brother, her eyes shining.

So, they were driven back to Chiakariga in style, Muthoni's brother at the wheel. In what seemed like no time, they pulled up to the *chai* shop in a puff of red dust.

A different *cucu* appeared at the door of the shop, two young children clinging to her dress. They looked out at the newcomers shyly. An older child in tattered shorts strutted boldly out to see what the ruckus was and surveyed the vehicle with a quizzical look on his face. Gatiria disappeared inside to talk with the owner of the shop and make arrangements for renting a room. When she returned, she had a key in her hand. She led Kanini, Muthoni and her brother to the back of the building and unlocked the door to her new abode.

Kanini poked her head in and let her eyes adjust. It was a tiny room, less than a quarter the size of the hut she slept in with Kathenge and little Gati. The walls were made entirely of tin, there was a dirt floor, a corrugated roof and no windows. The only light coming in was from the doorway. At least no snakes or scorpions could slither in, though this place would steam like a teapot in the afternoons.

It took no time to unload the table, two chairs, iron bed frame and mattress and situate them in the room. Then Gatiria invited everyone to the adjoining shop for *chai* and freshly made *mandazzi*, which smelled so savory no one could resist. She was in such high spirits that she bought tea and fritters for the *cucu* and her grandchildren as well. She found out the older boy would be one of her primary students. Everyone chatted freely. Then Kanini and Gatiria waved their new friends off and returned to Gatiria's quarters.

There was already a wire looped from one hook to another across one of the corners. Gatiria shook out her dresses and hung them over the line to air them out. She unfolded her crocheted doilies and placed them around, over the backs of the chairs and in the center of the table. She then laid her sheets and blanket over the bed.

"We'll have to find some flowers to put on the table. It looks much better anyway, don't you think?" asked Gatiria.

"Yes," Kanini agreed. "I'm glad you're feeling better about things, Gatiria. Yesterday, you seemed a little depressed."

"Well, I'm still worried. I'll feel better after I've met the headmaster. Brother John seems to think well of him."

"He does, and that makes me feel better. To have a single man living so near, Gatiria. What if he starts bothering you?"

Gatiria turned quickly to face Kanini. "I know how to take care of myself, Kanini. I will put him off, politely but firmly. There's no way I would get involved with any local man, even a headmaster. Especially not until I see a negative AIDS test with his name on it!" Kanini knew that her sister was trying to joke, but it was hard for her. Even if she saw such a test, Kanini was sure Gatiria would not get involved.

Kanini stayed as long as she dared, though she knew if she lingered too long, she might miss a vehicle back to Ishiara. Now, Gatiria escorted her. They rambled back through town under the blazing sun, no umbrella to shade their heads. A young boy, wearing only shorts, was just leaving his compound to take the goats out. Kanini noticed his protruding belly and patchy light hair, indications of kwashiorkor. He stared at them. They waved and smiled at him in return.

"I wish you could stay just one night," Gatiria admitted as they walked. "I'm sort of scared to sleep here by myself."

Imagine! Gatiria admitting to being scared of something! Kanini could hardly believe it.

"I wish I could stay till the day you start teaching," Kanini responded ardently.

Gatiria smiled. "That's in three days. Or three days if the pupils all show up. Sometimes they don't come the whole first week, if there's a lot to harvest or something."

"I know. Kathenge is always complaining about how so many of them get behind in their studies right away."

"Isn't it interesting, "Gatiria mused. "Right now, at least, your husband and I have the same profession. So, if he starts condemning me too much, remind him of that." She smiled at Kanini, then shook her head. "Not that it'll make any difference."

"He won't condemn you. I'm sure he's just amazed by your nerve, Gatiria. He's never met anyone like you before, even in Nairobi. It makes him uneasy when a woman knows more than he does...about anything."

"That's pretty typical," said Gatiria. "You can assure him that I won't be bothering him with a visit anytime soon."

"When do you think you'll come back?" Kanini asked.

Gatiria gave her usual shrug. "I'm not sure, Kanini. I don't want to commit to a time. This job could end up being a lot more than I've bargained for."

They arrived at the main road and sat under the shelter. Kanini scrutinized the long dusty road in each direction, but could see nothing except a circling vulture.

"What about a visit to Kajuki?" she blurted. She'd hoped to discuss this during Gatiria's visit, but it had never come up.

"To Kajuki? I don't think they're ready to see me there," said Gatiria. "Maybe you can go for a visit one of these days and check it out for me. I'd feel a little nervous just barging in on Mama and Baba."

Kanini nodded. She peered up the road, thinking she saw a dust devil, which could indicate a vehicle. It was only the wind kicking up a whorl of dirt and scattering tumbleweeds off into the bush. "Well, Gatiria, I should probably get going. I'll walk, and if I don't get a vehicle, I'll stop by one of Cucu's nieces and spend the night there."

"They live a long way from here, Kanini! You'll get a vehicle before then, I'm sure."

"I hope so," Kanini said with a shaky smile. She stood up and smoothed her skirt. As they embraced, Kanini buried her face in Gatiria's neck, hoping to take with her that floral scent her sister always wore. Then she broke away, collected her bag and set off down the hot gravel road, facing south. She looked back once to see Gatiria waving at her from under the shelter. The second time she looked, Gatiria was gone.

Chapter 4

The only view was the surrounding green hills dotted with acacia trees. Periodically a Thompson's gazelle glided by in the distance or a lizard scuttled across her path, but very little broke the stillness that enfolded her. Kanini fell into a reverie as she crunched along.

Despite the month they had spent together, Kanini hardly felt closer to her sister than when they were first reunited at the Ishiara market. After writing back and forth for nearly four years, Kanini thought they should have attained a certain level of intimacy, but instead, there was still a distance between them that she felt couldn't be bridged. Having never fully understood the motivation behind Gatiria's actions, at least now she perceived a glimmering of where her righteous indignation was directed. For all that Gatiria had always seemed so selfish, she was now driven to help others, people whose names she did not even know.

Kanini walked for only a few hours. By the time the sun began sliding down in the sky, she had flagged down a passing *matatu*, which landed her in Ishiara. From there she ambled the rest of the way home.

Upon arrival *mucii* a little after sunset, Kanini was comforted by the homey scene. The evening had grown slightly cool and Kathenge had built a fire outside. The children were running around and poking their sticks at it. She could see strips of Stefanie's orange skirt through the chinks of the *riko* and the aroma of *githeri*, fried with curry, onions, tomatoes and greens, wafted through the bamboo and made her stomach growl. Gachwe must have been in the hut she now resided in alone, since Kanini could see that a lamp was lit. She was probably preparing for secondary where she would return in a few days. Njoka was nowhere about, but it could be he was out with the livestock, since Kanini could not see any animals. She wondered about that; usually Gachwe or Stefanie took them out.

Kanini entered the gate of thorns and Gati ran to her. "Mama! Mama!" Kanini scooped her up and held her close. She'd never been apart from her daughter for more than a day before and hadn't realized how much she would miss her. She sat on one of the stones by the fire to breastfeed. Gati murmured contentedly, popping her mother lightly on the chest with her little fist. Kanini smoothed her nappy hair and wiped a damp smear from her face with her handkerchief. The sight of the little girl's curly eyelashes brushing her cheek filled Kanini with a buzz of contentment.

Kathenge meandered over from the chicken house and smiled good-naturedly. "*Muga*, Kanini." After she returned the greeting, he asked how her journey had been. She related most of her adventures, and he nodded with interest. He seemed impressed that they had spent the night at the mission.

"Where's Njoka?" asked Kanini.

"He's taken some goats to the house of a man near Kajuki. Not too far from your family's place," said Kathenge. "We need to pay Gachwe's school fees on Monday, you know."

Kanini noticed that a few of the animals remained in the pen, but not even half the herd. She hesitated before asking, "Why did you need to sell so many goats? Usually your salaries are enough to pay the fees."

Kathenge's look made her wish she hadn't asked. "The salaries weren't enough this time, Kanini. We had a lot of expenses with Mama's funeral, and the food we bought at Christmas. The fees have also gone up for next year..." He shook his head, making Kanini feel like a child. "Never mind; you wouldn't understand."

Kanini held her tongue, but she distinctly felt that he wasn't telling her everything. She knew that both the funeral and Christmas had not cost that much money—most of the food had come from their own farm or donations from friends and family. She wondered how much the men had used during their trip to Embu, however. She'd had arguments with Kathenge about financial issues before. He was so often loathe to give her even twenty shillings to use at market, while he went off to some big town or other and spent hundreds. Kanini had tried to tally the figures in her head, but not knowing how much Kathenge spent, she was unable to come up with any totals.

She did not want to spoil the evening, so she let the subject drop. When Stefanie came out of the *riko*, carrying a large steaming *sufuria*, Kanini set Gati down and went to help her. Stefanie smiled warmly in her direction.

Kanini was famished and quickly polished off a large bowl of *githeri*. She made sure there was enough for Njoka, before she helped herself to seconds. Glancing around the fire at her family members' golden faces, she tried to reclaim her earlier sense of contentment, but she was unable.

Later, lying on their mattress in the dark hut, she clenched her teeth as Kathenge moved towards her, his breathing growing heavier. There were no words spoken between them as he drew her *leso* off.

◯

Chiakariga Market
24 January, 1994

Dear Kanini,

Thanks for the letter I received from you last week. I'm only just getting time to reply it now. It's been so busy around here!

Many of the students arrived on time, that is, right after New Year's. In my class are fourteen Standard Ones, Twos and Threes. They are from seven to ten years old. Most of these kids, even the older ones, are completely illiterate! Some of them learned to read and write a little *Kimeru* last year, but by now they have mostly forgotten. So I am struggling to teach them.

They are at many different levels. Some read a little *Kiswahili*. I speak to them in that language for a short time everyday so they get used to it. Sometimes they act so bored. They start to behave badly, and then I have to discipline them. I never hit them, like Mr. Kiburu does. I only make them leave the class and stand outside for a while.

Mr. Kiburu started off okay, that is, he was polite and respectful to me. He is thirty-something and has never married. He has worked many different jobs in his life and has traveled all over Kenya. He never gets tired of telling stories about himself during lunch or after school. He followed me everyday to take a cup of *chai* for the first week. Finally I told him I needed to do some things of my own, so now he leaves me alone. I didn't want to make things uncomfortable, but I also didn't want his company all the time. I was also worried he might get a wrong idea about me. So now, things are a little awkward with him, but at least I am not bothered.

I will tell you more later. Right now it's too late and I'm very tired. I hope things are going well with you. Greet Stefanie and your husbands and give Gati a big hug for me!

Sincerely,

Gatiria

Ishiara Market
23 February, 1994

Dear Gatiria,

Thanks for your letter, which I received some weeks ago now. I don't have much time to write, but I just wanted to tell you some things about Njoka. He has not been doing well, at least for one week now. He is vomiting almost everyday and has high temperature. He feels very bad all over. Kathenge says it is a combination of malaria and dysentery, but I myself am thinking is a sign of the HIV disease that you told me. What do you think? He did not go out for all these days, just only lies in bed sometimes asleep. Stefanie is very worried for him, but really, Gatiria, I am more worried for her. Maybe she is infected too.

I talked with Gachwe and Stefanie in our house the other night while Kathenge was not there. I told them what I am thinking Njoka has, but they became too angry to listen after a little while. They are denying too much, just like you say the people always do. No one believes that healthy young men can die so easy from just fever and diarrhea or vomiting.

I wish we can all get tested—Stefanie, Njoka, Kathenge and myself. To know the facts can make someone feel much more secure, at least that's what I'm thinking. So far, the rest of us are doing okay. The children help keep our minds off our troubles. I don't know what we could do without them.

Love,
Kanini

Chiakariga Market
15 March, 1994

Dearest Kanini,

Thanks for telling me what is going on with your brother-in-law, Njoka. It surely sounds like he has HIV. Please keep me up-to-date about any new developments.

I want to tell you that during the April holiday, I will go to Meru by way of Materi mission, in order to do some research on the situation in this area. It seems that there is so much hunger here that the children do not have the strength to come to school. Our headmaster usually goes to the homes to talk to parents during the holiday, but this time I have offered to do it. I must first go and see if we can get some food relief, as well as some medicine. There is no dispensary in this area, and the people are obliged to walk all the way to Materi Boys'—that is the other Materi, which is not far—for *dawa*. If I could just keep some basic things in my room, I could be dispensing them now and then. As it is, I feel defeated by all these ailments and hunger pains.

Of course, to add insult to the injury, many of the adults around here have AIDS, this I am sure of. One boy who came for just only one week of school needed to return home to tend his mother who could not even get up in the morning. He's only seven years old, Kanini! His father has already died—of malaria, he said. But you and I know better.

Other children do not have any parents at all. Only grandparents who are looking after them, and these *wazee* are so old they can do very little to provide food. We have recently started a lunch program at the school so that children can be staying after their lessons to take boiled maize with a little beans. I went to Materi Girls' around a month ago to ask Brother John if it was a possibility, and he said he would see what he could do. Now, every week we receive a delivery of a large bag of maize and a small one of beans. I am buying Kimbo, salt and onions from my own pocket so at least the *githeri* can have some flavor.

Now, I need to go up to Meru town to find some information on AIDS that I can be dispensing to these people. I know many cannot read, but there is information with pictures that they can understand. I will explain it to them when I go to their homes. I will also try to get some condoms, though I doubt if anyone will use them.

I will stay with a friend in Meru, who finished Form Four when I was still in Form Three. She's working in one of the district offices there. I want to talk to her about how she got that job and how maybe I could get one too. Otherwise, this teaching is too depressing, and I feel very little satisfaction from it. Of course I feel bad to leave Chiakariga, but I need to think of my own future, don't I? I will be here for at least one year anyway.

I don't think I'll be able to make it to Ishiara this holiday. You could make a visit here, if you have the time. I know it is the harvest again. I will be returning here by 20 April at the latest. I hope all is going well.

Sincerely yours,
Lucy Gatiria

Ishiara Market
28 March, 1994

Dearest Sister,

I received your letter in good time and want to respond the soonest possible so that you get it before you leave. How's going there at Chiakariga? It sounds like there are a lot of problems at that school, at least as many as we were having at Kithinge sometimes.

I need to tell you the news that I may pregnant again. My month blood missed three times. I am worried to get another child, especially if Kathenge is infected with the HIV. What can happen to the child? If you know the answers, please tell me. Otherwise, you can get me some informations at Meru when you go.

On my side, I cannot understand why I even pregnant. Kathenge and I, we have followed that rhythm method you gave us in a careful way, since Gati was born. Do you know how it could happen, sister?

I want to go and visit Mama and the family. I would like to go before the baby inside gets bigger. Maybe I can visit them and then go to visit you at Chiakariga for a few. That will be at end of April, after we have planted most of the crop.

We are getting along OK, but we miss you very much. As I told you before, our lives are more bored without you here, sister.

Always,
Angela Kanini

Chapter 5

This pregnancy was far more difficult than her previous one. In late April, Kanini began dripping blood and feeling cramps, as though she were enduring another miscarriage. Kathenge brought Aunt Celina home with him one evening and the old woman advised her to stay in bed as much as possible to prevent another loss. Thus, for over two months Kanini could niether make any visits, nor do the work in the fields or the house. She felt like she had while recovering from circumcision: bored and idle. Finally, the blood and cramps stopped and the baby seemed to be growing. At this point, she was able to get up and move around again. She went back to doing light tasks and tending Gati. She did not do the heavy work in the field, even though it was harvest time.

By the time the next school holiday in August rolled around, they were behind in harvesting. Kathenge and Njoka rose to the occasion to help with the crop and even persuaded Gachwe to stoop over in the field. As Kanini watched her sister-in-law trudge out to the *munda*, *panga* in hand, a tiny kernal of satisfaction stole into the large *sufuria* of guilt and angst she was feeling over her condition.

Then one day in early September, Kanini's water broke, at least a month before it was time. With no time to arrange for assistance from Aunt Celina, she yelled from the compound, hoping Stefanie would hear and come to her aid. Her sister-in-law had not yet left for the field—luckily the children were already there with the men—then she hurried back to Kanini's hut, grabbing a pile of clean cloths from her own house on the way. She found Kanini on the bed, already struggling with intense contractions. Quickly she stoked the fire in the *riko* and put water on to boil.

Kanini was already at the pushing stage by the time Stefanie had things ready. Following her guidance, Kanini squatted on the floor over some towels and with a final thrust, pushed the baby out into her sister-in-law's waiting hands. A little boy! The cord was wrapped around his neck and his skin was a grayish color. A thick bluish-black substance stained his skin. His little mouth was open as though he was struggling for air, but there was no sound.

"I know he's dead, isn't he…isn't he?" Kanini gulped, breathless. Sweat was coursing down her face and she floundered for her handkerchief.

"No, he's trying to breathe, Kanini. But the cord...I don't know what to do." Stefanie held the slippery baby in both hands, a bewildered look on her face.

"Get a knife to cut it. I cleaned one over there, on the table."

Without hesitating, Stefanie seized the knife and sliced through the still pulsing cord. She immediately untangled it from around the baby's neck and thrust it away. When Kanini looked again she saw the baby resting on her stomach, his perfectly crafted eyes and mouth closed. Stefanie picked him up and turned him upside down, patting his back until tiny choking sounds emerged. A drop of spittle slipped out of his mouth.

"He'll live, Kanini, I know it. Have faith!" exclaimed Stefanie as she pried the baby's mouth open and, with her finger, removed a blob of discolored saliva. She laid the baby back on Kanini's breast. Looking down, Kanini got her first real look at the pathetic little mite. *This baby is not destined for this world*, she thought. *It will go where the other one went, the one that came out only blood.*

"He needs air, Stefanie. He can't breathe on his own. Maybe he's choking on something. What can we do?"

"I don't know. I wish Aunt Celina were here, or your mama—" Poor Stefanie sounded as though everything were her fault. She picked the baby up and felt under his nose. There was no air being expelled. The two women sat, exhausted and helpless, and watched the baby pass from this world to the next.

Stefanie began to weep as she laid the tiny body onto a nest of blankets and covered it with a *leso*. Kanini squeezed her eyes shut as a huge weight descended upon her chest, almost cutting off her own air supply. She could not cry. Guilt, dread and powerlessness overcame feelings of remorse. After the afterbirth spilled out, all she could do was cling to Stefanie and take deep breaths. Kathenge returned a short while later and found them there.

They buried the baby in a small grave near those of his paternal grandparents. They did not ask a priest or any neighbors or relatives to attend the ceremony. For the first time ever, Kanini saw Kathenge truly distraught, and she was touched by his show of emotion. She longed to reach out and touch him, to communicate that she felt as wretched as he did. Perhaps this traumatic event could begin the process of healing their torn relationship.

When he spoke at their little funeral, his words were cloaked in tears. "You were born too soon, little one...Your spirit wasn't ready for this world. It just wasn't your time." He blew his nose, turned and, without looking at anyone, walked into their hut and closed the door. Kanini ached to follow, but knew enough not to.

She felt like running into the hills where she could wail for hours into the wind. How could priests say that the dead were in a better place, especially when the dead one was a newborn baby who needed his mother?

She looked over and saw Stefanie weeping softly. Njoka too looked pained. Gati and Riunga squatted solemnly in the dust. Kanini had tried to explain to her daughter what had happened, but the child was too young to grasp it.

Stefanie and Njoka stood a moment longer before heaping dirt onto the little box. Kanini took her daughter into her arms and they stood and watched as the grave was filled in.

The next day, Kathenge did not return from school. Kanini found that she actually missed him and wanted him with her. At dusk, she was sitting outside her hut, where Gati was napping, when Stefanie and Riunga came in through the thorns with the herd of goats. Her sister-in-law handed her stick to Riunga, who was now able to herd them into their pen by himself.

"What are you thinking about, Kanini?" Stefanie asked. Kanini had been staring off into the hazy hills, unblinking, for a long while.

"I'm just thinking...It's been a hard day, Stefanie."

"I can't even imagine. I really feel for you, Kanini." Stefanie squatted beside Kanini's chair and squeezed her forearm. "I've wanted a second child myself and if I got pregnant and then lost it...I know I'd want to die."

"You want another child?" Kanini asked, her thoughts taking a sudden leap. "Is Njoka's condition—"

"I don't want to talk about it," Stefanie cut her off. "Where's Kathenge, by the way?"

Kanini shook her head. "I don't know. Njoka arrived home, didn't he?"

Stefanie nodded. "I saw him pass by while Riunga and I were out. Maybe Kathenge's out in the bush...even though there's no reason to celebrate."

Tears burned behind Kanini's lids. Her pelvic area had started to throb, as though reminding her freshly of her loss.

"I'm sorry I said that," Stefanie whispered. Kanini began to cry, the first time since the baby's death. She buried her face in her hands.

"Oh, Kanini, I'm so sorry," Stefanie crooned. "Why can't Kathenge—?"

"He doesn't comfort me, Stefanie," Kanini sobbed. "He doesn't care about me. All he wants is a son. I could be anyone—"

"I wish you two could have a real relationship," said Stefanie, her voice lowered. "He seems so proud, so unwilling to...to love you."

"I know. I always thought we'd grow to...grow to care more about each other." Kanini tried to muffle her sobs. "But, he's pulled away...now, of all times...We're supposed to be married. I'm his wife. But I can't imagine years and years with nothing more than this."

"Maybe he's just grieving in his own way. Things'll get better. You can get pregnant again—"

"No. I don't want to get pregnant again," stated Kanini, blowing her nose. She was glad she'd managed to keep a fresh handkerchief in her pocket. "Ever. I really don't. It's too much heartache."

"Well, if you tell Kathenge that, it'll only drive him further away from you," Stefanie reasoned.

"I'm not sure what I'll do...But I can't imagine having any more babies." Kanini hadn't realized she felt so resolute about this. Voicing her feelings to her sister-in-law made her all the more certain.

Over the next few days, Kanini wrote letters to Mama, Gatiria and Mukami, who was also pregnant. Mama had planned to attend this birth as she had the last one, and Gatiria wanted to come during December to help tend the newborn. Now, there would be no newborn. Kanini, who had worried so much about having a second child, now worried that it was her anxiety that had caused his early demise. Or maybe Ngai was angry because she had tried to alter destiny by preventing this child's conception.

At night, she prayed for the blissful relief of sleep, but when it did come, she had horrible dreams that haunted her all the next day. Exhausted and depressed, she found herself snapping at Gati and Stefanie, the two people closest to her. At night, she often lay on her side of the bed, crying softly so as not to disturb her daughter or husband. She wrote to Gatiria, beseeching her to come and visit during December anyway; she felt lonely and needed her comfort and wisdom.

Gatiria tried to come. The day she left Chiakariga, a freak rainstorm hit and completely washed out the Mati road. She had walked all the way to the road, then realized it was a futile effort; there was no way even a heavy lorry could get through the muck. She'd had only a week during which she could make the trip, and when the weather did not clear for four days, she could not justify the effort. Instead, she sent a letter in which she told Kanini that she was very sorry, but she would have to set aside another time to come, perhaps in April. The school situation was too difficult; she could not possibly forsake the people there.

Kanini felt despondent, the same way Aunt Njeri must have felt when her baby hadn't lived and Mama wasn't able to go up and tend her. She was also a little confused.

"I thought the pupils went home in December and there's no one left at school," she said to Kathenge the evening the letter came. Her family was eating alone, without Njoka and Stefanie. Kanini and Gati sat on metal folding chairs and Kathenge on his bowed wood chair. Gati smacked her lips as she ate, flicking tidbits of mashed plantains into the dirt.

Kathenge toyed with his food and shrugged. "Maybe her school is different. It sounds like she and that headmaster are trying to teach, administer, nurse and feed the children all at the same time." He took a small bite of his food, but chewed lethargically. "Maybe they have a special project going during this holiday."

"What sort of special project?" asked Kanini. "Your school never has these sorts of projects, does it?"

"Well, we're losing pupils, too, as I told you a while ago," he said gruffly. "Children can't leave their homes to come to school anymore. They're either caring for younger children because the parents are sick, or they're too weak or hungry to come. In the end, unless there are older siblings at home, these young kids become responsible for their households."

Kanini remembered the story of the fourteen year-old girl, who'd dropped out of Standard Six at Kathenge's school, in order to stay home and help her family. Her father had disappeared long before, and her mother was suffering with illness and could no longer care for the four or five younger siblings. Stefanie, whose cousin was married to this girl's brother, had told her later that the young girl had become a prostitute in Embu. Kanini wondered how many other girls were turning to this profession, the only one that paid them enough to put food on their families' tables.

"I wonder what project Gatiria has going," Kanini mused, almost to herself. "Is she teaching the pupils during the holiday? Or what? At least it sounds like she's going to stay another year." She sighed and set her own bowl down on the ground.

Kathenge got up abruptly, leaving his bowl on the chair. Without a word, he patted his pocket to make sure his cigarettes were there, then walked off. The darkness swallowed him whole.

I feel like I'm talking to myself, Kanini thought. *Why do I bother trying to engage with him at all?* She collected their bowls. *He's left his bowl half full of food. Why do I bother cooking either?*

"Can I have more, Mama?" asked Gati. Her daughter always had a good appetite. Kanini went to get her another spoonful from the pot, happy that at least Gati made it worth her while to cook.

Kanini hobbled to the year's end, her thoughts on the previous December when things had been so much better. Now, Gatiria was in a different town and too busy to visit, Gachwe was finished with secondary school and complaining about her lack of a future, Kathenge walked around silent and gloomy when he was around at all, and Njoka lay in bed, weak and sickly.

Stefanie's husband had recovered from his earlier illness and seemed as healthy as ever until the holiday ended in January. Then, right after school reopened, he came down with another fever. The aches and chills were unlike anything he had ever experienced before. He gave over the role of headmaster to Kathenge and remained in bed for over a month. By the end of February, he was able to limp back to school, to teach the class Kathenge had been teaching. He always returned home immediately, to rest in his hut. On weekends, he had little energy for anything more than tending to his most basic needs.

By the long rainy season in March, his strength had not yet fully returned. Stefanie was drained from catering to his demands, nursing and minding Riunga, as well as attending to the regular chores. Kanini was concerned about her sister-in-law more than ever these days. *Stefanie has truly become a dear friend*, Kanini thought. *We have become companions in our misery.*

Kanini volunteered to take over more of the farm chores, such as planting and weeding. When she asked Gachwe to help, the girl moaned that such work was beneath her; she needed to save her energy to start a career. Behind her back, Kanini told Stefanie that the girl needed to help support the family, either through a job or chores. So, Kanini came up with a plan.

"I'm glad you were able to convince Gachwe to help with the tomatoes," Stefanie said as they took a break one day after weeding the unripe fruits. She took a long draught of water from the gourd. "You were smart, Kanini, to convince her that selling tomatoes at market would be a good way to prepare to be a businesswoman. We always have so many, and there's no way either of us could go to town every week."

"The first ones should be ready next month." Kanini sloshed water on her sweaty face and threw a handful on Gati who squealed and dashed away. "I only wish we could divide the money in thirds. It doesn't seem right that you and I will be doing all the tending and harvesting and will only split half of the profit."

"That's Gachwe," sighed Stefanie. "She wouldn't do it unless she could get half of it herself. And what will she spend it on? Hair grease and those magazines—Or the fees for some course."

"At least we'll have enough tomatoes to sell this year. The plants look healthy so far and they shouldn't fail unless we all get sick and can't tend them."

Stefanie said nothing in response.

They walked home in companionable silence, the children chasing and arguing around them. Kanini's thoughts flitted to Gatiria's latest letter, which had been vague about her promised visit in April. Kanini had decided to make the journey to Chiakariga and was already planning it. She wrote to her sister that she would come in the middle of the month, with Gati. She wanted to see with her own eyes the "projects" that were going on at Gatiria's school.

"I wish I could go with you on your trip to Chiakariga," Stefanie said, as though reading her mind. She rubbed her gaunt cheeks. "I feel so old and tired, I can't believe it. I really need to take a break from here. I haven't seen my parents since Riunga was born!"

Kanini looked at her friend with pity. She knew Stefanie's parents lived much further away, in the town of Tharaka. It was only twenty kilometers east of Chiakariga as the crow flies, but the Tana river flowed between the towns, so there was no way to go directly without a boat. The overland route was long and circuitous.

"Maybe after I get back, you could go for a few days. I'd do all your work for you," offered Kanini.

"That's kind of you, Kanini, but Njoka could get sick again. He's so weak and thin...I don't know...maybe later in the year."

The next few weeks flew by. The rain fell and the weeds grew. They had not planted as much cotton this year, which was a relief. The tomato plants looked healthy; not a single one had the blight that sometimes occurred.

The night before Kanini's departure for Chiakariga, she bustled around, in the high spirits that characterized a *safari*. She prepared sacks of food to take to Gatiria and gathered clothes for her daughter and herself. Kathenge, slumped in his chair, eyed her with disdain. "It looks like you're going for a month," he growled.

"Don't worry. We won't be gone for more than three or four days."

"I don't know why you have to go at all. It's going to cost money." His words echoed Baba's from way back.

"Only forty shillings for transport there and back," said Kanini blithely. "I told you I'd pay you back after Gachwe starts selling tomatoes."

Kathenge went on as though she hadn't spoken. "You write enough letters to that sister of yours. You must have a good idea of what's going on there. Why do you need to visit?"

"We write in English, and I don't always understand all of it. Besides, I know there's a lot she's not telling me." Kanini had already discussed the journey with her husband. It annoyed her that he was questioning her now. She put her hand on her brow. "I feel so sorry for Gatiria. All she eats is *githeri*, day and night. They get no other food in that town. Only if she sends someone to Ishiara for something, but I'm sure she never thinks about her own needs. She's so busy helping those people there."

"I guess you think it's your business to feed your sister," Kathenge said with a short laugh, shaking his head. Then he got up and walked out of the house. *Of course it's my business to feed my sister, just as it's my business to feed you and Gati. You make no sense these days, husband.* Kanini shook her head as her eyes followed the orange glow of her husband's cigarette into the shadows.

Chapter 6

As she and Gati set off on their journey, Kanini's heart felt lighter than it had in the eight months since the baby's death. Gati, a small *kiondo* on her back, trotted along beside her mother. Despite lugging two heavy gunny sacks of food, as well as her satchel stuffed with clothes, Kanini's step was as lively as her daughter's. They arrived in Ishiara by the time the early *matatus* were pulling up to the stand.

In no time they arrived at the shelter near the Chiakariga trail, and within the hour stood at Gatiria's very doorstep. They knocked, but no one answered. Kanini tried the latch. "The door's locked."

"Where is she, Mama?" asked Gati, her eyes sleepy.

"Maybe she's taking *chai*." They went around and peered in the shop, but did not see Gatiria.

A *cucu* asked the little girl. "And who are you, little one?"

"I'm Gati." She lifted her chin and spoke with assurance.

"Ah," nodded the woman. "You must be related to the *mwalimu*."

"Gatiria is my sister," said Kanini. "We're wondering where she is right now."

"She's at the school working, of course," grinned the woman.

"What sort of work?" asked Kanini. "It's supposed to be the holiday!"

The *cucu* chuckled. "That teacher's always working. Especially on holidays! Go and see."

Kanini and Gati followed the tiny path to the school building where at least fifteen primary children were gathered. The smallest ones were playing with balls made of tape and cloth strips, while others gathered dry sticks, and still others sat in the shade stitching patches on the holes in their clothes. Standing a little apart from all the activity and talking to a man with glasses was her sister.

As Kanini waved, Gatiria turned and hurried over. "Kanini! You're here! *Habari ya safari?*"

"The journey was fine, Gatiria. Really fast. We're not even tired."

"I'm tired," piped up Gati.

"*Ngai*, look how big my niece has grown!" Gatiria scooped up Gati and swung her around. The little girl hunched her shoulders shyly, her eyes on the ground. "What? You don't remember me? Well, you'll get to know me again."

"What's going on, Gatiria? Why are all the pupils at the school during the holiday?" Kanini asked.

"They're always here, holiday or not. They have nowhere else to go."

"Nowhere else? Where are their homes?"

"These children don't have homes, Kanini. Their parents are either both dead, or one is dead and the other one can't be found or is too sick to care for them." She looked out over the clusters of children and tsk-ed with her tongue. "They've been living with grandparents or aunts and uncles...but many of them can't stay with these family members permanently, due to lack of food or various diseases...They're orphans, Kanini."

"But...There are so many! I would have thought two or three, but this looks like twenty!"

"Right now we have seventeen. They live right here on the school grounds. We've converted two of the classrooms into a dormitory. Didn't I tell you that in my letter?"

"You never told me! I only knew a few things; something about you helping out with some family's crisis, or taking a few children to one of the classrooms for a night while something got worked out at home. But, I never understood that you were starting an orphanage!"

"The need became so great, Kanini. All last August and December, we went to the homes, cared for the sick adults, babies and young kids. Then at the end of December, I got the idea that we should just let kids move into the school. I didn't want to let anyone know about it until it was approved." Gatiria's eyes danced as she spoke. "So I wrote up a proposal and presented it to Brother John. He approved it and sent some money and supplies to care for the kids, and now we have it. An actual orphanage."

"Why didn't you tell me? Your letters were so unclear...Or maybe my English is just so bad nowadays, I couldn't understand."

"Things only got worked out at the beginning of this holiday. Only a few kids were living here permanently during the school term. Most of them continued to walk from their homes. By the end of March, we had twelve, and two weeks later we had all seventeen."

"How are you caring for them? What do they do all day?" Kanini was still so flabbergasted she could hardly contain her questions.

"Oh, we have plenty to do. Right now, there are no lessons, but we've been planting a garden down by the river. Then there are building projects, washing, repairs—We keep very busy."

"Who cooks for them?"

"We take turns. Oh, I need to introduce you to Mr. Kiburu." Gatiria led Kanini back to where the man was overseeing some children weaving baskets. "Here he is. Mr. Kiburu, this is my older sister, Kanini."

Kanini shook hands with the man. He was a paunchy, homely man with pockmarks on his cheeks. His shaved jaw had the dark shadow of a man who could grow a full beard. The glasses made him look older and intelligent, if not completely trustworthy. "Nice to meet you," Kanini shook his outstretched hand. He eyed her up and down, as men often did, and smiled in return. More questions flashed across Kanini's mind. *How does Gatiria feel about this man? She seems happy enough to be working with him and giving up all her holidays to care for this big "family" of theirs. How is it between the two of them?*

For the next hour or so, Gatiria showed Kanini and her daughter around the compound and introduced her to the children. The last place they headed was down to the river, which was more of a narrow stream. Gati was shy and wouldn't join the other children as they splashed around, though at home she couldn't get enough of the water. She hid behind Kanini and clung to her skirt.

Back up at the school, Kanini noticed that some older children were cooking over a mud stove, out in the open compound.

"Will you build a *riko* to cook in at some point?" she asked.

"We get so little rain here that it hardly matters," Gatiria told her. "I'd still like to have one, so when it's windy, we could have some protection. We'll get to such projects in time."

Gati was hungry, so Kanini was relieved when her sister announced that lunch was ready. After she and Gati served themselves—first, since they were guests—she watched as the children formed a line and trooped over to receive heaping bowls of *githeri* and a spoon. "Salt?" Gatiria asked each one, a smile crinkling her eyes. She did not join Kanini and her daughter in the shade of an acacia tree until all the pupils were served.

A thin boy sat down beside them and struck up a conversation. "So, you are the *mwalimu's* sister?" He spoke in well-enunciated English, dimples indenting his cheeks.

"Yes I am. I'm Kanini and this is Gati. What's your name?" The sweet bright eyes of the child enchanted her.

"My name is Njeru."

"How do you like living here?" Kanini asked, wondering how much English he knew.

"Oh, this is a very good place to be," said the boy, his mouth full of maize and beans. "Mr. Kiburu and Miss Kagwima are good teachers and organizers. They've done everything for us."

"Do you have a mama and baba?" Gati asked in *Kimeru*. Kanini darted a glance at her daughter, and then looked back at the boy. She hoped Gati had not taken the boy aback.

"My baba went to Nairobi a long time ago to look for work and only came home a few times. Then my mama got sick and couldn't care for us anymore. My *cucu* is too old and no one else is around. So, I came here."

Gati stared at the boy, her eyes wide with wonder. Kanini said, "Well, I'm glad there was a place for you to go." She smiled at the boy, as Gatiria sat down next to them with her own bowl of *githeri*.

Before lunch was over, Gati grew irritable. Gatiria took them to her little room, and the child promptly fell asleep on the bed. Kanini left the door open so a faint breeze could blow in. Then Gatiria brought two chairs outside and unfolded them under a tree.

Kanini watched her sister's face. Although circled with shadows of fatigue, her eyes still shone with their old luster. "It must exhaust you to work all day everyday with all those children," Kanini said.

"It is a big responsibility to have them here all the time," Gatiria reflected. "I feel like a teacher, a parent and a nurse all at once! But, Kanini, this work really motivates me; I can't even tell you. Maybe I feel it's the best effort I can put forth right now in the fight against AIDS."

"Is that the main problem?" asked Kanini. "The parents of these kids have AIDS, or they've already died of AIDS?"

"Yes, I'm sure of it. Some of the children may even be infected. One thing I didn't know before is that if a woman is infected with the virus when she's pregnant, there's a good chance the baby will be born infected. And if not, breastmilk can even transfer the virus." She sighed and leaned back.

Kanini sat pensively for a minute. "I wondered if my baby had the virus." The familiar tight feeling constricted her chest. "He was so tiny and weak and died so quickly. I never talked to Kathenge about it, of course, but all the same—"

"It sounds like you're not able to talk to Kathenge about very much anymore," said Gatiria, covering Kanini's hand with her own. "I felt terrible after you told me what happened, Kanini…"

Kanini felt the old lump choke off her breath. She tried not to blink, so that her tears, always at the ready, wouldn't spill over. She wanted to talk to Gatiria about Kathenge, but didn't know where to start. How to confide in this sister, who'd never shown even the least interest in settling down with a husband and family, about the trauma she was experiencing?

Soon, Gatiria spoke again. "The hardest part is educating the people about AIDS and how to prevent it." She rubbed her temples and a furrow marred her smooth brow. "If they're infected, they need to keep themselves healthy. But of course, these people never boil their drinking water, they use unclean implements for circumcision and birth, the nutrition is awful—"

"How is their food different than at ours?" asked Kanini, welcoming the neutral topic.

"It's not so different. The people live on millet, sorghum, maize and a few beans or cow peas. They never eat any fresh greens or fruit, and the meat is saved for special occasions only." Gatiria raised her hands in a gesture of helplessness. "I can't convince people to fish out of the rivers either—they all see fish like Cucu did; like they're a kind of monster or something. At least the kids who are staying here have learned to fish a little."

"Ishiara isn't far. I can't believe you never come and buy fresh food for yourself, Gatiria. You're looking thinner than ever! You'll get sick yourself, and there won't be anything left of you!"

"I won't get sick, Kanini. I'll never put myself at risk."

Kanini stared at her sister. Did Gatiria think that the only sickness nowadays was AIDS? What about dysentery, malaria, TB, typhoid and cholera? Diseases you could get even if you weren't HIV positive?

Kanini took a deep breath. Then she asked bluntly, "So, you are still a virgin?"

Gatiria didn't miss a beat. "Of course, and I always will be, at least while I'm single. It's not so hard to remain like this. I know that the nuns at Materi have chosen this lifestyle." Gatiria waved her arm in the direction of the mission. "Though I don't share their religious views, I could take a vow of chastity easily enough. To me, it's worth not having to worry for my life."

Kanini nodded and looked into the shadows of Gatiria's little room. Her gaze fell on little Gati sleeping innocently and in her mind's eye she saw a man's form hovering over a grown-up version of her daughter. A demanding man, who wouldn't take no for an answer. She squeezed her eyes shut and prayed that Gati would follow in her aunt's footsteps. Even if it meant thwarting aspects of their culture like Gatiria had, she hoped Gati would be strong enough to make her own decisions, instead of feeling obligated to follow a host of traditions that Kanini wasn't sure had much meaning anymore.

She also prayed that Kathenge would stand by her in allowing Gati to live the life she chose for herself. She knew he would not obligate their daughter to be circumcised. If Kanini had her way, Gati would also not be forced into a prescribed marriage. Women had become more independent in Kenya. This was frightening to some, because it meant that men no longer had all the control. Kanini wanted to embrace these changes, if not for herself, then for Gati. She had to hope that her husband would stand by her, even if he would never stand with her.

Kanini pulled one of her bags onto her lap and rummaged through it. She pulled out two mangoes. "Your talk makes me hungry for fruit," she said.

"Look what you've brought, Angela Kanini! You are so good! I only wish I could make that fruit multiply one hundred times to feed the people in this place."

As they tore the peels off the mangos with their teeth, Kanini asked, "So, Gatiria, you've taken on such a project. You must be planning to stay here a while."

"It is hard work, Kanini. It's not what I want to do my whole life. But for now, it's the right thing to do, I'm sure of it. I have the support of the mission and my pay is enough to provide for myself and this community. At this point, I am satisfied."

Chapter 7

For weeks after her visit, thoughts of Gatiria and her life in Chiakariga followed Kanini as she went about her chores. She talked to Gati about her sister's work, as though the three year-old could comprehend. It helped to voice her thoughts to someone. She found it difficult to discuss Gatiria with Stefanie, since her sister-in-law was so preoccupied with her own problems.

The day after Kanini's return, Stefanie told her in private that she believed Njoka had AIDS. He had left the day before to get a malaria injection at the health center in Ishiara and was staying with an acquaintance in town. "He's already gotten so many injections," said Stefanie with a deep sigh. She lifted her hands to her chest then let them fall to her sides. "I think it can't be only malaria. He would be well by now if—"

"What does Kathenge say?" asked Kanini.

"He claims that it's just a continuing case of malaria, as though Njoka was always inclined to getting it, which he wasn't. It's a pattern that started with their father and continued with Bilibina. Now, it's happening to Njoka." Stefanie's voice lowered. "I think Gatiria is right. Njoka has this *ukimwi* and they are both denying it."

"I'm glad you see the truth now, Stefanie." Kanini took her sister-in-law's limp hands. "I just wish it were possible to get him the test...the one that shows whether he's positive for the disease."

"We'd have to drug him and drag him there for that to happen...and not tell Kathenge!" A bleak look ravaged Stefanie's face.

"How is Gachwe, by the way?"

"That one, she's off in her own world. I asked her to help me weed the tomatoes the other day, and she didn't even answer. She only thinks about herself." Stefanie shrugged. "If she's worried about Njoka, she doesn't show it. She's talking about going to Embu or Nairobi to look for work, maybe in a dress shop or something. You and I know that there are plenty of Form Four leavers who want jobs like that, and nothing out there for them."

"I thought she was going to sell our tomatoes!" Kanini's voice was bitter. "It'll serve her right if she goes all the way to Nairobi and can't find a job."

"I agree with you, but don't say that to anyone around here," whispered Stefanie. "I'm surprised you said that, Kanini. You've always been so willing to accept what others are doing."

"I'm frustrated, Stefanie. Gachwe just wants to get out of here and not fulfill her promise to us. After all the work you and I did to put her through secondary!" Kanini's voice rose in anger. "I feel like we're the only ones looking for solutions around here."

Stefanie strained the *chai* she'd been making and poured two cups. As Kanini sipped hers, she could see Riunga and Gati through the slats in the *riko*. They were batting a homemade ball back and forth with sticks.

"Stefanie, have you considered that you might also be infected?"

Without glancing away from the doorway, Stefanie set her cup down. "Yes, I have. I'd already thought about it last year when we had that discussion with Gachwe. I got annoyed because I didn't want to believe it could happen to us...to me...I didn't want to believe...that Njoka would be unfaithful to me." A large tear slipped from her eye and down her cheek.

"Oh, Stefanie..." Kanini folded her friend into her arms and held her. How slim she felt! "Maybe you and I should get the HIV test. It would be a relief to know that we weren't infected, at least. Then we would know that the children were free of it too."

"What if we find out we're positive for the disease?" asked Stefanie. "Then what? I'd just end up feeling more depressed. Maybe it's better *not* to know."

Hot tears burned in Kanini's eyes as well. Even after presenting him with a positive AIDS test, she doubted Kathenge would be any less derisive. If anything, he'd probably blame *her* for being unfaithful! She shook her head and brushed the tears away, then looked up at a sudden cry from her daughter. Riunga had just popped Gati over the head with his stick. Stefanie rushed out to deal with them, while Kanini continued watching from the doorway.

Weeks went by. The cotton was transported to Ishiara where the cooperative paid them for it. Kanini and Stefanie harvested onions and green vegetables down by the river. The peas ripened to the fresh stage. Kanini picked a number of them, which she cooked and served the children. They pinched the bright orbs between their fingers and ate each one as though it were a sliver of freshly roasted beef.

Each time Njoka returned from a visit to the clinic at Ishiara, he looked thinner and more wasted. He tired easily and could hardly walk to school once the term began in May. In the mornings, Kanini could hear his rasping cough as he rose from bed and went about washing and taking *chai*. He was determined to continue teaching, despite their pleas that he stay home and rest.

Kathenge said nothing about his brother's condition, continuing to accompany him to school on a daily basis. Kanini found out a few weeks into the term that her husband had begun teaching some subjects in Njoka's Standard Eight class. He also taught his own Standard Six class and was responsible for all of the discipline and other duties of Headmaster. Kathenge did not tell Kanini how much he had taken over at school. She learned about it from the mother of one of his pupils whom she met at market one day. After her discussion with this woman, she returned *mucii* and wrote to Gatiria about it.

Her relationship with her husband became more and more distant. She was afraid to bring up anything having to do with Kathenge's job or Njoka's illness, and thus it seemed that their discussions merely danced around these issues. They made superficial conversation about the animals, Gati and the crops that would need harvesting. Kathenge never related stories about school as he once had.

One day, he entered the compound just as Kanini was hanging out the last of the laundry. After draping the wet garments over the thorn bushes, she straightened to find him watching her. She wiped her damp hands on her skirt and took a deep breath.

"Can we sit and talk a minute, Kathenge? I want to tell you something I've been thinking about for a while." It felt unnatural to broach a subject to her husband in this formal way, but if she didn't speak directly, he might drift off and she wouldn't see him for another day or more.

Kathenge said nothing, but he pulled his chair into the shade and sat down. "I want to tell you, husband, that I...that I would like to travel to a hospital and get that operation done. The one that would make me unable to have more children." She breathed deeply, trying to catch an expression on his face, but it remained impassive. "After what happened the last time—and the first time—I don't want to go through it again."

Her husband stared straight ahead, as though he had not heard her. She noted how much he had aged in the past year: new creases were grooved into the skin around his eyes and mouth, and gray hair edged his temples. He had been so handsome when they first got married, his eyes laughing and his teeth bright. Now, his face held very little appeal for her. The only person to whom he flashed his smile was Gati, and Kanini hadn't seen him do that in weeks.

She had worried that he would fly into a rage at the very notion of her getting permanently "closed"; this silence was almost more sinister.

"I know you must want more children—a son," she continued. "I would have liked more too, but...but I can't go through that pain again—"

"It is a woman's duty to go through pain!" Kathenge's voice broke through like a bull from a pen. "What did you expect when you got married, Kanini?"

She was ready for this. "It's not the physical pain, Kathenge. It's the heartache of losing these children—when they die—Of not knowing what to do when they come so early."

There was another silence. He seemed to be weighing what to say, or perhaps he was feeling his own pain. "You could stay with my Aunt Celina during the last months of your pregnancy." He struggled to keep his tone steady. "She'd be able to help you..."

Kanini hesitated. She wanted to voice her real fear, her worry about Kathenge's possible HIV infection. Why bring babies, who might die at birth or soon afterward, into the world? She thought she saw a slight sneer curl his lip. She faced him squarely, breathed deeply and said, "Well, I appreciate that idea, but—but I think I would still like to get this operation."

Kathenge's eyes blazed and he gripped the armrests of the wooden chair. His knuckles turned gray. Kanini held his gaze, her heart beating hard in her chest. Then his eyes fell and he muttered, "This marriage is nothing like what I thought it would be."

Kanini took a deep breath. "It is not what either of us thought it would be, husband."

Kanini began to think of the misery in which she was immersed as an entity called Despair. It was an ugly troll with a huge nose and missing teeth, and its intent was to follow her family around, pulling them down into its hideous hole in the ground, until they were unable to scramble back out of it alive. Kanini felt trapped in the same dark, numb place she had lived in after the baby's death. How to get out of it and begin life anew?

Then she received a letter from her brother, Njagi. He told her that he and Mukami were the proud parents of a healthy son, whom they had named Mbuba. Everyone was doing fine, but they would love a visit from her as soon as she could make it. Little Josefina—the family still referred to Gati exclusively by her Christian name—needed to meet her new cousin.

The good news and lively tone of the letter made Kanini cry. She wanted desperately to go to Kajuki to visit her family. She felt lost, frightened and unloved here in this place where everyone walked around afraid to talk to each other. Finally she sniffed back her tears and blew her nose. Maybe in the cool month of June she would go. She would take both Gati and Riunga. After her visit, she could continue on to the clinic either at Materi or Meru to get the operation done.

Ishiara Market
19 May, 1995

Dearest Gatiria,

Please forgive me writing another letter so soon after the last one, not even receiving anything from you. It is only that I need to tell you my latest plan.

I will like to go to Kajuki again, maybe early next month, whereby I will travel to Meru to have that operation done. This is the one you told me I can be closed *kabisa*. Also, I want to have an AIDS test, if they will give it to me, so I can be certain my health is in stable condition. So, please you tell me the better place to go and when is good time to have that thing done.

Life is so difficult here nowadays, sister. Even the ones who are not sick, they are acting somehow miserable, eg. Kathenge. Everyone is made to feel bad, especially Stefanie, and even myself. How are you coping there where you have no family, where you get so little support yourself and must be the support for everyone? I can only admire you. Myself, I would be having a hard time of it. Look at the time I am having here, and these are my own family members!

Anyway, I must be going now, dearest. I hope to hear from you very soon!

Sincerely,
Angela Kanini

Chiakariga Market
28 May, 1995

Dearest Kanini,

How are you doing there at yours? I've been thinking about you since the time I received your letter of 10 May, up to the present time when I got the other one. I am feeling so sorry for everything happening there. It sounds like Njoka may not last much longer—I feel very bad about that. What will they do at that school without him? Will they hire another teacher? It sounds like too much for Kathenge to keep doing his work.

I am glad that at least Stefanie admits what is really affecting her husband. She sounds so strong and fearless. Did you talk to her about getting an AIDS test? Maybe she could go with you to hospital.

I agree with your idea to get sterilized—that is "closed *kabisa*". Why should you have more children who might be affected by AIDS? The only problem is they might not want to do the operation on someone so young, especially having only one child. I will set it up for you at Meru hospital, since I know one doctor there. I will tell him that you already had two miscarriages and are not in good health. He should be able to do it for you. My next letter will contain the information about when you can go.

Compared to your life, mine is somewhat easy. Despite so much suffering here, a lot of work with people I don't know well and no good food, at least everything I do is well appreciated. If I don't like Mr. Kiburu's attitude one day, I can leave him alone and not see him again until the next day. Not like you who have to sleep with Kathenge. I feel somehow lucky about that. Myself, I would rather deal with strangers who are friendly, than loved ones who I cannot talk to.

We have been very busy. One boy—that little Njeru who you talked to your first day visiting—lost his mother just last week. Now he has only an uncle, but that man has five children of his own and cannot take Njeru even overnight. So he is with us permanently. At least ten others are with us most of the time, only leaving now and then to visit grandparents or relatives here and there. Some of the others that you saw when you were here have gone to live in other places, with relatives who sent for them. They may be returning, we don't know.

So, Kanini, here I am a mother with eleven adopted children, though I am not even married. Life can be so ironic, can't it? We have become a close family, though it is usually just me caring for these kids. Sometimes I get help from Muthoni, the nurse from Materi. I'm sure you remember her. Our headmaster is here during the day to teach classes, but he usually goes *kupiga maji* in the evenings and I don't see him again until the next morning. Some weekends he has been here, but others he goes visiting in the area or on longer trips. He does bring a lot of our food from the mission and also Meru. He's not a bad man, just a little boring. I would rather be with Muthoni, who is very interesting to talk to, moreover hard-working! We have so much in common, just like you and Stefanie. It is very nice to have women friends, but of course, sisters are the nicest.

I must go, dear sister. Please greet all the family members for me. I will write to you soon about the appointment at Meru hospital.

Sincerely,
Auntie Gatiria

Gatiria's letter also brought tears to Kanini's eyes. She knew it was probably the uncertain nature of their lives that was making her so emotional. She couldn't wait to see Mama and the rest of her family again and looked forward to Gatiria's next letter.

When it came, she began planning her trip. She wrote to Mama and Baba telling them she would be at Kajuki within nine or ten days. When she asked her sister-in-law about taking Riunga along, Stefanie hardly needed persuasion. Kanini had been nervous about mentioning the trip to Kathenge. After their discussion about the operation, he seemed to be avoiding her at all costs. She worried that at the last minute he might forbid her to go.

Early on the day of the journey, a cloudy Monday in mid-June, Kanini awoke to find that Kathenge had already vacated the bed. Relieved, she quickly fixed breakfast then set off with the children along the path that led to Kajuki. She carried a burlap sack of green grams and a large sisal *kiondo* stuffed with fresh produce. The air was crisp and the children, their faces freshly scrubbed, had on their cardigans.

As they walked, Kanini told them about Cucu's house. "My little brother's just a little bigger than you, Riunga. He'll probably take you out with the goats."

"What's his name?"

"Mutwiri. He's...he's your uncle, Gati." She smiled to herself at the thought of the fussy baby Mutwiri now an uncle.

"Maybe he can be my friend," said Riunga. The chubby little boy stopped to scoop up a lizard that was slithering along the trail. He carried it along as he jumped over rocks and skirted bushes, hiding it from Gati when she clamored to see it.

As always, Kanini felt uplifted to be on a trip. The children amused her and the feeling of carrying a load as she walked warmed her limbs and cleared her head. Despite the clouds overhead, there was very little chance that it would rain. They so rarely walked without the glare of the sun in their eyes, that this weather presented a most refreshing change.

They arrived *mucii* in the warmth of the afternoon. The children were sleepy, so Kanini lay them down on her *leso* in the shade of the old acacia that still grew near the main hut. She was surprised to see no one about. It was still a shock not to find Cucu at the corner of the hut, warming her bones in the sun.

Through the branches of the acacias, she glimpsed a figure heading up the hill from the river. Was it Mama or Mukami? The slow, halting gait told her who it was. She hurried out the gate to greet her mother. Mama set the heavy *mtungi* down in relief and her face split into a quarter moon, floating on its back. After greeting her, Mama explained that Mukami was still down at the river, bathing little Mbuba. She would be up soon.

Gazing upon her old home from the familiar river path, Kanini felt as if nothing had changed. No one was any sicker than usual, the crops were doing better and her family seemed happy and healthy. Why couldn't her husband be like Njagi, a stable family man, who never ran around with other women, infecting himself and his wife with insidious viruses? Of course, she only presumed Njagi was faithful; perhaps he did go with other women in his spare time. Most men seemed to.

"How long will you and the children be with us, daughter?" Mama asked.

"Two days, Mama. On Wednesday I have an appointment at Meru hospital for a procedure. Gatiria will meet us there."

The smile faded from Mama's face. "What sort of procedure?"

"It's something to steralize me..." She dropped her eyes from her mother's searching look. "I don't want any more children, Mama...The doctors there can make it so that I'll never get pregnant again."

Mama continued to stare at Kanini, shock overtaking her face. She wrung her hands together. "Why don't you want any more children? You only have one."

"But I've been pregnant three times. Two of the pregnancies ended early, with the babies dead. That was so hard for me, Mama. I don't want it to happen again."

"You're so young still, my daughter. You could have many more healthy babies who would help on the *munda*, who would take care of you when you're old—" Mama's tone turned beseeching. "What will you do without a son?"

"Mama, life is so hard already. If I want to parent children, there are so many others—I can help Gatiria with her orphans, *mungu akipenda*. I could probably even adopt one as my own child if I wanted to." Mama gaped at Kanini, as though she were speaking a different language. Kanini continued unabashedly, pulling the produce she'd brought out of her *kiondo* and setting it on the shelf in the kitchen. "There's also Riunga. Stefanie needs so much help with him. His father is very ill and may die."

Her mother still looked unconvinced. Kanini thought, *how can she relate to what I'm talking about? Her life seems so far removed from all these unfortunate events.* "I know I never had my own son, Mama, and that makes me sad. But it scares me to get pregnant; I never want to do it again." She surprised herself with how decisive she sounded. Like Gatiria.

Mama turned and started stowing the onions and cabbage away, muttering something unintelligible. After a moment, she whirled to face her daughter again. "Where do you get such strange ideas, Kanini? What you intend to do horrifies me...The spirits will not be pleased with your choices, my child."

Kanini poured water into a *sufuria*, trying to calm her throbbing nerves. She wanted to change the subject. She would have liked to tell Mama about Gatiria's work, but she couldn't remember how much she had already told her, or if she was even interested. She felt at a loss for anything to say.

They heard voices in the compound. Mukami had just arrived from the river and was chatting with Gati and Riunga. Kanini fled the *riko* and greeted her with open arms. Tears filled her eyes as she embraced her friend and the tiny baby swaddled to her back.

"Mukami, I have been dreaming of this day. Look at you! A mother now! I am so happy for you!"

"Yes, and Mbuba is a healthy and smart boy already, like his father and his aunts," Mukami answered proudly. "He notices everything."

"He is my very own nephew," Kanini said wonderingly, taking the little mite's hand in her own. She slipped the baby out of the *leso* and sat on a rock with him in her lap. "Gati! Riunga! Come take a look at your little cousin!"

The grubby children had just sat up and still looked dazed from their short nap. They got up and went over to stare at the wizened face of the baby, their eyes wide. The two of them had always seemed so small to Kanini, but now they looked huge and bulky by comparison. Squinting in the sun, the baby turned his face to Kanini's bodice.

"He wants to nurse, Mama!" exclaimed Gati. "He knows how to find *iria*!"

Mukami and Kanini laughed as Kanini handed little Mbuba back to her childhood friend and sister-in-law.

The two days Kanini spent at home were some of the most pleasant she had experienced in a long time. The children sensed her relaxed attitude and played cheerfully, delighting in the new surroundings, their baby cousin and the doting attention they got from their relatives. Baba, especially, took quite an interest in them. He sat them on his lap one night, telling them stories by the fire. Njagi engaged with them as well, though he showered most of his attention on his wife and new son. She couldn't help but feel envious of Mukami. Would Kathenge have treated her better if his own baby son hadn't died?

Kanini took the children out on an excursion with Gitonga on the second day. As they rambled around the countryside, Kanini showed them all her old haunts. The large baobab tree down by the river was a favorite; thirteen year-old Gitonga was the only one able to climb it, but the younger ones tried as well.

As they headed home, Kanini asked her brother if he was making plans for *nyambura*.

"Didn't Mama tell you?" Gitonga asked. "I've made an appointment at Chogoria hospital to have it done surgically. In December, after the KCPE. I'll stay overnight, and then when I come home, we'll roast a goat and have a feast. You're all welcome, of course."

"You're going to get circumcised surgically?" Kanini was astounded. "I can't believe it."

"I started reading up on all the infections and diseases you can get by letting an untrained circumcisor do it with a knife or a razor blade out in a field. It scared me. I don't want to get that HIV I keep hearing about."

"Finally!" Kanini breathed. "Someone around here who talks sensibly. So, you've heard about HIV?"

"Oh yes. Njagi's found out a lot from the big towns he's been to. A lot of the people here in Kajuki don't believe it's a problem—they probably just don't understand it—but what else can explain all the deaths?"

"So, you've had deaths around here too," said Kanini. "Are there many orphans, do you know?"

Her brother shrugged. "There aren't as many primary kids in school as there used to be. You hear stories about how their babas just never came home from Mombasa or Nairobi. Then there are the mothers who've died as well. You wonder who's at home taking care of these kids."

"Do the teachers at school talk about HIV at all?" asked Kanini.

"No, they're not supposed to. It's still such a taboo subject. But we find out one way or the other."

Kanini told Gitonga all about Gatiria's work in Chiakariga. He'd heard a little about it, but didn't know the details.

"Leave it to Gatiria to use her energy in such an unusual way," Gitonga grinned. "I still picture her trying to become the first woman president of Kenya."

"She might try to do that someday," Kanini reflected. "Just give her time."

On the morning of the third day, Kanini repacked her bag and walked to the Mati road by herself. Her mother had offered to keep the children while she attended the hospital; hopefully, she had come to at least partially accept the operation.

Kanini waited a short while, then boarded the OTC bus and was whisked up to Meru in less than three hours. At the Chiakariga stop, she was disappointed not to see Gatiria, since her sister had written that she would be there. Kanini was glad she did not have the children to deal with. She was still feeling nervous, however.

Once in Meru, she alighted and looked around, wondering if Gatiria had perhaps taken an earlier vehicle. She decided she would get some lunch, and then return to the vehicle yard, to await her sister.

She wandered through the streets of the town, marveling at how it had grown. She had not been there since 1983, the year before the terrible drought, when she had come on an excursion with school. It amazed her that Gatiria came here all the time. The buildings were large and close together. There was so much traffic that Kanini was obliged to edge along the buildings, so nervous was she that the barreling vehicles might swipe her off the road. She knew Meru was no match for the capital, Nairobi, but it was the largest town she'd ever been to.

The marketplace sprawled before her, five times larger than the one at Ishiara, even on a market day. The vendors had every possible item for sale: tire sandals, homemade soap, plastic carry-alls, dishes and basins, machinery, metal *jikos* and sacks of charcoal, *sufurias* of all sizes, squawking chickens, furniture, colorful clothing and all sorts of cloth, as well as an infinite variety of food. She could smell the delicious scent of roasting goat coming from a food stall and stopped to order lunch. As she ate, she felt the market pulse with the bleating of goats, the tinkling of Swahili music and the loud voices of vendors bargaining with their customers. She ate her meal quickly, as the flies began to swarm around her.

She headed back to the *matatu* stand and waited on a bench in the shade of a eucalyptus tree. Kanini did not regularly crochet or knit as many women did, but she often brought a skein of yarn along on trips. From her bag, she pulled out her needles, which were attached to the piece of a sweater she had begun long ago for Gati. She set to work on it, noting how she would have to alter it to fit her growing daughter.

She had hoped knitting would take her mind off the operation, but she became obsessed thinking about it. Time passed slowly as her mind flitted about. What would the doctors do to her? She couldn't imagine someone cutting into her and fiddling with her tubes so that her body couldn't make any more babies. Although she trusted her sister and the doctor she was acquainted with, these fears reminded her of the ones that had preceded *nyambura*.

Kanini looked up every time a vehicle pulled into the yard. Finally, Gatiria appeared at the door of a battered yellow *matatu*. Kanini hailed her, stuffed her knitting back in her bag and hurried over.

"I'm sorry I'm late, sister!" breathed Gatiria. "I was so worried about you with the children. I hurried as fast as I could, but I couldn't leave the compound until noon, and then there was no vehicle for nearly an hour! Finally I got this thing coming from Embu."

"No problem," said Kanini, trying to sound calm. "Mama and Mukami are keeping the children."

"Oh good! So...Mama understands what you're doing here in Meru?" Gatiria led the way out of the yard and onto a road that headed up a steep hill. She linked arms with Kanini.

"Yes, I told her. It upset her, of course. I gave her some of my reasons for not wanting more children, but—she thinks this sort of thing angers the spirits. She thinks I'm trying to take too much control." She tried to keep her tone light. "You know how she is. I'm sure she wouldn't have approved of me using that family planning method. I think she would love to have twenty grandchildren, at least!"

Gatiria squinted up at the sun and tsk-ed with her tongue. "Well, it's typical of older people. They don't understand that if we don't do something to control the birth rate, this country will be full of unemployed, desperate people, or people dying of disease, within just a few years. We already have too many desperate and dying people!" Gariria shook her head and rolled her eyes. "Even younger people, most of them, believe we should just keep having children. We used to have debates in secondary about population control, and so many of the students claimed that if Kenya only had more people we would develop faster, like Switzerland or something. It was crazy."

"It does sound like they weren't thinking very much about our actual situation here," agreed Kanini, though she didn't know what Switzerland was.

The walk on the backroad to the hospital was pleasant. The air was cool and dry, and a breeze ruffled the undersides of the silvery eucalyptus leaves high above them.

"I like this area, Kanini," Gatiria commented. "People are much more motivated to work where the climate is cooler and there's more shade and greenery. You wonder why the *wazungu* claimed the White Highlands? I'd still like to get a job here sometime."

As they approached the hospital, Kanini felt shy and guarded. Outside on the trampled lawn, in the blazing sunlight, sat dozens of *wazee*, as well as mamas and their children. From the looks on their faces, it seemed that most had been there all day.

"It's too bad," Gatiria mumbled, as they threaded their way through the camped out families. "None of these people has an appointment."

They entered the stuffy building and walked past the long lines of people, directly to a small desk in a corner, where a youngish woman sat. It was obvious that Gatiria had been here before, a fact that lowered Kanini's anxiety level immensely. Gatiria spoke to the woman, received a form on a clipboard and guided Kanini to an unoccupied corner off to one side to fill it out. They returned the form and waited a short while. Then they were led down a hall to a white-washed room—dingy and in need of paint—where two long lines of beds, jutted out from the wall, only a few meters apart. In each bed was a woman and between them were tables laid with various implements.

Gatiria pointed to an empty bed and the two sat down side by side. Kanini looked around at all the quizzical faces suddenly turned their way. "I need to tell you, Gatiria," she said under her breath. I'm a little nervous about all this. No one we know has ever had such an operation. What if... what if something happens? What if something goes wrong?" She felt like a weakling with her complaints and questions. But if she could voice her concerns to anyone, it should be her sister.

"What can possibly happen, Kanini? It's a very safe procedure, much safer than giving birth out in the bush like you did with no one to help you. Or going through *nyambura*." Gatiria's face radiated assurance. "These people are professionals. They know what they're doing. Don't worry."

"I trust you, Gatiria. I'm so happy not to have to worry about getting pregnant again. After the first one, it always frightened me, and with the situation now, it'd be even worse." Kanini paused. "Only tell me, Gatiria. How much pain will there be? I know you haven't had the operation, but you might know—"

Gatiria's smile was wide. "Kanini, they put you to sleep! You didn't know that? You breathe in a hose and go right to sleep, so that when the doctor is operating, you feel nothing! It's so easy!" Gatiria stroked Kanini's arm with an air of confidence. "When you wake up, it's all done, and you're totally closed! I'll be right here with you, so if you need anything, I'll do it for you."

"So, there really will be no pain? I thought it would at least be like having a baby."

"Of course not. There is some cramping you feel afterward, stomach pains that last for a few days. That's why you'll stay here until Friday. But nothing like what you've already experienced."

Kanini breathed deeply and lay her head back on the pillow. She felt much better.

"I'm so glad you made this decision for yourself and your family," Gatiria was saying. "It's so good...and responsible. Oh yes, I've also arranged for you to have an AIDS test. The doctor will just take a little blood from you to analyze in the laboratory. It won't be any different from an inoculation." Gatiria patted Kanini's knee. "It'll take awhile for the results to come, but you'll be very relieved to know the truth of your condition. I wish Stefanie had come for one too."

"Stefanie isn't doing well. She worries so much about Njoka that she doesn't eat and she's lost a lot of weight."

The foreign sounds of the hospital room clinked around them as Gatiria weighed her words. "If he dies, Kathenge wouldn't take Stefanie as his second wife, would he?"

"I hope not! Kathenge talks so proudly about what a modern man he is. Wife inheritance is such a backward custom...I can't imagine Stefanie standing for it, anyway." Kanini's heart beat hard at the thought. "That would probably be the thing that kills her."

"She's always cared so much about Njoka...I really feel sorry for her," said Gatiria, shaking her head.

"Yes," whispered Kanini. "It would be kinder of Ngai to take Kathenge from me than Njoka from her."

Gatiria drew her breath in sharply and their eyes locked. Kanini knew they were thinking the same thing: thoughts such as this one shouldn't be voiced aloud.

"It sounds like you really dislike Kathenge these days, Kanini," Gatiria said.

"How can I not, Gatiria? He's changed so much. I know he was depressed when our son died. I was too. He wouldn't come near me during the day, wouldn't even talk to me. He gets colder all the time. What sort of marriage do we have, anyway?" Despair, the evil troll, was tapping at her shoulder again. It had been so wonderful to experience freedom from her ugly comrade during the past few days. Now, its return started her head throbbing and her eyes burning with unshed tears.

Gatiria took her hand and squeezed it. "I didn't want to upset you, Kanini. Let's not think about all that. I'm sure you're right; Kathenge won't marry Stefanie. And even if he does, isn't there a certain amount of time after the funeral where the new husband can't touch the widow of his brother? Like six months or something?"

"Traditionally, these brothers were not supposed to touch the widows at all!" exclaimed Kanini. She was surprised that Gatiria didn't know this. "It's only recently, with so many more widows around, that the brothers have been taking them as wives. Before, they just kept them at home and protected them, at least that's what the Meru people did. I think what they're doing now is very corrupt."

"Corrupt and unhealthy!" said Gatiria. "It spreads AIDS to the partners who didn't have it before! *Allah!* What is happening in our country, Kanini? The bad traditions continue, while the good traditions are changed for the worse. I dread how things will be once Gati is grown up."

Kanini swallowed the lump in her throat. She snorted into her handkerchief, hoping the noise would scare Despair away.

"Well, Kanini, I should go to greet my friend, *akina* Karimi, who I'm staying with tonight. I'll be back after you eat supper. I want to say good night to you. And, let's not talk about anything upsetting, alright?"

Kanini nodded, astonished that Gatiria had suggested such a thing. She blew her nose one more time and stuffed her handkerchief into her pocket.

Gatiria helped her get settled. She changed out of her dress and into a clean hospital gown. Then she got into the bed, which felt strange at this time of day, especially since she wasn't sick or recovering from anything.

After Gatiria left, Kanini noticed the woman in the next bed watching her. Kanini smiled thinly and the woman grinned in return.

"Do you speak *Kitharaka?*" asked Kanini.

"Yes. I'm from down by Materi," the woman answered. "What's your name?"

"Angela Kanini Kathenge. What's yours?"

"Mary Wanja Kithinji."

"How long have you been here?"

"Just two days. I was having trouble giving birth at home. When I got here, I had twins!"

"Twins!" Kanini breathed. "Did they both live?"

"Yes! Two boys! They're in a box keeping warm, since they're very small."

"A box!" breathed Kanini. "Where is this box?"

"In a room down the hall. It's called a *nini*, an... 'Intensive Care Unit'." The woman had a hard time pronouncing the English words.

"How do the babies eat if they're in a box?" asked Kanini.

"They're being fed through a tube since they can't breastfeed yet. It's very strange."

Kanini didn't know what to say. Tiny babies being kept alive through a tube in a box! She wondered if her own son might have lived had she given birth in a hospital.

"How did you get here on time?" asked Kanini, her eyes wide. "I mean, in time to have the babies?"

"I got a *matatu*. It was horrible." The woman cackled a little, remembering. "The first baby was stuck inside me. At that time we didn't even know I was having two! It felt like I would break apart with all the pain. I was lucky to get a vehicle, but the ride was so bumpy I nearly died! At least we got to the hospital on time."

"Did the babies come out...all right?" Kanini didn't know how to ask a stranger such a question.

"They came out healthy, if that's what you mean. But they didn't come out in the normal way. The doctors had to operate."

"Operate!" exclaimed Kanini. "To give birth? How did they operate?"

"They cut my stomach open and took the babies out," the woman explained.

"Cut you open!" Kanini was horrified. What would Mama say about that? What would the spirits think? "The cut must've been huge!"

"It's actually not so big." The woman showed Kanini with her fingers how big her incision was. "The doctors are used to doing these operations. They're able to save babies who would die otherwise. Also mothers."

"So, it didn't hurt you when they cut you open like that?" Kanini was still incredulous.

"No, I was asleep. I heard your sister telling you about that. The operation doesn't hurt at all. Of course, when you wake up–" The woman smiled a little and patted her midsection, which was covered with a blanket. "It's pretty sore."

"My sister told me I would probably be sore too," said Kanini. "I'm getting sterilized. At first I thought they'd take everything out. Then my sister told me the doctor just goes in and pinches my...*nini*. I don't really understand it–"

"There's so much that's difficult to understand these days." The woman laughed shortly. "It can make your head spin."

Kanini was eating a dish of watery *uji* for supper when Gatiria returned to keep her company. The sisters kept their conversation light and in the moment, which Kanini was thankful for. She had never thought of Gatiria as a comforting person, but some aspects of her sister's character had either changed or were still revealing themselves.

As Gatiria left, she patted Kanini's shoulder and whispered the Swahili words, *"Lala salama."*

Kanini thought she might lie awake for many hours, with all the strange sounds and lights, not to mention the thoughts that cluttered her mind. In the end, however, she was able to take her sister's advice and sleep peacefully throughout the entire night.

Chapter 8

Kanini returned to Kajuki two days later still feeling weak and nauseous from her operation. The ride on OTC made her cramps worse. After careening over the bumps, Kanini's insides felt as though they'd been shaken around in a gourd and left to ferment, like *ucuru*.

Gatiria had remained with her throughout the day of her operation. The hospital had overwhelmed her, with its endless bustle of nurses and aides and patients coming and going. At night, it was never truly dark, since dim electric lights had to be left on along the walls. The cramping had made it hard to sleep during the night following the operation, though it was nothing compared to the night following *nyambura*. She'd also been hard-pressed to eat the food that was given her. Did they think she had lost her teeth? Gruel and soft, thin foods for every meal? Gatiria told her it was because these foods were more easily digested. Now that she was going home, Kanini couldn't wait to sink her teeth into Mama's *githeri*, chock full of chewy greens, onions and plantains.

Tramping along the Kajuki road, she could not avoid the town, and was thus greeted by *wazee* and mamas, many of whom she hadn't seen in years. She stopped by the *duka* of Florence—still the best in town—and found her relative negotiating a disagreement between two of her toddlers. Her children now numbered five or six; Kanini couldn't keep track. She gave some candy to Kanini to take back to Mutwiri, Riunga and Gati.

That evening, Kanini accompanied Mukami down to the river, a *mtungi* in her hand. "How I envy you, Mukami," Kanini admitted with a sigh as they moved down the familiar path.

"You envy me? Why, Kanini?"

"Well, you had a hard life growing up," Kanini began. "But now you live with my brother, who acts nicer than he ever did, and you get the love and support of my parents, who are so proud of their new grandson. Things are working out much better for them now that they're older. And you get to share it with them."

"I guess I am lucky. Your mama is wonderful, Kanini. She really appreciates me! I wish you could have such a mother-in-law...I'm so sorry yours died."

"Yes, a lot of people at our place have died. It all seems so far away when I'm here. Then I get back there and it hits me like a rock in my face."

"It sounds very sad. You should come here and visit more often, Kanini. I've missed you since you got married."

"I would also like to come and visit more often…" Kanini debated for two seconds whether to voice all her thoughts, then her words tumbled forth. "Actually…I want to leave that place for good, Mukami. Maybe move to Chiakariga where my sister is living and help her with her work there."

Mukami looked at her sharply as they reached the river's edge. She sat down on a rock, her eyebrows knit and her lips pursed. "How could you leave your place for good, Kanini? You would leave your child behind?"

"Well, no, I couldn't do that. I would take her with me."

"What about Kathenge? He's your husband, Kanini! And Josefina's—Gati's—father!"

"I know it's hard to understand, but I don't want to live there anymore, Mukami. Kathenge doesn't like living with me either. It would be better for both of us if I leave."

Mukami appeared truly shocked. "How can you talk this way? He would never allow it!"

Kanini wondered if she should have opened up to her friend. "I know his family paid a good bride price for me—"

"Yes, and both you and Gati are his legal property. How can you think he would ever let you go?"

Kanini had no response. She sighed as she filled her *mtungi* and swung it onto her back.

"Anyway, I think things will get better for you there," Mukami said in a resolved tone as they headed up the hill. "Sometimes the situation is tough and you just have to get through it. You need to look past the present to the lifelong commitment of your marriage. It's all worth it in the end."

Kanini glanced quickly at her friend, but Mukami was faced forward, headed up the hill. *She sounds just like she did before* nyambura, Kanini thought. She had to respect her friend's constancy; in contrast, her own belief system was on the other end of the spectrum from what it had been. How fickle and contradictory she must seem to someone as steadfast as Mukami!

It felt so good to be with her friend that it didn't bother Kanini that they couldn't see eye to eye as they once had. Kanini had not even told her friend why she went to Meru. She took Mukami's hand as they climbed up the path, their jugs bumping lightly against their backs.

Kanini arose the next day, feeling healthy enough to begin the long trek back to Ishiara. She knew the children's slow pace would keep her from getting too tired. They would take their time and enjoy the journey. Mukami gave her a beautiful new doilie she had crocheted, from brilliant pink yarn. It looked so bright and cheerful that Kanini immediately placed it over her *kiondo* so that she could see it with every step she took. As she hugged her friend, Mukami whispered, "I will pray for you, Kanini. And please come back and visit us again soon!"

Mama loaded her down with millet meal and cowpeas, since she had plenty more in the stores. It felt good to have so much food in the family. And it also seemed, barring another terrible drought as had affected them in the 1980's, that Gitonga would be able to attend four years of secondary school beginning the following year. Kanini felt very happy for her family.

Baba, Mama, Njagi, Mukami, Gitonga and Mutwiri all waved the travelers off and wished them well. In good spirits, Kanini and the children headed through the bush along the path that led to Ishiara. On the way, they felt some sprinkles of rain, and Kanini thought, as she often did, that it must be a good omen. Despair would be gone, swept away in the drops that fell like tears upon their faces.

But, after a week away, Kanini arrived home to find that Despair had spawned; wretched little trolls with their wicked grins now dwelt wherever she set foot on the compound. Njoka was so ill he was unable to get up to walk to the toilet, let alone do his job. It was apparent to the entire family that he would not live to see the next harvest. His once brawny, muscular body was now shrunken and emaciated. Kanini was shocked at how the bones poked through his shoulders and chest. Stefanie too looked unhealthy. She waited on her husband every minute, wiping up his spittle after he coughed and cleaning him after he used the waste bucket. It seemed she hardly got any sleep, so ashy and distraught did she look. Despite only being twenty-four or twenty-five years old, Stefanie looked closer to forty.

In private, Kanini told her sister-in-law that she needed to rest; she herself would take over some of the endless tasks. Stefanie laughed caustically. "Oh, Kanini, believe me, there's plenty for both of us to do. There's the grinding, gourds to fix, clothes to wash, firewood to gather—I've done hardly any of it in days. Then there are the tomatoes! They're just getting ripe and someone has to harvest them. I tried to get Gachwe to do it on her own, but she needs constant encouragement."

"Who's been taking the animals out?" Kanini asked, noting that they were all still in their pen.

"Kathenge takes what's left of them, then he gets the fire going so that I can cook something. It's all I can do to keep enough water up here. I don't know how we can keep living like this. We need to hire someone. Maybe one of your brothers could come help us—" Her voice drifted off. She dragged her fingers through her nappy hair then roughly tied a head square over it. "Look at me! I'm a mess. I haven't bathed or washed this hair since before you left."

"Stefanie, you have to keep up your strength," Kanini squeezed Stefanie's arms between her hands. "If you've been infected with what Njoka has, getting weak will make the disease infect you sooner. You've got to get more sleep and not work so hard. Maybe Gitonga could come down. I'll write to see if he's free during the August holiday."

The next month flew by, there was so much to get caught up on. Gachwe was finally able to take loads of tomatoes to market, which brought them some very welcome cash. She complained about the work, but Kanini knew she liked the contact with outsiders; what better way to keep up her business acumen?

Gitonga, helpful as ever, agreed to help them during the month of August. He took a *matatu* to Ishiara on a Tuesday and accompanied Gachwe home, humbly hauling her sack of leftover produce. His shiny face and sunny disposition created a striking contrast to the solemn mood that pervaded their home. Despite his youth and good health, Gitonga had experienced suffering in the past and understood what it was like to be at the end of your rope. He therefore dived into the work with a level of vigor only the very motivated can muster. He took care of the goats and the one cow they had left. He played with Gati and Riunga, keeping them out of their parents' way. Having not yet been circumcised, it was still considered appropriate for him to do women's work, such as hauling water and firewood. He thus freed Stefanie up to tend her husband exclusively. Kanini still had plenty to do, but she could now oversee the goings on and delegate tasks to whoever could perform them.

Now that Gitonga was there to help, Kathenge did not stick around as much. He went off in the mornings to ramble and recreate, much like he and Njoka had done during previous holidays. Sometimes he would stay away all day and into the night. No one but Gati seemed to miss him. Kanini felt the entire farm heave a collective sigh of relief whenever his form disappeared out the gate.

One afternoon after he had returned from his wanderings, Kanini approached him about a minor repair.

"I'm glad you're home earlier than usual, Kathenge. Part of the fence needs to be fixed, and no one around here can do it."

Kathenge glanced at her and then walked past as if she had not even spoken. He entered their hut, letting the bamboo door swing shut in Kanini's face. Stung, she followed him inside.

"Kathenge, what's going on? You won't even talk to me these days. I'm trying to keep this farm running, there's so much to do...Yet, you go off as though things were the way they always were before. As though Njoka weren't dying—"

"He is not dying!" croaked Kathenge, his voice betraying rare emotion. "Why do you say that? He has malaria, that's all. You ask what's going on with me? What's wrong with *you*, woman, talking to me like this?"

He brushed past her again and left their hut, walking stiffly toward Njoka's. He knocked on the door and Kanini heard Stefanie answer. She then heard his rough voice as he shouted at his brother. Minutes later, Stefanie appeared at Kanini's doorway.

"Why is Kathenge so cross today? He's in there telling Njoka that he'd better be up and healthy by the first of September so he can help teach school. What is he thinking?"

Kanini sighed deeply. "Kathenge is in extreme denial, Stefanie. It's like he thinks Njoka just decided to get sick, as though he can recover if he feels like it...Kathenge is such a fool. I can't even talk to him."

"Niether can I. He becomes crazier every time I see him."

Kathenge disappeared for the rest of the evening and the next day. Gitonga and a neighbor finally got the fence mended.

Gachwe had been selling tomatoes at the Ishiara market for less than two months when an old acquaintance from secondary school stopped at her spot one Tuesday morning. They struck up a conversation and by the time Gachwe came home that evening, she had been offered a job in Embu at the *duka* of the friend's mother. She would be employed with a very small wage, but also given room and board at her friend's home. She excitedly made plans to vacate within the week and travel to Embu. The tomato season was nearing its end, but there were still a few more weeks Gachwe could have sold them. Kanini and Stefanie talked about how once again, Gachwe's motives were solely for her own advancement.

Njoka faded away gradually and within a month of Gitonga's return to Kajuki, he had passed into the realm of the ancestors. Kanini awoke one morning to hear Stefanie's muffled sobs coming from their hut. She had known this would come to pass. Now their family would suffer through the aftermath of yet another death. With a deep sigh, she arose to help Stefanie make preparations.

A month after the funeral, Kanini came upon her sister-in-law crying softly in the *riko* at suppertime. The *githeri* was bubbling away and the swinging lantern cast shadows on her shimmering face.

"What's wrong, Stefanie?" Kanini hissed, trying to keep her tone low. Stefanie had been tearful for weeks, but she did most of her crying where no one could see her.

"Something I never thought would happen." Stefanie looked up at Kanini from her haunches, her soggy handkerchief covering most of her face. "Kathenge wants to inherit me."

"What?" Kanini gasped. "I just told Gatiria in June that no way would he do that. How can he be so ignorant?"

"I guess he wants a second wife...I don't know, Kanini. I can't even imagine it. What is my life coming to?" Kanini handed her a fresh handkerchief.

"Just don't tell me he's going to have you cleansed. If that's the case, I'll help you run away," Kanini muttered. She remembered the day she finally found out what this deplorable custom entailed. Kathenge and Njoka had been laughing over the fate of a female teacher who taught at their school. The woman's husband had recently died and she was about to marry another man, one of her own choosing. They overheard her in the staff room telling another female teacher that the man had demanded she be cleansed, so she wouldn't infect him with any diseases. So she would return to "virgin status", was how they put it. Later, Kanini had asked Kathenge more about the custom and he'd told her, as though it were a joke. Just the thought of it nauseated her.

If a woman had not been infected with HIV yet, cleansing would surely expedite the process. Cleansers were known as some of the least decent men in town, their job being to have sex with a widow so that she could then be "clean enough" to be married by another man. The cleanser who lived near Ishiara had "cleansed" an untold number of women in his day; it was astounding that he himself had not been claimed by AIDS.

What an awful prospect for her poor, weak sister-in-law, to have to deal with all of this after Njoka, whom she had truly loved, had so recently been laid in the ground.

"Don't even say it, Kanini," whispered Stefanie. "I don't think he would be so barbaric as all that."

"At least we have to hope not," said Kanini.

For the next few days, she walked around numb, stunned at what Kathenge was demanding. She now regretted her wish from long ago that he would take a second wife; who knew it would end up being her own dear sister-in-law?

One day out in the field, Kanini couldn't bear her thoughts anymore. As they hoed the plants, she began rambling, "Stefanie, we can't let this happen. I don't care if you get cleansed or not. We have to get away from this place, before he takes you against your will."

Stefanie sighed and said in a small voice. "Your husband has become a different person, Kanini. He's not as he once was…I don't want to think about it." Her head sank into her hunched shoulders and all Kanini could see was the green triangle of her headsquare.

A lump formed in Kanini's parched throat. She stopped working and gazed off into the cloud-streaked sky. "I didn't want this to happen, Stefanie. I prayed that Kathenge would take pity…that he would come back to me. Anything. It's like he's taking out his anger, his helplessness…on you. As though you were the one who made—or kept—Njoka sick."

Stefanie just shook her head. Her lip quivered and she tried to speak, though only small gasps emerged. When she finally spoke, her voice sounded dead. "I don't know what he's doing…My life has become only suffering, nothing more. I've stopped feeling, Kanini, really. He can do what he wants to me. I can't imagine feeling anything ever again."

Stefanie plodded through the days. It seemed that she took very little joy in her son, and no joy in anything else. Kathenge no longer slept with Kanini—what she had yearned for, but which now brought her no relief. She lay awake next to her sleeping daughter, trying to contrive plans to get away.

The best idea would be to go to Chiakariga and live with Gatiria; not only she and her daughter, but if possible, Stefanie and Riunga as well. It could grow to be a community for the victims of the AIDS disease. It seemed like a dream. And indeed, there was no way to make it a reality; not as long as Kathenge was alive.

Part of her wished he would get sick and die of an AIDS-related illness, as Njoka had, but then her better judgment told her that Kathenge dying of AIDS presented her own death sentence as well. No, she sincerely hoped

Kathenge was not HIV-positive. Meanwhile, she wondered when her test results would be ready. Gatiria had arranged for them to be sent to the clinic at Materi, whereupon her sister would pick them up for her. Then she would write Kanini and inform her.

Kanini's heart thudded as she imagined herself opening that fateful letter. She prayed that the results would be in her favor; Ngai had to forgive her for her wicked thoughts about Kathenge, for the sake of her daughter, if nothing else. She would do anything to be allowed the chance to live long enough to see Gati grow up.

Kanini was waiting for something, some sort of sign or message, she didn't know what. In late November, she went to the market, made her usual purchases and went to the tiny post office for the mail. The only item was a letter from Gatiria, the first since she'd seen her in Meru. She tore it open and found no test results. Her racing heart melted into a heap of relief, though she knew they probably just weren't ready yet. She hungrily read the letter.

Chiakariga Market
24 November, 1995

Dear Kanini,

I hope this letter finds you in good spirits, considering the recent events. I received the letter, which gave news of Njoka's death. I'm very sorry. I hope Kathenge did not force Stefanie to be inherited, like we talked about in Meru. At any rate, I feel very concerned for Stefanie's welfare.

We have also had some bad luck here. Our headmaster has quit and joined a course in Nairobi to teach secondary school. I wonder how he can quit when thirteen children depend on him for 24-hour care and sixteen others depend on him for an education. Now it is just only me who is here, and Kanini, I NEED HELP!! Really! What we talked about in Meru has become something urgent. If you could come and help here, even for a month or so until another teacher or headmaster is found, we would appreciate it so much! I am exhausted, though I know you must be too with all you're doing. If you came here, we could work together, and you would even be paid by the mission.

I have to give Muthoni credit for coming nearly every weekend to help out. She is an angel, Kanini! I see why she decided to become a nurse. She cares so much for others; never gives a thought about herself. She brings medicine, food, storybooks, exercise books, chalks, everything we need. Plus, she gives me company. Sometimes she stays the whole day on a Saturday, for supper even! Her brother always brings her down. They are truly wonderful, and I could not do this work without their support.

Please think about coming here, Kanini, just only for a month. I know it is the planting season, but maybe you can leave it just this one time. You have so few mouths to feed there now, and I know you must have stores left from the last harvest. I feel terrible even asking this of you, but we are desperate, sister. See what Kathenge says about this. Perhaps he could spare you for three or four weeks, you and Gati.

I did not include your test results since the mission has not yet received them.

Sincerely,

Gatiria

Kanini tucked the letter into a pocket and stared off into space. It was true that she and Stefanie had recently planted their crop for the next season, and it would need to be weeded soon. Maybe if Gitonga could come again in December to help! But he always helped Mama with their harvest and this December he would be planning his post-*nyambura* celebration. What to do? She was determined to go to Chiakariga and answer her sister's plea. But she was torn; how could she leave Stefanie in her pathetic state, to take care of the entire *munda* on her own? Maybe one of Stefanie's own siblings could come. If only Gachwe would be willing to help. What good was she? Working at a *duka* in Embu, when her own family was rapidly disintegrating.

It was a Tuesday and she was standing under a tree at Ishiara market. She had come to get their mail and buy fresh produce. Gati was there with her, as usual, hauling the *mtungi* of kerosene for the lamps. As Kanini stood there holding the letter, an idea took root in her mind. She watched as the old OTC bus rattled up to the *matatu* stand and thought, *I could get on that vehicle and go to Chiakariga without any permission from Kathenge. He would hardly miss me; he never pays me any attention when we're together anyway. He would have Stefanie to himself.* At the thought of her sister-in-law, a guilt reflex kicked in and Kanini reconsidered. "We can go for one week only," she told Gati. "I'll leave a note at the *hoteli—*"

Almost in a daze, Kanini took her daughter's hand and walked to the restaurant, wrote and left the note, and then headed toward the vehicle stand. They boarded the bus going to Meru, squeezed in next to the countless bodies and hugged their bags on their laps. Gati was full of questions, but Kanini hardly heard herself answering them.

On the walk to Chiakariga, Kanini squeezed Gati's hand. She pictured her sister teaching when they arrived, or perhaps serving lunch. She and the orphans would look up and everyone's face would glow with joy and surprise.

No one was around in the town center, which was not unusual. Kanini walked to the school, still holding her daughter's hand. She could see Gatiria through the window of a classroom. She knelt down and pointed her out to her daughter. In another classroom, the younger pupils sat quietly, studying on their own, awaiting the time when the teacher would visit their class. Having only one teacher struck her as ludicrous. "Why, if we lived here with Gatiria, maybe I could help teach!" Kanini exclaimed aloud. Then she checked herself. "That is, I could teach until they got someone else."

Kanini took Gati back to town and they sat in the *chai* shop, each with a cup. There were no *mandazzi*, however, Kanini shared some bananas she'd brought from Ishiara with her daughter. Within the hour, she heard Gatiria's key in the lock at the back of the shop. She grasped her daughter's hand and they hurried out to greet her sister.

Gatiria stood rooted in the doorway; she made no move to invite them in. As though they were strangers.

"What is it, Gatiria?" asked Kanini, frightened and perplexed. "We're here! We didn't even tell Kathenge; no one knows. We can only stay a week or so, but–"

"Kanini." Her voice wavered. Gatiria's voice! Wavering! "Come in… We need to talk."

"What is it, Gatiria?"

Gatiria went to the table and picked up a folded paper. Wordlessly, she handed it to Kanini.

Before she even looked at it, Kanini knew what it was. A heavy hand seemed to press down on her heart. She took a deep breath as she opened the paper and read the results of her HIV test. As though she had been told in a dream, they stated what she had known all along. She had only refused to think about it. Denial. Like Kathenge and Njoka, she too had been in denial.

Gatiria gave her a long hug, as only Gatiria could. "I'm so sorry, my sister." She began to cry. Bewildered, Gati started crying too. Then, Kanini herself cried.

Chapter 9

It took them a long time to overcome their grief. Finally they were able to clasp each other's hands and sit calmly on the bed. Gati lay across her mother's lap. "I need to consider my future now," Kanini said as she stroked her child's head. "And hers." Her voice was raspy. "You told me that an infected person could maybe live eight to ten more years. If she takes care of herself—"

"I know you can live that long, sister." Gatiria wiped the moisture from her face with a scrap of fabric. It wasn't a real handkerchief, but it was something. "You can probably live even longer. There may soon be a medicine that will prevent people with HIV from getting AIDS. We're just waiting for its development."

"Will it be developed within the next few years?" Kanini looked at her with hopeful eyes.

"I don't know. In some countries, they have it even now. Only it's very expensive."

"I guess I just need to wait...and pray." Kanini mumbled to herself. There was a long silence, broken only by Gati's occasional sniffle. Kanini bent over and hugged her. Though her eyes blurred again with tears, she laughed a little. "Look at my daughter, Gatiria. She doesn't even know what we're crying about, yet here she is, full of sympathy."

"She has a strong and compassionate heart, that one." Gatiria gently squeezed the child's arm. Then she sat up straight. "Kanini, I want you to stay here with me. I can take good care of you, despite our lack of fresh food. You'll be surrounded by loving souls: Muthoni, myself and all the children, who will appreciate you so much—"

"But, how—" Kanini wrung her hands together. "...What will we tell Kathenge?"

"We'll tell him that you're HIV-positive and need to take good care of yourself in order to stay healthy. The situation with him is not healthy. Look what happened to Bilibina, Njoka...and now with Stefanie—"

"Stefanie!" exclaimed Kanini. "I'm sure she has the virus too, but she's not taking care of herself and she could get really sick—"

"Would it be better for both of you to get really sick, Kanini? You need to tell Kathenge that you will not stop being his wife, but this is the best place for you to be right now."

"But, Stefanie...She's become his wife too, Gatiria. Kathenge inherited her. She's miserable right now. I couldn't leave her. If I did, she'd give up all hope."

Gatiria shook her head. "I wish Stefanie could come here too. But that'd be impossible. Maybe Gachwe could help out for a while until things are better over there."

"Gachwe's gone. She doesn't care what happens to us, Gatiria. Kathenge wrote her about Njoka's death, and she never even wrote back."

"Well, there's lots to think about, isn't there?" Gatiria shook her head and reached over to draw Gati onto her lap. "Meanwhile, I'll get this cooker lit so we can have some food. What do you think, Gati?" The little girl smiled for the first time since they had entered the house.

For Kanini, the next three days passed in a bittersweet blur. Each morning she awoke and helped her sister prepare *chai* for their breakfast. Then they would go out to oversee the cooking of *uji* for the orphans. She often did not remember her condition for hours. Then the memory of it would creep into her mind and she would feel a heaviness rest on her shoulders, as though Despair had dropped a shroud over her. She would shake the memory away as well as she could and return to thinking about her sister, her daughter or the orphans as they interacted, played or worked together. She focused on banning thoughts of Kathenge and even Stefanie from her mind as she savored each moment and prayed that she and Gati could spend their future in Chiakariga.

Kanini enjoyed spending time with the thirteen orphans. Each had his or her own tasks to perform and knew the routine inside and out. They were well-disciplined and polite, as though they understood and appreciated the huge effort that was being put out on their behalf. Gatiria and Muthoni had begun some cottage industries, which helped the children earn money for their own upkeep. Many were skilled at making tire sandals, which Muthoni's brother took up to Meru and sold at the market. Some were good at weaving small baskets out of sisal, to be sold at the markets in Meru and Ishiara. Gatiria had confidence that at some point in the future their motivation and industry would make it unnecessary to take as much charity from the mission.

Gatiria invited Kanini to help teach, since the school was so understaffed. Kanini was delighted to go over lessons all morning in the younger pupils' classroom. She was patient with their questions and a natural at explaining the science and literacy material. She thought she'd forgotten most of her

Swahili, but it soon came back to her. Gati was usually able to sit patiently for the first few hours, then Kanini would take her out into the sunshine to play.

On Thursday afternoon, Muthoni and her brother drove up in the mission Landrover and hauled out burlap sacks of maize, maize meal and beans, which they set inside a covered storeroom near the school. The orphans gathered wood and hauled jugs of water back from the river. As Muthoni was opening the sack of maize, Kanini approached her. Muthoni wiped her hands on her dress and clasped Kanini's hand.

"It's so good to have you here, sister. I only hope you can stay permanently."

"Thank-you, Muthoni. It's nice to see you again." It was clear Muthoni knew about Kanini's medical condition. Kanini glanced away from the gaze of this striking woman, knowing that if she met her eyes, she might start to cry. At Gati's call, she smiled at Muthoni and hurried away.

After supper, the adults and some of the older children sat around the fire, talking and enjoying the mild evening air. Gati joined a group of younger kids in a game of hide and seek; she romped with them as if they'd known each other for years. Their merry voices soothed Kanini's soul like balm to a wound.

Kanini had not felt this contented since her visit to Kajuki, back in June. But this was more than mere contentment; she felt released from something she couldn't put her finger on, something that had restricted her before. She knew it wasn't just Kathenge who'd been keeping her prisoner; it was her own sense of duty, her self-inflicted obligations and responsibilities. Now that she knew the years left to her were finite, there was no reason to adhere rigidly to what had always dictated so much of her life. She was able to break free.

Muthoni and her brother left after the moon was high in the sky and the orphans were getting into their beds. Gati had fallen asleep on Kanini's lap. She carried her sleeping daughter inside Gatiria's tin room and laid her on her mat in the corner. Then she and her sister sat outside in the shadows and talked.

"You've been here two days, Kanini. It seems like Kathenge has maybe not missed you. I'm hoping he's willing to leave you to the life you want."

"I wish I felt confident about that, Gatiria. I'm afraid that he'll come for me just to spite me, not because he really wants me. Even after he finds out that I'm infected with the virus...it won't make any difference."

"If only there was a place you could go...somewhere we could hide you."

"Oh, Gatiria, you're mad. He's a man. He has all the power. He would find me; he could even hire soldiers to track me down." Kanini's tongue tsk-ed at Gatiria's naivete. "And Gati...There's no question that he has the law on his side when it comes to her."

"What if you were given the choice to be granted your freedom from Kathenge, but you also had to give up your daughter? What would you do?"

Kanini stared at her sister. Gatiria really was naive!

"I would never give her up, Gatiria." Kanini shook her head. "Even if I had to live with Kathenge and be beaten by him everyday for twenty years...I could never do that." The thought of losing Gati made her feel physically sick.

"I thought you felt that way." Gatiria laid her hand on Kanini's knee. "A woman can never give up her child."

A silence fell between them as Kanini thought about how Mama had given up Gatiria. Kanini knew her sister was thinking the same thing.

"Have you given any more thought to going to Kajuki?"

"I have, actually. I want to see Mama and Baba. Do you think they would see me, Kanini?"

"I think so. With everything that's happened, especially after my sterilization, I think Mama realizes that the world has changed so much. You can't stay angry with one of your family members forever." Kanini's eyes traveled up to the smattering of stars blinking through the spidery branches. "The townspeople were angry with us, but they forgave us. I'm sure Mama and Baba would forgive you, too. They probably have already."

"I hope so. I miss them. I need the strength I could get from them. Your stories have made it sound like things are going so well at Kajuki."

"You won't believe how Njagi has changed, Gatiria," said Kanini grinning. "He's so good to Mukami and the baby—"

"I want to be there with them during these good times. And I'd like to meet their little one."

"We should take a trip to Kajuki sometime soon," Kanini exclaimed. "Maybe Muthoni could come and stay with the orphans for a weekend and we could go then. It's really so close to this place, we could even walk."

"Let's write a letter—or you write one—and ask them what they think. Then we'll wait for the reply. We'll write it tomorrow."

Kanini lay on her side of Gatiria's bed that night, her heart uplifted.

How strange to feel so carefree, considering she had this virus that would cut her life short by many years. Life was dear, she knew. There was so much to do, so many new experiences to be had. There were people to get to know and her child to raise, all in such a brief time. She wanted to live each day to the fullest; she wanted never to waste time again dwelling in misery or anger. Life was too short—especially now—for any of that.

Resolute, she banished Despair from her life forever.

She could hear huge beetles crashing around the lantern that was still lit on the table. Though her eyes were closed, she knew her sister was beating the insects away as she sat working. Kanini smiled to herself. This was a life she could live for a long time.

Friday was spent following the daily routine. Kanini taught the pupils in the morning, helped cook a big lunch, and then settled down to some quiet time in the heat of the afternoon. It had not rained once since their arrival at Chiakariga, which Gatiria said was common, even during the rainy season. After supper, everyone turned in early since the next day they would need all their energy for the wide range of activities that Gatiria had planned.

Kanini awoke refreshed to experience a Saturday in action. After breakfast, she listened as her sister explained the day's schedule to the children. First, half the group would go to the river, accompanied by Kanini and Gati, to wash clothes and bathe. Meanwhile, Gatiria had organized some repair jobs with the other half, as well as the various craft projects. The groups would switch activities after lunch.

When everyone reconvened at around eleven, Gatiria announced that the children could play netball and soccer for an hour before lunch. They let out a whoop and immediately started organizing the games. The boys grabbed their soccer ball—a real one that had recently been purchased in Meru—while most of the girls lined up on either side of the net for netball. Kanini had started cooking lunch, so that when everyone was completely worn out, it would be time to eat.

A few hours later, Kanini was just dipping a spoon into her bowl of *githeri*, when she looked up to see a smartly dressed man enter the compound. The sun was behind him, so she couldn't see his face. She thought it might be the old headmaster and was just turning to call Gatiria, when the man strode directly over and stopped in front of her. She looked up to meet the flashing eyes of her husband, Kathenge.

The sight of him caused her to cough up the spoonful of food she had just swallowed. Kathenge grabbed her arm and pulled her roughly to her feet. Her bowl and spoon clattered to the ground.

"Kathenge! Stop! What are you doing?" Gatiria was beside them, attempting to block his way. "You can't grab her like that!"

Kathenge pushed past her and pulled Kanini along with him to the edge of the schoolyard. Gatiria hurried after them. Kanini tried to catch her eye, but could not.

"This is *my* wife!" He snarled at Gatiria like an animal. "What do you mean by sending for her without my permission? She belongs with me! With us! She's coming home *now*!" Kanini felt his grip tighten on her arm. She felt like an object being fought over by these two driving forces.

Suddenly, her husband began to shout, "Where's my daughter, Josefina? Josefina, come to Baba!" Gati did not seem to be around. Gatiria turned to head back. Was she going to find Gati and hide her? Gatiria was capable of anything, Kanini knew.

"Kathenge!" Kanini finally found her voice, though it hardly sounded like her own. "Gatiria didn't send for me. I came because I wanted to. I can't...live with you anymore. I want to stay here—Here with people who need and care about me...us...Gati and me."

Though they were some distance from the pupils, Kanini could see their bright uniforms out of the corner of her eye. She was sure their attention was riveted on the two of them.

"What are you saying? Stefanie, Riunga and I don't care about you or need you?" He shook her shoulders roughly. "Josefina is my daughter. Of course I care about her, and she needs me. You don't belong here, Kanini. You belong with me. You belong to me."

Then Kathenge did something he had never done before. He struck her. She saw the flash of his hand as he raised it and then felt it slam into her face. She caught herself from falling to the ground, as his words throbbed in her ears: "...lack of respect...causing me to lose face...in front of a bunch of school kids—"

"You can't get away with hitting her, Kathenge," Gatiria's voice hovered nearby, though Kanini couldn't see her. She wished her sister would stop. "She'll run away again and you'll never find her!"

Her face stung, but her heart felt nothing; it had encased itself in a protective coating. Even though she knew she could never run off again, she was certain she would break away from Kathenge's grip somehow. Her determination steadied her as much as Gatiria's hand on her arm.

"I will return with you, husband. But—" Her voice shook; it did not sound full of resolve. The faint taste of blood was in her mouth. She felt the scene swirl around her in a kaleidoscope of heat and color, much like she remembered *nyambura*. "—I need to get my things." Gatiria's strong hand helped keep her on her feet. Her sister strode alongside her towards the room they had shared.

A whimper from Gati snapped Kanini around. There she was, standing with the boy, Njeru, clinging to his hand for dear life. Their faces blurred as Kanini scooped her daughter up and carried her into the little house.

"You can't go with him, Kanini," Gatiria begged. "It'll be terrible. What will you do?"

"Gatiria, I have no choice. I've never had a choice. Choices have been made for me ever since...ever since I got circumcised." As usual, Gatiria was blubbering with no handkerchief in hand. Kanini thrust the one she was packing at her sister. "You...you've always had more choices; you've taken choices for yourself. You might be able to do something different right now if it were you. But it isn't. It's me. And...I have to go. You know I have to go—"

Gatiria blew her nose and stared at her. Kanini's tears had dried and as she faced her sister, she hesitated. Then she held out a hand, fearing that to initiate a hug would rip all the protection from her heart. Gatiria grasped her hand with both of her own.

A shadow in the doorway blocked out the sun. Kanini withdrew her hand from her sister's and collected her satchel from the bed. Then she took Gati's hand and strode from the room without looking back.

Keeping her eyes down, Kanini followed her husband out of town and down the track toward the Mati road. Gati clung to one of her fingers, panting as she struggled to keep up. As they followed Kathenge's straight back, Kanini glanced down at the soft sand on the path. The large impressions of her husband's leather shoes were spaced widely apart, but she had been struggling to place her feet into them, out of habit. She veered to one side of the trail and, one foot after the other, began to make her own footprints in the sand.

Glossary

Meru/English

Cucu (sho-sho)—grandmother
Gasukari (ga-soo-ka-di)—tiny sweet bananas
Githeri (gi-the-di)—staple food made with boiled maize and beans
Iria (ee-ree-ah)—milk
Irio (ee-ree-oh)—food made with mashed potatoes and vegetables
Kigiri (kee-gi-ri)—field for performing boys' circumcision ceremonies
Kiondo (kee-ohn-do)—hand-woven bag made from sisal or yarn
Leso (lay-so)—light, decorated cotton cloth with a Swahili saying printed on one edge
Mburu (m-boo-doo)—starchy black fruits
Mono (mo-no)—a lot, very much
Mpumiro (m-poo-mee-do)—coming out ceremony, held a few weeks after circumcision
Mucii (moo-see)—home
Muga (moo-gah)—greeting (to one person)
Mugeni (moo-gen-ee)—greeting (to more than one person)
Mugwatani (moo-gwa-ta-nee)—caregiver
Munda (moon-da)—farm
Mutaani (moo-tah-nee")—circumciser
"Ndathie" (n-dah-thee-ay)—"I'm going"
Ngai (n-guy)—God
Nikwega (ni-kway-gah)—thank-you
Nimwega (nim-way-gah)—greeting (in Chuka dialect)
Nthoroko (n-tho-ro-ko)—cow peas
Nyambura (nyahm-boo-da)—circumcision
Riko (ree-ko)—kitchen
Ucuru (oh-sho-ro)—fermented millet gruel
"Wathieco" (wa-thee-ay-ko)—"Where are you going?

Swahili/English

Akina (ah-kee-na)—that person
Allah (a-lah)—the God, Allah
Baba (ba-ba)—father
Bahati (ba-hah-tee)—luck
Bibi (bee-bee)—ma'am, Mrs.

Boma (bo-mah)—stall made for one or two animals, usually from bamboo
Bwana (bwah-na")—sir, Mr.
Chai (chy)—tea, usually made with milk
Chapati (cha-pah-tee)—flat bread made from wheat flour
Choo (cho)—toilet
Dada (da-da)—sister
Dawa (da-wa)—medicine (or pesticide)
Duka (doo-kah)—shop
"Fuata nyayo" (foo-ah-ta nya-yo)—literally "to follow in the footsteps", a Kenyan expression
"Habari gani?"—(ha-bah-dee gah-nee) "How's it going?" (literally, "What's the news of the day?")
Hoteli (ho-tel-ee)—small restaurant or cafe
Hoti (ho-tee)—greeting to announce arrival
"Huko tuu"—(hoo-ko too) "Just there."
Jiko (jee-ko)—cook stove
Kabisa (ka-bee-sa)—exactly, the most
Karibu (kar-ee-boo)—welcome
Kipindupindu (kee-pin-doo-pin-doo)—cholera
Kimeru (kee-may-roo)—Meru language
Kiswahili (kee-swa-hee-lee)—Swahili language
Kitharaka (kee-tha-ra-ka)—Tharaka dialect
Kizungu (kee-zoong-goo)—language of the white people (usually English)
"Kupiga maji" (koo-pee-gah ma-ji)—to go out drinking (literally, "to beat water")
Kuzaa (koo-za)—give birth
Kuzaliwa (koo-za-lee-wa)—was born
"Lala salama" (la-la sa-lah-ma)—sleep peacefully
Mandazzi (man-dahz-ee)—a bland fritter, often eaten with chai.
Matatu (ma-ta-too)—public transport vehicle, usually a covered pick-up or small van
Mavi (ma-vee)—excrement
Maziwa (ma-zee-wah)—milk, breasts
Mimba (mim-bah)—pregnant
Miraa (mi-rah)—type of plant that when chewed produces a mild high
Mkubwa (m-koob-wah)—big
Mtharaka (m-tha-ra-ka)—person from Tharaka
Mtungi (m-toong-gee)—plastic or earthenware water jug
"Mungu akipenda" (moong-goo ah-kee-pen-da)—"if God wills"
Mwalimu (mwa-lee-moo)—teacher
Mzee (m-zay)—old man

Mzungu (m-zoong-goo)—white person (literally, a person who goes around in circles)
Nini (ni-nee)—thing-a-ma-jig, whatever, what?
Panga (pahng-ga)—machete
Pikipiki (pik-ee-pik-ee)—motorbike
Pombe (pohm-bay)—beer
Rais (rah-ees)—president
Safari (sa-fa-dee)—trip
Sawasawa (sa-wa-sa-wa)—the same, okay, all right
Sufuria (soo-foo-ree-ah)—cooking pot
Ugali (oo-ga-lee)—stiff cornmeal porridge
Uji (oo-jee)—watery cornmeal porridge
Uki (oo-kee)—honey wine, usually homemade
Ukimwi (oo-kim-wee)—AIDS
"Unafahamu" (oo-na-fa-ha-moo)—"Do you understand?"
Unga (oong-ga)—flour
Wazee (wah-zay)—old men
Wazungu (wa-zoong-goo)—white people

About the Author

Kirsten Johnson graduated from Carleton College with a BA in English literature. She then traveled to Kenya in 1982 with the Peace Corps to teach English at a rural "Harambee" school, where she met Celina Kanini Kinoti, a fellow teacher. She has taught refugees in Thailand and elementary schoolchildren at an international school in Bolivia. Currently, she teaches

English as a Second Language in Madison, Wisconsin.

She has been selling hand-woven bags and hats made by the Gatumi women's group—the women of her Kenyan village—for many of the intervening years since returning to the U.S. Most of the money earned from this project goes to pay the school fees for the children of these women. *Footsteps* is intended to both raise awareness of the lives of girls from Tharaka, Kenya, as well as help earn funds for their education.